The Untime

The Untime Revisited

Novels of 19th Century Paris

Hugh Ashton

J-Views Publishing, Lichfield, England

Epigraph

"What then is time? If no one asks me, I know what it is. If I wish to explain it to him who asks, I do not know."

Augustine of Hippo, Confessions

THE UNTIME – WHAT DID READERS SAY?

HAT did people say about *The Untime*, the first book in this series?

This novel definitely gives the feeling of a late nineteenth-century adventure story, with labs full of apparatuses and Leyden jars, daring reporters, mad scientists, and travel through time and space. The characters speak with charming formality, my favorite phrase being, "No, no, and a thousand times, no!"

As usual, Hugh Ashton exhibits a wonderful command of language, and this time there is a new twist – the characters are supposed to be speaking French. So, added to the usual punctilious Victorian turns of phrase, it is possible to pick up a hint of Gallic flavor as well!

At first this book was hard for me to get into because it is so different from Mr. Ashton's other books (which I really like). However, the more I read, the more I wanted to know what was going to happen. At the end, I was saying, "I need to know what happens after this!"

The Untime & The Untime Revisited: Novels of
19th Century Paris
Hugh Ashton

ISBN-13: 978-1-912605-42-2
ISBN-10: 1-91-260542-2

Published by j-views Publishing 2018
© 2014, 2015, 2018 Hugh Ashton
All rights reserved. Without limiting the rights
under copyright reserved above, no part of this
publication may be reproduced, stored in or
introduced into a retrieval system, or transmitted, in any form, or by any means (electronic,
mechanical, photocopying, recording, or otherwise) without the prior written permission of
both the copyright owner and the above publisher of this book.

This is a work of fiction. Names, characters,
places, brands, media, and incidents are the
product of the author's imagination.

j-views Publishing, 26 Lombard Street,
Lichfield, England
www.j-views.biz
publish@j-views.biz

Foreword by John Paul Catton

WHAT Ashton is particularly good at is to invent universes that are based on fictional creations we've seen before, but given original twists. He did it with the Sherlock Holmes canon, and now he's done it again with H.G. Wells. *The Untime* is a monstrous fountain of invention, a fictional universe based on Wellsian scientific romances and incorporating elements of Jules Verne, H.G. Wells, H.P. Lovecraft, Arthur Machen, and Frank Belknap Long.

Despite its short length, being the length of a novelette, the tale has a sprawling, epic quality that could hardly have been produced in any other fashion. It accurately captures the writing of that historical era. It's a style that becomes intriguing, then engaging, then enthralling. *The Untime* is rooted in its era and incredibly well-researched – but it also stretches the late Victorian scientific paradigm, dropping the names of all sorts of theories that belong to quantum physics at a time before quantum physics had been conceived, and so fleshing out a relatively slight plot with all manner of scientific concepts, speculations and discussions.

Despite all these intriguing concepts, it is the strong leading and peripheral characters that drive the densely written story, and provide the best shocks and twists. What is really shocking is how little the antagonist actually appears. In most stories this would be a problem, but here, because of the nature of the story, the threat to the time-space continuum posed by Professor Rémy Lamartine becomes more sinister, as he has the power to appear and strike at any place, any time.

The portrayal of the protagonist Jules Gauthier is linked with the concept of the entire story; he is an everyman, an observer thrown into a situation beyond his understanding, and as such serves as the reader's viewpoint, as was common in the scientific romances of the time. The most intriguing character is probably Agathe

Lamartine, who plays the role of the daughter of the – quite literally – mad scientist. At first she seems an 19th century damsel in distress, but turns out to be more than capable of taking care of herself. There is also Professor Schneider from the Sorbonne, an academic rival of Lamartine's, who seems a typical sceptic at first, but becomes a mentor and staunch supporter of Gauthier's mission as the plot unfolds.

A lot goes on that I cannot really discuss because of spoilers, and that gives you a clue as to The Untime's scale and depth. The plot begins when journalist Jules Gauthier makes the acquaintance of Professor Rémy Lamartine, and becomes the audience to the professor's theories on time, reality and the existence of other dimensions. On a visit to Lamartine's house, Gauthier is invited to inspect the machine that the professor has constructed, and together the two venture into the Untime – the nebulous dimension that exists outside of our reality and encompasses all of time and space. The two time travelers return – but Lamartine seems strangely changed by the experience, and over the days that follow his behavior becomes increasingly bizarre and erratic. Gauthier suspects that Lamartine has become a danger to those around him ... and he's right. Lamartine, however, poses a threat not only to Gauthier and his own family, but also to the continued existence of the perceived consensus reality that we call 'our world'.

One of the delights of this book is the amount of fascinating scientific concepts packed in, blurred into the fiction with invisible ease. It's worth commenting on Ashton's skill in narrative construction considering the difficulty of constructing plausible time paradoxes that don't hopelessly confuse the reader. The Lovecraftian elements, while not entirely unexpected, are extremely well done and a vivid depiction of cosmic horror. These sections achieve a very chilling feel; the atmosphere is shockingly effective at times.

The 19th century French settings are extremely well evoked, and despite the fantastical nature of the majority of the events, a feeling of realism is brought across to the reader. The historical "age" of the story is made much more concrete by creating the story in this manner. The book is able to play with the concepts of paradox and the vastness of eternity, but it doesn't allow itself to become confusing.

A beautifully written piece, then, with a

superbly characterized cast and a hugely satisfying ending. An astonishing book, powered by symbolism and striking imagery, and wrapped up in bold, experimental narration. Looking over the Steampunk/Alternative History range as a whole there are few books that have this much impact, or that break the rules with such verve and distinction.

JOHN Paul Catton is the author of *Tales From Beyond Tomorrow!*, *Moonlight, Murder & Machinery*, and the YA trilogy *Sword, Mirror, Jewel*.

Acknowledgments

As always, I want to thank other people who have made this book possible. Only one name appears on the cover, but a book is always the fruit of more than one person's labours.

First and foremost, Yoshiko, who has had to cope with the perils of the Untime while this book has been written.

Next, all who have commented and made suggestions regarding the story and its development. I have not always adopted these ideas, but they have all provided stimulation and inspiration.

John Paul Catton, for his unduly (in my opinion) flattering Foreword and evaluation of my work. Coming from another writer whose work I greatly admire, this is praise indeed.

And Jo at Inknbeans, who was always more than an editor and publisher – she became a true guide, philosopher, and friend, who generously gave her time and support to me during the (un)time while I wrote this.

To all those whom I love, who have explored the Untime with me and helped to uncover its mysteries.

THE UNTIME

Introduction

THE events I am about to describe may seem preposterous and incredible to some, but you may be assured of their veracity. Though I did not take detailed notes of all the conversations and activities recorded here, my relation of them is, to the best of my recollection, accurate.

I am supported in this assertion by my wife, Agathe Gauthier (née Lamartine), who was present at many of the events described here, and has been able to refresh my memory regarding many of them.

However, notwithstanding the truth of what I am setting down, I feel it inadvisable to make these facts public at this stage. I admit that the commotion and concern in the popular press surrounding the reported death of Professor Lamartine, who up to that time had occupied a prominent position in the public eye, tempted me at the time to give an open account of the savant's actions, but wiser counsels than mine prevailed.

I have therefore prepared this manuscript, and propose that it be kept in some safe place, unopened until such time as I, and all connected with the events described here, have passed from this life. It may be that at some time in the future, eyes, as yet unknown to me, will discover and read these words, which will finally put an end to the mystery surrounding the Lamartine Affair, as it was then known.

Jules Gauthier
Paris, 1905

Chapter I

IT was a fine spring day in 189– when I visited my friend, the famous Professor Rémy
Lamartine, at his laboratory in the suburbs
of Paris. Lamartine had resigned his Chair at
the University at some years ago, following
a disagreement with a colleague as to who
should have pre-eminence; the Professor of
Greek Poetry, or the Professor of Astronomical
Science. Lamartine himself, though a leading
member of the department of physics, with an
international reputation in that field, held that
the classical scholar should precede the scientist, as the art of poetry had preceded the science of astronomy in the history of ideas.

However, there were those within the Regents of the University who disagreed with Lamartine, and he with them, to such a degree of violence that he was forced to step down from his post, and conduct such researches as he pleased as a private individual, while retaining the title of "Professor", to which, some who were opposed to him argued, he was not fully entitled as no longer being connected with the University.

I might add that this release from Academia was not a particularly onerous restriction upon him, financially or in any other way. Lamartine had married a wealthy woman, and her family's wealth would have enabled him to live on a luxurious scale, should he have a wish to do so. As it happened, his cupidity was directed only towards knowledge, and the money that might have been spent on frivolous gewgaws and knick-knacks was instead spent on mysterious apparatuses and the materials needed to construct them, as well as the generous salaries with which he rewarded his loyal assistants.

The house which contained his laboratories was a large one, and had formerly been the family residence of his wife's family. He now occupied it through right of inheritance, and, standing in its own extensive grounds, it was perfectly located as regards his neighbours, who were seldom inconvenienced by the noises, fumes, and occasional small explosions that proceeded from the rear outbuildings where the practical portions of the experiments took place.

I had come to know Professor Lamartine through our mutual membership of a musical society, which sold subscriptions to concerts. I had myself subscribed, as one of the promised concerts was to give us Johann Sebastian Bach's Goldberg Variations, which comprise some of my favourite pieces of music. At the concert, which took place about a year before the events related in this story, I discovered myself seated next to a man of advanced middle age, with a shock of black wiry hair, and a short beard, clad in evening dress which showed that the wearer had enjoyed many dinners in it, if the stains thereupon were any guide.

To my astonishment, before the recital started, my neighbour produced a large pad of artist's sketching paper and a roll of coloured pencils. As the music started, he began drawing, and my astonishment increased when I saw he was producing a visual representation of the themes and development of the variations, from the first Air, through the Variations, to the final

Quodlibet and the reprise of the Air. All this was done almost as a mathematical graph, but one which acted as a perfect guide to the music.

Though what he had produced was far from being standard musical notation, and a musician would be unable to play the exact notes from his drawing, what I beheld on the paper, to my mind, completely captured the complexity of Bach's thoughts as expressed in the music.

I said as much to my companion, and he appeared pleased.

"You think so? Well, I am glad to hear you say that. This is an idea that came to me only this morning, and I fear it needs more thought and rigour before I can call myself pleased with it. However, not a bad start, though I say it myself. I am pleased to discover that you appreciate the theory behind the imperfect practice. Maybe you will join me at my club for a drink after this concert?"

I was later to discover that this was a typical utterance of Lamartine. Whatever work he was engaged upon never seemed to be exactly as he wanted it to be. His mind built up the most elaborate edifices, many of which were doomed to failure even before the first attempt was made to put them into practice, and many more of which had to be abandoned part-way through their implementation. However, such failures were hardly ever the result of a lack of rigour or precision on the part of their inventor. Rather, the thoughts behind them were of so advanced and complex a nature that our present age lacks the means to put them into practice.

I have heard Lamartine expound for some time, for example, on the method by which men could be sent to the Moon, and then return. Every step of the process that he explained was perfectly sound, but with our present abilities in the field of manufacturing, for example, we could never produce the kind of machinery that he described.

"Nor is that all, my dear Gauthier," he added. "To reach the Moon, to land safely upon it, and then return to our Earth, requires the kind of calculations that would tax even the Analytical Engine designed by the Englishman Charles Babbage and never completed. Before we could even think of launching our craft into the æther, we would need reams of paper and forests of pencils to determine the exact date and time, to the very second, when the voyage should begin. And that process would have to be repeated for every significant event on the voyage. Some day, perhaps, a new Babbage will invent a machine that will perform these calculations."

"Not you?" I asked.

Lamartine shook his head. "The design and construction of such a machine, though complex, would be tedious in the extreme. It is a matter for a mechanic, or an engineer, not a scientist. Though I applaud Babbage's efforts, I cannot help but consider that his talents would have been better spent in another direction."

"So we will never reach the Moon because of our inability to perform the calculations that will take us there?"

"That is merely one of the factors which may impede our efforts. Another is the lack of suitable materials. Even my primitive calculations show that the steel we now use would be too heavy, and there is not enough aluminium in the world to construct such a vehicle. We must await the development of suitable metals. It is sad," he sighed. "When I was a lad, I had dreams that Man might fly to the Moon. Perhaps I would not be the very first, I felt, but I might be among the first men to travel to another world. But it is not to be. The task is too much for one man, and will require the resources of a whole government."

"And no government is interested in such a thing, of course."

Lamartine laughed bitterly. "They are interested in explosives and armour plate, faster ships, and longer ranges for their guns. If the Moon were a naval coaling station, our government, as well as those of the British and Germans, would be racing to get there. But as it is..." His voice tailed off and he took a sip of his cognac.

We held many conversations following the concert. He speedily discovered that I am a journalist, writing regularly for one of the more serious weekly magazines, and he was kind enough to act as my advisor when I was asked by my editors to write on scientific subjects. Not only did he most generously provide advice and knowledge, but his own researches often formed the centrepiece of my column, being as they were both bold and original.

On the occasion of which I am writing, I had been summoned by a telegram from Lamartine.

"Come at once. Astounding discovery. Lamartine." I showed this to my editor, old Simon, who audibly sniffed his scepticism, but allowed me to accept the invitation at the magazine's expense.

"The old boy" (old, indeed! Simon had ten years, if not more, on Lamartine) "has sometimes come through with the goods. I want seven hundred words off you by Tuesday, and this will do as well as anything, if there's any substance to it whatsoever. And no cab to the station. You can walk. It will be good for you." And this, mark you, coming from a man whose sole notion of exercise was standing up to light his cigar.

As I mentioned earlier, it was a fine day, and it was a positive pleasure for me to walk to the station. Little did I know what I would experience before I beheld the streets of Paris once more.

Chapter II

ON arrival at the suburban station serving the village in which Lamartine resided, I decided to walk to Lamartine's house, and on the way there, I purchased a bottle of Armagnac, of a brand to which I knew him to be particularly partial. My visits to Lamartine almost invariably included a meal prepared for me, and I felt it incumbent upon me to return the hospitality in some fashion. Sometimes this took the form of a box of cigars, a bouquet of flowers or box of chocolates for Mme. Lamartine, or on others, such as this, a small bottle of spirits. My gifts were always accepted, with protestations, but it seemed to me to be a poor return for the

Professor's generosity of time and spirit.

I was delighted to see Agathe, the Professor's daughter, walking in the garden as I approached the house. In her early twenties, she had inherited her mother's good looks, with fiery hair in which Titian would have gloried, and striking green eyes, rather than her father's slightly eccentric appearance, and it seemed to me that whenever I entered into conversation with her, that she had inherited many qualities of the scientific mind of the Professor, as she almost invariably referred to her father.

On several occasions, she had done me the favour of accompanying me to the theatre or to a restaurant, with the approval of her father, and though it would not be accurate to say that we had an understanding, there was something between us that went deeper than simple friendship. I doffed my hat and asked after her health and that of her mother before asking the whereabouts of her father.

"The Professor is round at the back. Shall I take you, or will you make your own way? I warn you, he's very excited about things. No, I can't spoil his fun and tell you what it's all about, because he has yet to inform even his own family of what he has been up to," she smiled after we had exchanged greetings. "I'll let him have the pleasure of telling you himself. But it's great news, he tells us."

Intrigued, I told her that I would find my own way to the Professor, and started around the house to the laboratories at the back. As I made my way, I was nearly knocked over by a small child, pedalling a tricycle as fast as her little legs would make the machine move.

"Hello, Marie," I said, recognising the infant as the child of the Lamartines' housekeeper. "That's a lovely tricycle," I told her, rubbing my bruised shin as I did so.

"The P'ofessor and Mrs P'ofessor gave it to me as a p'esent. Sorry about your leg," she lisped, pulling out a tiny handkerchief and gently rubbing my trouser leg with it.

"Thank you," I replied. "It's much better now. I'm just going to see the Professor."

"I shall take you there myself," she announced gravely, turning her vehicle as handily as an experienced coachman turns a carriage. She made her slow, dignified way beside me, acting as a kind of guard of honour as I reached the laboratories, which had formerly served the household as stables. "He's in there," she told me gravely, pointing to one of the doors.

"Thank you, Marie," I said to her, and knocked on the door.

"Enter!" came the familiar tones, and I opened the door to discover Lamartine sitting at a desk covered with papers, in their turn covered with his sprawling handwriting. "What kept you, Gauthier?" he demanded, hardly looking up from his work. "I telegraphed you over four hours ago."

I smiled to myself. This was typical of the man, who, while hospitable and considerate in most things, somehow seemed to be unable to grasp the concept that there were matters in the world which were of more importance to others than the affairs of Professor Rémy Lamartine.

"My dear sir," I gently reminded him, "it is not always as easy for me to make the journey to appreciate your discoveries, as it is for you to make the discoveries themselves."

He chuckled. "Very well, then. By the way, I see that you enjoyed little Marie's company on the way here. It is a joy to see her making her rounds, and acting as a guide for the benefit of my visitors."

"May I ask how your researches into the nature of the new gases are progressing?" When I had last visited Lamartine, he was engaged in the pursuit of knowledge regarding some of the rarer elements, such as helium and the recently discovered argon.

"I was hoping that these would combine with other elements to create valuable compounds, but so far, they have resisted my attempts at a forced marriage. No, the reason why I have called you here today is of far more interest and importance than a handful of exotic elements. I determined that you shall be the first to experience this new discovery at first hand. Come with me." He rose, and led the way through a door leading to the next room. "There, what do you make of that?" he declaimed with a flourish.

I gazed at the mechanism before me. Polished brass struts formed a framework supporting a labyrinth of glass tubing connected to shining metal vats, with dials and gauges which no doubt informed the cognoscenti of the status of the liquids or gases contained therein. Polished mahogany rails, at about waist height and supported on more brass rods, stood in the centre of this complex mass of piping, enclosing a horizontal square sheet of thick glass, about a metre on a side, and raised about thirty centimetres from the floor. On the side of the glass platform furthest from us I recognised some electrical apparatus, with Leyden jars and accumulator coils. Copper cables connected these to some of the vats. A white cloth covered a part of the machinery, and more cables led from under the cloth to the electrical part of the assembly. Everything seemed to be of the highest possible quality, as regards both materials and construction, and it was clear that much effort, not to mention considerable expense, had been spent on the construction of this thing, whatever it might be.

"I can make nothing of it," I confessed. "It is hardly one of those constructions where the function is determined by the form."

Lamartine laughed. "I would be amazed if you had been able to work out the purpose of this machinery from its appearance. Allow me to show you how it works." He reached in his pocket and pulled out a watch. "Observe the hour," he said, pointing to the hands of the timepiece.

"A little after three o'clock." I took out my own watch and regarded the face. "I have the same hour."

"Very good," he said. "Perhaps you would do the honours? Please place the watch in its proper location, which is the centre of the glass platform." I took the watch from his hand, and with some trepidation advanced towards the apparatus. "It is perfectly safe at the moment," the Professor called to me. "Simply place the watch, face-uppermost, in the centre of the glass. Excellent," he told me as I did so, and I stepped away. "I will now demonstrate to you the capabilities of this machine." He moved to the cloth-shrouded part of the machinery, and with the showmanship of a stage magician, removed the covering.

Beneath was a mass of controls, reminding me of the engine room of a large steamship. Dials, levers and knobs abounded, the purposes of which were a mystery to me. I expressed my wonderment.

"It may seem to be complex," Lamartine admitted, "but it is actually more simple than it appears. Here, you should wear these." He passed a pair of smoked glass goggles to me, donning a pair himself. "The machine also makes a loud noise when in action, so this may be of use," handing me a wad of cotton-wool. "Use this to block your ears. I trust you are now ready?"

He bent to the controls and made adjustments. A faint buzzing sound started, which grew in pitch and intensity until it became an almost unbearable high-pitched whine, despite the cotton-wool with which I had stuffed my ears.

"On the count of three," said Lamartine, grasping a large brass lever. "One ... Two ... Three ..." He pulled the lever, and there was a blinding flash of light, from which I turned away instinctively. The lightning was accompanied by a thunderous crash. "Look!" cried Lamartine, pointing to the apparatus. There was no trace of the watch on the glass plate. It had vanished from the spot where I had placed it!

Chapter III

"**Y**ou can hardly expect me to be astounded that it has gone," I said, removing the goggles, and pulling the cotton-wool from my ears, "after the noise and thunderstorm you have just created. It is probably in thousands of pieces by now, shivered by the shock of the blast."

Lamartine said nothing to me, but merely smiled.

"And," I added, "I am surprised that the neighbours have not made their feelings known to you if this is the nature of the experiments that you have been conducting." I confess to having been more than a little annoyed by the inconveniences to which I had just been subjected, and despite my respect for Lamartine and his knowledge and abilities, I could not help but show this irritation.

"I confess that their desire to expand the boundaries of knowledge is not as great as my own," he answered me. "However, on this occasion, the effect was considerably more violent than previously, and I anticipate the worst – at least, as regards the non-scientific aspects of the experiment."

As if to confirm his words, there was a knock on the laboratory door, and his daughter entered. "Excuse me, father, but Colonel Legrasse's butler has just called to express Mme. Legrasse's displeasure at the noise of the recent explosion."

"Please pass on my sincere apologies, and explain that I am otherwise engaged, and am therefore unable to express my regret in person. Oh, and," as Agathe turned to go, "ensure that Mme. Legrasse receives a bunch of the finest grapes from the hothouse."

"Very good."

"And the same goes for any other complaints," Lamartine called after her. "You may also add that I do not anticipate any more such disturbances today."

My ears were still ringing from the sudden

explosion, and black spots still danced before my eyes. "What was that?" I demanded of Professor Lamartine. "It sounded like a thunderbolt."

"That, my dear fellow, is precisely what it was. A large quantity of electrical force making its way through the atmosphere in the form of a spark, accompanied by the noise which appears to have irritated my neighbours. If it had come from the heavens, they would, I am sure, have raised no objection, but as it is, my production of a perfectly natural phenomenon appears to have caused them some distress."

"And the watch? What has happened to that?"

"That, Gauthier, requires some explanation. I trust that my little lightning bolt has not jarred your mental faculties?"

I shook my head.

"Good. Then let us go to the other room for," here he pulled out another watch from his waistcoat, "another fifty minutes or so. While we are gone, it may be as well to open the windows and release the smell of ozone."

"It is indeed rather strong," I agreed, assisting Lamartine to open the casements. Following this, he covered the controls once more with the cloth and led the way into the room where I had earlier encountered him.

When we were seated facing each other across the desk, he hospitably offered me a cigar, which I accepted with pleasure. "I do apologise to you for the inconvenience. To tell you the truth, I was more than a little startled myself," he added with a smile. "Though there is always something of a discharge on these occasions, today it was somewhat greater than usual."

"And what, precisely, are 'these occasions', if I may ask?"

"You may need your thinking cap here." His eyes twinkled as he took a blank sheet of paper, and a pencil, which he used to place an almost invisible dot in the centre of the paper. "What do we have here?"

"A dot."

"Let us rather refer to it as a Euclidean point. How many dimensions does a point possess?"

"Why, none, I suppose."

"You suppose correctly. Now look." He took up the pencil again and drew a line. "A Euclidean line. How many dimensions?"

"One."

"Imagine yourself to be a creature living in this universe, which consists only of this line. The concept of here," and he placed the pencil point on the paper, some one inch away from the line, "would be incomprehensible to you, would it not?"

I agreed, and he continued, drawing two more lines, connected to the first line and to each other, to form a triangle on the paper. "And here we have?"

"Two dimensions," I replied dutifully.

"Indeed so. Our little flatlander can move this way, and that way. And of course, we know these as the x and y axes of a graph. But here," and he waved the pencil above the paper, "is an area that is totally unknown to our little flatlander. He cannot conceive of it, any more than we can conceive of the fourth dimension."

"There are only three dimensions, are there not?"

"You see, my little flatlander, that you are indeed bounded by what you can perceive. But what I have been able to discover through the art of mathematics that there is indeed a fourth dimension, and most probably, though I have yet to confirm it with mathematical certainty, a fifth."

I puzzled over his words and, try as I might, I was unable to picture in my mind what manner of world could contain four dimensions, let alone five.

Lamartine observed my puzzlement and smiled. "We – that is to say – we poor flatlanders trapped in a world of three dimensions, find it hard, if not impossible, to imagine more. Our mistake comes in imagining that these extra dimensions are to be measured with rulers in metres and centimetres. We can, of course, imagine them to be similar to ours, but that is more a matter of convenience than an actual representation, just as this drawing here is a matter of convenience for our two-dimensional flatlanders." Here he sketched a perspective rendering of a cube.

I considered his words for a minute. "May I assume that I would not understand the mathematics that led you to this conclusion of there being more dimensions than the ones we perceive every day?"

"I think that is a very reasonable assumption indeed. I mean no disrespect to your mental faculties, or to your intellectual abilities, which are undoubtedly superior to those of the average blockhead calling himself a journalist, but I think it is fair for me to say that there are very few people in the world – perhaps only one or two – who would be capable of following my mathematical train of thought. If you wish, however, I will be happy to show you some of my working papers." He smiled, knowing what my answer would be.

"I am sure that these are beautiful, of their kind," I said, smiling in reply, "but their subtlety would be wasted on me. What, though, is the link between these extra dimensions and your thunder-machine in the next room?"

"It is considerably more than a 'thunder-machine'," he exclaimed, somewhat impatiently. "Believe me, if I wished to create a device which was no more than a producer of flashes and bangs, I am sure that I could do better than what is in the next room. No, what I have produced is the practical, tangible fruit of many hours of calculations, and it is nothing more or less than a gateway to the fourth dimension, and possibly to the fifth, and even possibly dimensions beyond that."

"You mean that the watch disappeared into the fourth dimension?" I asked incredulously.

"Yes, in exactly the same way that this pencil point disappears from Flatland when I lift it from the surface of the paper."

"So the watch is now in the fourth dimension?"

"And possibly the fifth and sixth as well," he added, smilingly. "Shall we return to the 'thunder-machine', as you were unkind enough to refer to it?" His tone, as well as his faint smile, persuaded me that he was not seriously annoyed by my describing his brainchild in such terms.

We rose, and made our way into the adjoining room. "Keep your eyes on the glass platform," Lamartine advised me. "If my calculations are correct, and if I adjusted the controls correctly, we should see a result in the next minute at the outside."

Indeed, he had hardly finished speaking before there was a soft "pop" sound, accompanied by a shimmer of light in the centre of the glass plate which lasted for less than a second. When the light had faded, the watch had appeared in the centre of the plate, as I had placed it there an hour earlier.

Chapter IV

"THE famous English magician Maskelyne would be proud of you," I said. "That is as neat a piece of conjuring as I have seen in a while." I spoke light-heartedly, but in this instance Lamartine chose to take my words seriously.

"This is no mere stage illusion," he said, with some heat. "It is the result of my researches into the very nature of the universe. What you have just beheld marks a new chapter in our understanding of the world which we inhabit."

"I apologise for my ill-timed jest," I said. "Believe me, I respect you too well to believe that you would ever resort to such trickery.

Perhaps you can explain to me in simple terms what has happened just now?”

“I accept your apology,” Lamartine answered, with some magnanimity. “I should have known better than to assume that your words were in earnest. I will do my best to explain what you have just witnessed, without resorting to mathematics, that is to say, as far as this is possible.

“To begin my explanation,” he continued, “do you remember that I told you that these new dimensions were not to be measured in metres and centimetres?”

“I do. In what should they be measured, then?”

“In seconds, minutes and hours.”

I considered this briefly. “You mean, then, that these new dimensions are time itself?”

“Yes, indeed. They are temporal, rather than spatial dimensions.”

“No wonder that I cannot imagine them, since they are invisible to me.”

“But you can see their effects, can you not? You are aware of the passage of time and of its effects, surely? And what I have done is to render these dimensions visible, or at least tangible, in such a way that we can move freely along them.”

“But how?”

"I can give you an analogy," Lamartine told me. "Let us return to Flatland, and its inhabitants. For our flatlander to travel from one side of his world to the other, he must traverse the width of the paper, must he not?"

"That much seems obvious."

"But what if the paper on which his world exists is folded in half? Then he is able to move directly from one side to the other."

"I begin to grasp your meaning."

"What I have done, I believe, is to bend or fold the fifth dimension so that the relations between the three spatial dimensions and time become flexible. I was able just now to manipulate that watch so that it moved forward in our time, while not moving in space, or its own time."

"What do you mean by 'its own time'?"

"Look at that watch, and tell me what time it shows."

I moved gingerly towards the glass slab on which the watch reposed.

"There is no need for any anxiety on your part," called out Lamartine. "I am hardly likely to set off the thunder and lightning while you are there."

I was somewhat reassured, and put out my

hand to touch the watch. "Why, it is cold," I exclaimed. And indeed it was; condensation, if not ice, was starting to form on the watch's surface, and the glass under it.

"Why, yes. I have observed such a phenomenon previously," answered Lamartine. "I am assuming that all the energy, including much of the heat, has been absorbed by the process. Now have the goodness to examine the time shown on the face."

I did so, and remarked with some surprise that the time appeared to have advanced by only a minute or so since I laid the watch on the glass an hour previously.

"But that is easily explained," I said. "The shock of the lightning and the thunder may well have stopped the mechanism."

"I doubt it very much," Lamartine told me. "Hold the watch to your ear."

I did so, and was amazed to hear it ticking. "Then the shock of its reappearance, however it was accomplished, was sufficient to restart it."

"My dear Gauthier, you must believe me when I say that watches and clocks do not conveniently start and stop in this fashion. I have carried out such a trial with a number of timepieces, including hourglasses, which are not susceptible to shock in the same way, and in every case, the setting of the timepiece is the same on its reappearance as it was when it disappeared. You must believe me on this."

"How many times have you performed this experiment, then?"

"This is my sixth attempt."

"And in every case, the timepiece has returned at the time you expected? That is to say, according to our time, since there seem to be two different times involved."

"Other than some initial slight inaccuracies in the settings of the machinery, which caused some slight discrepancies, that is so. In this last instance, I believe that there was a discrepancy of about thirty seconds in a total time of one hour. That is less than one per cent, and I am certain that this can be made more accurate as my trials progress."

My head was spinning with the implications of this. "I now believe that you have sent an object into the future," I said. "But could you send such an object into the past in the same way?"

"I have successfully done so," he told me. "I have observed an hourglass appear on this glass platform, taken it off the machine, and an hour or so later, sent it back into the past at the time when I saw it appear."

I considered this. "You are telling me that an hourglass that you had never seen before appeared on the plate, you then sent it back into the past, and you never saw it again? And you are sure that it was the same hourglass?"

"That is all perfectly correct."

My head was spinning. "What was the initial source of this hourglass? Had you seen it before? I do not see how it can ever have existed, given that you no longer possess it, and you had never seen it before its miraculous appearance. I fail to understand this puzzle."

"Aha! I knew I had invited the right man to share my discovery," he exclaimed. "You have put your finger on the very point that has been puzzling me also. Where did this object appear from? How was it created, and what existence does it have outside the dimensions that I have discovered?"

"You cannot explain this in terms of the Flatland paper?"

"Try as I will, I find it impossible to fold the paper of Flatland in such a way as to provide an explanation. Only by piercing the paper with the pencil can I come close to an analogy."

I shuddered. "If you are indeed piercing holes

in time by sending things into the past, I have many concerns regarding the results of such actions."

"I, too," he confessed. "I have only set the controls to the past that one time, being fearful of any future outcome. However, I am hopeful that this can be overcome as I come to a fuller understanding of the nature of the problem."

"Do you intend to go further into the mathematics to discover the answer?" I asked. "Or to seek help from another?"

"There is no-one in this country who would be able to assist me," he answered. "There are, perhaps, a few in Germany who might understand a little of my methods, but I am unwilling to share my work at this stage. No, there is only one way in which I feel that I can understand it fully. My researches so far seem to indicate that living matter will behave in a different fashion to mere dumb inanimate matter. According to all that I can predict, the vital protoplasm that gives us life, and the spark of consciousness that ignites us, seem to be factors that will influence the way in which the new dimensions operate. Consider for yourself how time seems to pass. Sometimes quickly, sometimes slowly."

A dreadful suspicion came over me. "I think

I know what you are proposing. I believe that you wish a human being to take the path that the watches and hourglass have taken before."

"Indeed so. I am prepared to become the first chrononaut in history, sailing into the unknown seas of time."

"It is a risk you should not take alone!" I exclaimed. "If any accident were to befall you in that mysterious dimension, then there would be no help for you."

"Precisely so," he replied, with a sardonic smile. "This is one of the reasons why I invited you here today. When I make my first voyage into the unknown dimensions, I will have a companion by my side. A companion I can trust – that is to say, you, my friend!"

Chapter V

Y OU may imagine my astonishment when I heard these words. As a journalist, I had sometimes found myself in strange situations, which at times had placed me in some danger, but never had I expected to encounter anything of this nature.

"Surely," I stammered, "there must be another whom you can trust to accompany you? One of your assistants, for example, with a knowledge of science and your work that are infinitely superior to mine."

"You surely are not afraid?" Lamartine rebuked me.

"I am more than a little concerned about

various matters," I told him. "For example, who will operate the controls when we set off on our travels through time? Who will determine where and when we will exit your new dimensions?"

"Why, no-one will operate the controls." He smiled enigmatically, and stroked his short black beard while waiting for my response to his pronouncement.

"So you are proposing that we wander through the unknown world without any control over our destination?"

"By no means. Allow me to explain. An inanimate object, such as the watch that you have just seen, requires its time and place to be set with the control panel. It is unable to make decisions of its own."

"That much is obvious."

"But where does it go when we no longer see it? It is axiomatic, is it not, that matter can neither be created nor destroyed?"

"Very true."

"I believe that it passes into what I call the 'Untime' – that is to say, a state in which neither time nor space have any meaning in the everyday accepted sense. It is a state which is unimaginable to us."

"And yet you have imagined it?"

"I have done more than imagine it, my dear Gauthier. I have proved it mathematically."

I laughed. "I suppose I must take your word for it. You know well that I am unable to follow your steps in your dance through the abstract world of mathematics. But you have proved it, you say? You are certain of this?"

"As certain as I am of any scientific theory," he told me, with great conviction ringing in his voice.

"And you can assure me that there is no danger?"

"I can assure you of no such thing. What I am offering you, as a man and as a journalist, is a unique opportunity to be the first to experience a completely new world. Of course there is danger! What would life be without it?"

"I must consider this," I said. "If I venture into the Apache districts of Paris, or if I fly in a balloon, or attend Army manoeuvres, there is danger. But these are known dangers. I may assess them and provide against them in a way that removes the risk from my actions. But here? You are asking me to place my head in the cage of an animal of unknown temperament. I do not know if I will be embraced or decapitated.

Give me time, Professor."

"A day at most," he replied brusquely. "There are others who might not be as cautious, shall I say, as you. There is Daniel from *Le Monde*, for example."

"That scribbler!" I exclaimed. "All he is good for is the reports of the police-courts. Why, the man has all the poetry of a German sausage."

"Or," he continued, ignoring my outburst, "perhaps I might invite Rousseau from *Le Figaro* to accompany me."

"You cannot be serious," I told him. "Rousseau perhaps has imagination, and I confess that he possesses a certain literary style, but he is a raging Socialist. Who knows what kind of complexion he might place on your Untime and his experiences?"

"Who indeed?" replied Lamartine calmly.

"Damn you, Lamartine!" I cried. "You have decided me. I am not prepared to let such rascals as Daniel or Rousseau to introduce your work to the world. I am your man, Professor." He extended his hand to me, and I clasped it warmly.

"I knew I could depend on your friendship," he told me. His smile by now was no longer secretive, but instead betokened a genuine pleasure.

"When do you wish to start?"

"There is no time like the present," he retorted smartly. "We can start at once."

Once again, I was taken aback by the sudden nature of Lamartine's demands.

"At least give me time to prepare my last will and testament," I said to him.

Lamartine laughed in my face. "By all means, my dear fellow," he answered me. "Though I confess to being somewhat offended by your lack of faith in my calculations, which assure me that such a precaution is completely unnecessary."

"Nonetheless," I retorted in as firm a tone as I was able, "I would welcome the opportunity to set my affairs in order. It is high time that I did so, in any case."

"Very well, since it seems to be of some concern to you. Here is a pen and paper. Shall I call in my daughter to witness the document along with myself?"

This was an eventuality that had not occurred to me, and I had no wish for Agathe to be aware of my lack of faith in her father's abilities. "Maybe, on second thoughts, I will put my trust in your calculations," I told Lamartine.

"Then let us make preparations," he said. "If you do not wish to be frozen on your return, as was the watch, I advise you remove all metal from your person. Your watch, keys, coins, and the like."

"My waistcoat has brass buttons," I told him.

"Off with it, then. The risk of carrying any metal on your person is too great, not only on account of the extreme cold, but of other matters connected with the electric fields."

On searching my pockets for other metallic objects, I came across the half-bottle of Armagnac that I had purchased earlier as a gift for the Professor, and held it out to him.

"Excellent," he said, inspecting the label. "You came well-prepared, I see. Remove the foil covering the cork, and we can then take this with us. Where would we Frenchmen be without this nectar of the gods, eh?"

While he was thus talking, he was divesting himself of his braces, his belt, and his boots, having first emptied his pockets of their contents. When I questioned the boots, he pointed to the hobnails on the soles. My shoes, however, were of the newer, rubber-soled type, and contained no metal as part of their construction.

"Do not expect to be comfortable," he warned

me. "I would remove your cravat and collar," taking his own advice as he spoke. "I do not anticipate pain, but we may suffer some discomfort. But we will never know until we experience it, will we?" His eyes sparkled, and there was a joy in his voice like that of a schoolboy who is about to start exploring a forbidden attic rumoured to be full of mysterious treasures.

At length we were both satisfied that we were free of any metallic encumbrances, and in our shirt-sleeves made our way to the other room, where the mysterious apparatus stood, gleaming in the rays of the setting sun.

I remembered Lamartine's earlier words. "You promised that there would be no further explosions tonight, when you talked to your daughter earlier."

"Why, so I did," he replied. "And I intend to keep that promise. You and I are free agents, with our own sources of energy – our bodies – are we not? Unlike the watch, which required a powerful external stimulus to take it into the unknown dimensions, we will travel there largely under our own power, aided by the peculiar conditions provided by my machine."

"So the smoked glasses and cotton-wool are not needed this time?"

"You may wear the glasses if you like – they contain no metal parts – but I am sure they will prove unnecessary. The cotton-wool may well serve to protect our ears from the noise of the gas in the pipes, though."

He darted to the control panel. "Stand on the glass platform. It will certainly bear your weight, Gauthier. There is no call for you to appear so dubious. Ensure that you leave enough room for me to stand beside you." He turned controls and moved levels. "Thirty seconds from now," he said calmly, stepping away from the panel and joining me on the platform.

That half minute was the longest of my life.

Chapter VI

During the thirty seconds that Lamartine had allotted for the apparatus to become active, I hardly dared breathe, as the noise once again rose to an ear-splitting whine. I noted the exact hour displayed by the clock on the wall. Beside me, Lamartine was coolly counting to himself, "Twenty-eight, twenty-nine, thirty—"

And as he reached the final figure, a dramatic change took place.

I may say, with all due modesty, that I am accounted as one of the better writers for the Paris journals, and I have indeed been praised for my powers of description. However, what I encountered on this occasion would have

defeated a Balzac or a Victor Hugo, let alone a
mere journalist.

I will try to give you some account of what
Lamartine and I experienced, but I fear that it
will fall short of the reality.

My first impression was that my body had
disappeared, and I was pure mind, such as one
sometimes experiences in a dreaming state.
Naturally, the sudden way in which this had
occurred caused me to cry out, but again, as in
a dream, my cries were inaudible.

Also, even though I had the sensation of being
incorporeal, I had a strong sensation of choking, and extreme heat, which caused me to cry
out inaudibly once more. The overall impression was one of terror and panic, but this did
not last for long, and I was left in a state of calm.

Somehow, though I was still unconscious
of my body, I was aware, as I had never been
before, of my location. Not only my location
on the platform, or in Lamartine's laboratory,
or even in France, but in relation to the whole
of the Universe, absurd as it might seem. Not
only that, but all parts of the Universe seemed
equally close, or equally distant. A single step
(as it were) might take me to the furthest stars,
or to the next room. It was a dizzying prospect,

and it seems to be insanity when I write it in this way. How, you ask me, could I choose whether to visit Orion or Orleans? The Milky Way or the Parc Monceau? The answer is simply that I could make my choice, with ease. I knew with certainty where I was and how I could transport myself elsewhere.

And this, mark you, without my being able to see anything. If I was conscious of anything at all in my vision, it was of a pale green glow, almost uniform, and surrounding me on all sides. I could not tell from where the glow proceeded, or on what it was shining to produce the slight variations in intensity.

As I mentally explored the whole of the Universe, sending my mind this way and that, from the Chamber of Deputies in Paris to a planet in a nearby galaxy inhabited by strange tripod-like creatures resembling three-legged cockroaches more than anything else, I became aware of something else about my surroundings which was, if possible, even stranger than my omnipresence. I was now out of the flow of Time. Time passed me by in the same way that a locomotive passes a passenger waiting on a station platform. The passenger knows full well the nature of a train. He may board it if he chooses. But if he does not choose, he may stand and watch the magnificent machine sweep past him.

Can you conceive of a world without Time? And I begin the word with a capital letter to impress upon you the majestic ineffable nature of the concept. Throughout our lives, we are conscious of the passage of this invisible, intangible force, but we never trap it, or even begin to slow it, and it resists all our efforts to master it. Even in our dreams, we are aware of its presence.

To be free of Time! Can you imagine the sensation? It is almost impossible to describe in words what I felt when I realised that I was Time's master, rather than the other way around. I was suddenly free of the dictator that had oppressed me all my life, and now it was I, Jules Gauthier, who was in control, with an almost god-like power over this most puissant of forces.

Just as I was aware of exactly where I was, I was also aware of when I was. I knew, with the same certainty that told me I could step onto the surface of Pluto, that I could move myself into next week, next year, next century, even. For just an instant, I was tempted to take myself into the land of the Hottentots, at a time two hundred years hence, merely on a whim.

To be master of space and Time! I luxuriated

in the moment. Of course, you will say, since I was experiencing no such thing as Time, there could be no moment in which I could luxuriate. Very well, then, I luxuriated.

But what of Lamartine? Where was he? Though I might be outside the reach of Time, memory still had its hold over me, and I remembered that I had arrived in my present state with a companion. As I had discovered earlier, I was mute, and therefore shouting for Lamartine would be a waste of time and energy. Nor, being effectively earless, would it aid me to listen for sounds of the Professor.

Nonetheless, I adopted a state which might be termed as "listening", and to my relief, I could discern a faint mumbling which, though the words were indistinct, still carried something of my companion's mode of speech. I knew it was useless for me to consider shouting, but I forced my mind to send out a telegraphic signal, as it were, informing my companion of my presence.

To my intense relief, I received what could only be an answer.

"I ... here ..." I perceived.

I continued to send my mental beacon out into the void, and was rewarded by the sensation of

Lamartine's voice, with its distinctive timbre, sounding clearly in my ear.

"Well?"

"It is ... awe-inspiring," I replied. You must imagine this conversation as taking place without voices, and possibly even without words. However, there was no lack of clarity in our communications.

"Where shall we go? I have a fancy to observe our legislators in the Chamber of Deputies," he said to me.

"Very well. At the present time?"

"I think that would be best," he agreed. "For this first journey in the Untime, maybe we would do well to limit ourselves."

Accordingly we stepped (if the action we undertook may be so described) into the Chamber of Deputies in Paris, where we were located at the rear of the chamber behind the seats of the Deputies. The mist that surrounded us thinned, so that we were observing the proceedings through a thin greenish haze. I wished to see more clearly, and prepared to leave the mist, but was interrupted in my intention by Professor Lamartine's thoughts.

"Once you leave the Untime, how will you ever return into it?" he asked me, and the question was a good one. I therefore restrained myself, and observed the Deputies at their work, if so it may be termed.

Some were asleep, some were unobtrusively buried in the perusal of documents that appeared to be closer to sporting journals than papers of state. A few appeared to be alert, and listening to the Deputy at the front, who was facing slightly to our left as he addressed the Chamber.

As we watched and listened, the speaker turned slowly in our direction to face us. A look of horror came over his face, and his words came more slowly, until he eventually ceased to speak, and his face turned pale.

Several of the Deputies (those who appeared to be awake, at any event) turned to follow his slack-mouthed gaze, but even though they were looking directly at us, appeared not to perceive us.

Beside me, I had the sensation of Lamartine chuckling. "Ha! The fools!" he exclaimed. "Let us see." Immediately he had spoken, a small ball of rolled-up paper shot from where I perceived the Professor to be located, and struck one of the Deputies on the forehead. The poor man gave a cry of surprise. Since he could see

no-one ahead of him who could have thrown
the paper at him, his shock at the assault was
perfectly understandable.

CHAPTER VII

"**D**ID you do that?" I asked Lamartine, scarcely able to believe what had just happened. "Was it you who threw the paper just now?"

"It was indeed," he answered me. The chuckle had not yet left his voice. "And so is this," he added, as another ball of paper seemed to leave our misty envelope and struck another sleeping Deputy behind the ear. This last woke up with a start, and glared furiously around him before standing up and stamping noisily out of the Chamber, shouting loudly that he would have his revenge on those who dared disturb the sanctity of the Chamber.

I could hardly credit my senses. Lamartine, though no longer teaching at the University, was regarded as one of the foremost men of science of the country, and he was behaving like a child, flicking inkblots around the classroom.

"You should not be doing this," I thought to him. "This is unworthy of you and your position in the world of science."

"Why not? It amuses me," he answered me, and a third ball of paper made its way into the midst of our legislators. This time, its destination was not a human being, but an inkwell being used by one of the Deputies, who was writing what appeared to be a very unofficial document on pink notepaper. The ink splashed over the apparent billet-doux, and onto the cuff of the indignant Deputy, who turned behind him to discover the source of the missile, only to find all other heads in the Chamber turned in our direction.

I noticed that several of those on our left (that is to say, to the right of the political field) were crossing themselves and muttering, presumably prayers to protect them from the invisible presences that were tormenting them.

"You should stop this," I told Lamartine, as severely as I dared. "These are schoolboy antics.”

“Maybe I will cease now,” he said, but it appeared to me to be with some reluctance. “You must admit, however, that they are Where shall we turn to next?”

“Perhaps the British House of Lords?” I suggested. “Surely they will have more dignity than our Deputies, with the weight of centuries behind them.”

Accordingly, we moved, and were observing the crimson benches of the Mother of Parliaments through the green mist. I say we were observing the benches, as the place was nearly empty. In addition to the Lord Chancellor, who presides over the House, a total of three of the noble lords graced the hall with their presence. One was speaking, but due to his age, and the apparent loss of his teeth, his words were so indistinct that it was impossible for me to distinguish what he was saying, though my abilities in English are generally considered to be above the average.

The other two peers were snoring softly, oblivious to him, and seemingly to everything else around them.

“Have you seen enough?” Lamartine asked me, and there appeared to be a little mockery in his words.

"I have seen enough," I said, more than somewhat disappointed by what I had just seen. "Maybe it is now time to leave the Untime."

" 'Time to leave the Untime,' you say? I hope you are well aware of the irony in your words," he answered. "Very well. We have made two successful excursions into space, have we not? What say you to a little excursion in time?"

I confess that this idea was a little disturbing to me, and I told him so.

"Nonsense, man!" he rebuked me. "As you can perceive for yourself, in the Untime, Time itself is merely another dimension – one which we may bend at will, or even ignore at our leisure, should we so desire."

"Then let us take a short journey only," I said. "Let us return to your laboratory an hour's time from when we started."

"I agree with the time, but let us deposit ourselves outside my front gate," suggested Lamartine. "Are you confident of your ability to do so?"

"As sure as I am of anything in my life."

"Very well, then. On the count of three. One ... two ... three ..."

I took my incorporeal steps in time and space

and found myself tumbled on the grass verge outside the gates of Lamartine's house. The sun was considerably lower in the sky than at the time of our "departure" – indeed, it had almost set. I was clad in shirtsleeves, but it was not on account of that, I was sure, that my teeth were chattering with cold. Professor Lamartine was beside me, and it was clear that he, too, was suffering in the same way as was I.

He looked over to me and extended his hand, which I grasped with some affection and not a little relief. "My heartiest congratulations, my brave fellow chrononaut!" he exclaimed. "My God, I am cold! Do you have the brandy with you still?"

I reached in my pocket and produced the bottle, withdrawing the cork before handing it to him.

"Here's to Time! Here's to Untime! Here's to you! Here's to me! Here's to us!" he exclaimed. He took a long pull at the bottle and sighed deeply. "Many thanks, my faithful friend." He took another drink before passing the bottle back to me. I drank in my turn, and felt the fiery liquid burn its way down my throat. Now the burden of Time was laid upon me once more, I felt much as does a swimmer who has emerged from the water and feels the earth's pull again.

"Well?" he said, lying on the grassy bank, propped up on his elbows.

I adopted the same posture, regardless of the sight we would present to any passers-by; two middle-aged gentlemen of somewhat full habit, dressed in their shirtsleeves, and lying by the side of the road.

"It is an amazing sensation, to be sure. Almost god-like."

"God-like, yes. Indeed, god-like," mused the Professor, his eyes half-closed.

CHAPTER VIII

WHEN I heard these words, and looked at his face, I feared for my friend's state of mind. An almost idiotic grin of infantile pleasure seemed to possess him, and his hands twitched almost feverishly, as he repeated the phrase "god-like" to himself over and over again. Possibly, I told myself, the Armagnac had proved to be too much for his system, following the extraordinary experience which we had just undergone.

"Come," I said, and helped him to his feet. "We are neither of us decently attired, and I, for my part, am still cold, despite the brandy."

"Very well," he answered. "God-like," he

muttered once again, and then to me, "Do you now understand the concept of eternity?"

I considered for a moment. "Is that what we experienced?"

"Can you think of a better term to describe it? Or perhaps you did not perceive it in the same way as did I. What exactly did you experience?"

I told him, as best I could, in somewhat halting language, the sensations I had felt throughout the time I had spent in the mysterious dimensions. As I spoke, Lamartine nodded in confirmation at each point.

When I had finished, he burst out with, "You and I, my dear friend, are the only ones who know of this. Let us keep it so at present. Later the world must know of this – the world will know of this," he repeated with some ferocity and a glint in his eyes. "But the time is not yet ripe. I must ask you to say nothing of this to anyone else as yet, and certainly you must refrain from giving any details of any of this in your magazine."

"Old Simon will believe I have come on a wild-goose chase, then," I smiled.

"Oh, pah! I can present you with some discovery or other that will make it worth your editor's while to have sent you here," he said.

"An improved diving-apparatus, for example? I recently perfected such a one, which the British Admiralty is currently inspecting. Our own Navy dismissed it as unworthy of their attention, the fools."

"That will do very well. But what do you propose doing about the Untime, as you call it, that we have just experienced?"

"Why, to refine it and to make practical use of it, of course. Do you not see that the man who harnesses these dimensions will have a place in history that will rival the great Alexander, or Julius Caesar, or even our own Napoleon, our mighty Emperor?"

"And you intend to be that man?" I asked. I was now somewhat concerned that the recent exposure to these new dimensions had turned my friend's wits. He had never talked in the past using such a tone, or expressed such ambitions.

"Why should it not be me? You have just seen the fools we and others elect now to govern us. You must surely admit that my intelligence exceeds theirs by a considerable amount."

"I agree, but—"

"The sooner that France is ruled by a man of true intellect, the better the world will be. France will take her place as the mistress of the civilised world, and the man who rules France will perforce rule the world."

His words sent a chill down my spine. Despite all my respect for Lamartine and his scientific ability, I could hardly conceive of him as the supreme leader of the planet. "Come," I said to him, "I will take you to the house, and then I must return to Paris."

"No, no, I will not hear of it," he said. "You must stay to dinner. There will be champagne to celebrate our success."

I was actually happier to hear that I was invited to dinner than to consider leaving the Professor in this state. I was unsure how I was going to explain his mental state to Mme. Lamartine, but I was saved that task when we were informed by the maid that she had retired to bed with a headache. I retrieved my waistcoat and other garments and impedimenta from the laboratory, and made my toilet before meeting the Professor in the dining-room. Agathe was attending her mother, and did not join us.

Dinner, with the promised champagne, proceeded calmly enough. Lamartine seemed to have put his dreams of glory on one side, though I detected something in his eye that was not usually a part of his character and gave me pause for thought.

At the end of the meal we sat with our brandy (the remains of the same Armagnac that I had brought with me and which had restored us after our journey into the Untime) and cigars, and discoursed on general matters. By unspoken consent, it seemed that we were not to discuss the events of the day. However, when I stood up to take my leave of my host, he placed his hands on my shoulders and gazed earnestly into my face.

"I will remind you, my friend, that what you have seen today and what you have experienced is unique. Only one other in this world has undergone such a revelation – that is to say, me. I want you to swear, on your honour as a Frenchman and as a gentleman, that you will not reveal what has happened today without my express permission. May I have your word on this?"

Naturally, in my profession as a journalist, I was accustomed to keeping secrets. Such a request was hardly unknown to me. And yet, given the momentous nature of the Professor's discovery, and his extraordinary state of mind, there was something about this demand that made it unique. The hesitation in my acquiescence was visible, and a look of anger, almost of rage, swept across my companion's face.

"If you cannot give me your word on this, I will be forced to take some kind of appropriate action," he said. The smile which accompanied these words was no doubt intended to reassure me that they were intended in jest, but the tone of voice in which they were uttered gave the lie to this.

"Of course I will give you my word," I answered him. I thereupon swore a solemn oath to him that I would not reveal his secrets.

"Excellent, excellent," he smiled at me. "You relieve my mind mightily. I will send you the details of the diving-apparatus tomorrow by post. I think that this will satisfy your editor, will it not?"

"It will, indeed," I assured him, and made my way from his house to the railway station, where I took the slow train back to Paris. The journey gave me ample time to reflect on the events of the day, and on the strange behaviour of my friend the Professor. I had never beheld him in such a secretive mood in the past. Typically, he was only too eager to share his new discoveries with the world, and I could only ascribe the strangeness of his behaviour to the extraordinary events of the day. But his strange and unaccustomed mood was nothing when compared to the turmoil in which I found my own mind. How could I start to describe the feeling of omnipotence that I had sensed while in the Untime discovered by Lamartine? However ineffable the experience, it was one that I found myself anxious to experience once again. The sense of timelessness that I had experienced there was likewise one for which I entertained a fond memory. In the same way that some drugs reportedly take hold of their users, these feelings gave me the strongest desire to repeat them at the earliest possible opportunity. I hasten to add that I had no desire to use these immense powers for my own personal gain or aggrandisement, as it appeared did Lamartine, but the temptation to explore worlds and times which were otherwise unreachable was one which nagged powerfully at my curiosity.

When I at last reached my apartment and took myself to bed, it was a long time before I was able to fall asleep. The words that Lamartine had spoken to me kept going through my head. I could only hope that they were the effects of a temporary delirium caused by the strange journey that we had undertaken. Although I was in agreement with him that the government of the day was in need of improvement, I was far from being convinced that Professor Lamartine was the man who would constitute a suitable replacement.

I could not rid myself of the memories of the timeless state in which I had found myself, and the immense powers which had been bestowed on those who entered the Untime. These powers, should they be exercised inappropriately, would surely cause havoc of the worst kind. At length, I fell into a deep sleep from which I woke almost a full twenty-four hours later.

Chapter IX

I AWOKE, refreshed in body and mind, some twenty hours after I had retired. My sleep had been deep and dreamless, and I was somewhat chagrined to discover that my alarm clock had rung, and I had been unconscious of its call. Obviously I had missed a day at the office of the magazine, but I proposed to inform my editor that I had suffered from a sudden summer chill, which had prevented me from attending to my duties.

On checking my post, I found that Professor Lamartine had been as good as his word, and had dispatched a sheaf of documents related to his diving-apparatus. I determined to produce

an article for the magazine, which would explain
the advantages of this new invention, and also
provide me with the pleasure of castigating our
government for their stupidity in ignoring its
merits, and allowing the British to take advantage of them.

To create such an article was the work of a few
hours only, and I hoped that it would soften the
heart of old Simon when I went into the office
the next day.

When I finished my labours, my stomach
reminded me that I had not attended to the
inner man for some time, and I took myself to
a restaurant. To my surprise, I recognised the
familiar face of Agathe Lamartine, who was eat-
ing her meal alone at the next table. At the same
time that I saw her, she appeared to notice me,
and hailed me with some relief.

"Will you do me the honour of joining me at
my table?" she requested.

"I would be delighted," I replied. I am by
nature somewhat gregarious, and it gives me no
joy to eat my meals in solitary splendour. It was
a pleasure for me to share my meal with this
charming young lady.

As I raised my glass in salute, I noted that her
usually cheerful face had taken on a serious

aspect, and I felt compelled to ask if anything was amiss.

"Why, yes. The Professor is far from being his usual self, and I confess that I came to Paris – to this very restaurant – on the off-chance of finding you here, to discuss the matter. I knew that you lived in this district, but I do not know the exact address, and had heard from the Professor that you and he had sometimes taken meals at this establishment. I confess that I had few expectations of my expedition's success, and it must appear to be very shameless of me, I admit, but my little adventure seems to have borne the fruit I had hoped for."

"Well, you have found me," I smiled. "But please tell me more of your concerns regarding your father."

"I have never before seen him in such a state," she told me. "Today he appeared to be a madman, unable to control his emotions. In the space of only a few minutes he seemed to move from a state of extreme depression to one of wild elation."

"What were the subjects of his conversation?"

"That is the other extraordinary thing. You know that the Professor has never displayed a keen interest in the political world in the past.

But this morning, he read the political news in three newspapers as soon as they were delivered. I have never seen him do such a thing before."

I laughed, though inwardly I was concerned at hearing this news. "Then you need look no further for the cause of his depression," I said. "The news from our politicians is enough to make one laugh and weep by turns."

"There is some truth in what you say," she admitted, "but there is more to it than that. Have you ever heard my father discuss economic theory?"

I shook my head. "No, never."

"And yet this morning he talked of little else other than bimetallism, a topic about which I know little, and have no wish to learn more."

I agreed. "It is strange for him to discuss such matters."

"May I ask what transpired yesterday in the laboratory? When I ask the Professor, he refuses to answer my questions on the matter."

"I fear that I am unable to tell you. My lips are sealed by oath."

A pretty little moue came to her face as she heard my words. "I was hoping that you would satisfy my curiosity on the matter. Perhaps you may at the least inform me whether the explosion yesterday that has disturbed his wits?"

"I do not think so." A thought struck me. "You say that the Professor has been like this since the morning. Do you happen to know at what time he arose?"

"For all I know, he never went to bed last night. At any event, when I arose a little before six this morning, he was awake and had obviously been in the laboratory for some time," was the astounding answer. Astounding to me, since I had felt fatigued since our little adventure, and I had just slept soundly and without dreaming for a full twenty hours.

"Then it is no doubt a lack of sleep which has caused these mental aberrations," I said. "Tomorrow will no doubt see him returned to his normal self after he has rested."

"There is more, though," Agathe told me with a note of concern in her voice. "I noticed yesterday that you were greeted by our little pet, Marie."

I smiled at the memory. "Indeed I was, and my shin still remembers it. What of her?"

"Of course, the Professor has acknowledged her existence in the past. Indeed, it is he and my mother who presented her with her tricycle.

But today, in the intervals between his almost compulsive new-found interest – one might almost say obsession – with political affairs, I observed him staring fixedly at the little mite, who was on the other side of the garden. If this had happened just once, I would have said that he was in a brown study, and was merely refreshing his mind. However, this occurred on at least five occasions that I noted, and only in connection with little Marie. On at least three of these occasions, he was taking notes, which appeared to be of a mathematical nature. I was unable to see any details."

"I am sure that there is some perfectly natural explanation for all of these things," I said, though I was far from convinced of the truth of my own statement. "Though I cannot give you all the details, I am able to tell you that what took place yesterday was physically demanding, and also was a sore trial to the spirit. Indeed, I myself have only just awakened from a sleep of some twenty hours," I confessed.

This produced a charming little smile, which I confess that I found so attractive that I covered her hand with my own. She did not seem to object to its presence, but suffered my hand to remain there. "You say that you have slept for twenty hours? I take it this is somewhat unusual?" she smiled.

"I have no recollection of its ever having happened previously," I replied. "Eight hours is typically the maximum length of time I spend asleep."

"And yet the Professor would seem to have slept very little, if at all," she mused. "You yourself have not experienced any fascination with previously unremarked subjects?"

"I think not. I can tell you that between my awakening some hours ago and my coming here I have been engaged on the production of an article related to the improved Lamartine diving-apparatus, the details of which he was good enough to send me, and which were delivered to me while I slept."

"Ah, that diving-apparatus," she smiled. "Perhaps that has put him in mind of the politicians, causing his sudden interest in that direction. Did he tell you that those fools at the Hôtel de Brienne had rejected his invention? He is now in communication with the British, much to his disgust."

"Yes, he informed me of that, and I am about to lash and lacerate those responsible in my column, you will be pleased to hear. Maybe you

are correct as regards the source of the interest
in politics."

"It does not explain differences between my
sleeping habits and his, or the interest in the
little girl, though."

"Indeed it does not."

"But let us talk of more cheerful things," she
suggested, and the conversation passed to the
opera, a diversion for which we both shared a
passion.

Chapter X

O^N my return to my apartment after escorting Agathe Lamartine to the station where she was to catch the train to her home, I pondered the matters we had discussed. I had not, for obvious reasons, informed her of her father's strange words and behaviour immediately following our sojourn in the Untime. It was strange, to my mind, that I had sunk exhausted into a long slumber, while Lamartine had apparently been able to do without sleep. The obsession with politics might well have resulted from the diving-apparatus having been brought to the Professor's attention, but I was more inclined to ascribe another reason, connected with the wild words uttered by Lamartine the previous day.

Then there was the question of little Marie, and the seeming interest taken in her by the Professor. What was the meaning of this? I was unable to come to any conclusion in my mind, try as I might to find a solution.

Before taking my leave of Agathe, I had given her the address of my apartment, and requested her to contact me by telegram or any means that seemed appropriate, should there be any further developments that he felt should be brought to my attention.

For a few days, I heard nothing. Old Simon took my piece on the diving-apparatus, and to my disgust, pruned it of many of the passages wherein I took the government to task for its stupidity.

"We cannot afford a libel suit, Gauthier," he told me. "And with the government in its current precarious state, such criticism would be unwise."

When, I asked myself, was the government ever in a state other than precarious? But I held my peace on the matter.

However, four days after our meeting at the restaurant, I was awakened in the morning by the delivery of a telegram from Agathe. In it, she positively demanded my attendance at Lamartine's house. I confess to having been slightly reluctant to accept the invitation, but calculated that I could persuade Simon that my visit would result in another article. Accordingly, I wired my acceptance, and set off for the suburbs once more.

This time, there was no welcome outside the house, and when I rang the bell, the door was answered by the housekeeper, who held a handkerchief to her reddened eyes.

"It's the Professor you'll be after, then, sir?" she enquired. "He's not here, you know."

"In fact, it is Mlle. Agathe who is expecting me," I told her, giving her my hat and stick.

"This way, sir," she told me, admitting me to the drawing-room, where Agathe was waiting. She stood and held out her arms to me as I entered the room.

"I am glad you have come, Gauthier," he told me. "The house is at sixes and sevens. You saw Mathilde, the housekeeper, just now?"

"I noticed that she appeared to be upset. What is the matter?"

"Little Marie has gone missing. The last time that anyone saw anything of her was yesterday afternoon."

"And there is no trace of her?"

"The only sign of her is her tricycle, which was discovered standing by the laboratory."

"And where is the Professor? I was informed just now that he was not here."

Agathe sighed. "The Professor is away. He is visiting a manufactory in Geneva, which is producing parts for one of his inventions. He left yesterday morning, before Marie was discovered to be missing."

"Before he left, how was he?" I asked. "Was he still concerned with politics?"

"No, that enthusiasm faded the next day. I made discreet enquiries of my mother, and discovered that on the evening that we talked in the restaurant, the Professor retired a little after nine o'clock, and arose at half-past seven the next morning, after apparently sleeping soundly throughout the night. The next morning, as far as I was able to tell, he behaved in his usual fashion, and there was nothing untoward in his behaviour for the rest of the day."

I confess I was relieved by this news. "Then we may attribute his earlier eccentricity to a lack of sleep, perhaps?" I suggested. "The news comes as somewhat of a relief to me. I had feared that—" I held my peace, fearing to say more of my fear that the balance of his mind had become disturbed, and she, sensing my embarrassment, forbore from questioning me further.

There was an awkward silence, during which my companion's attention appeared to be entirely focussed on a tree outside the window. "I called you here, because you requested me to call you should any further events occur," she said at length. "I was aware that your interest was primarily with the Professor, of course, but it struck me that the disappearance of this little girl fell into the category of the unusual."

"And so it does," I replied. "I cannot possibly conceive a connection between a missing child and the Professor's eccentricities, but I thank you for your invitation, nonetheless. Was Marie much given to running away and hiding, do you know?"

"By no means. She is always – let us hope and pray that the present tense is still appropriate here – a charming and friendly little child. According to Mathilde, she has never given any trouble or cause for worry or concern."

"You have searched everywhere, I take it?"

"Everywhere, save the Professor's private study in the laboratory."

"Why not there?"

"In the first place, because it is the Professor's private study, and secondly, because it is locked, and there is no way that Marie could have entered it."

I shrugged. "Both would appear to be excellent reasons for excluding the chamber from your search. Perhaps I could make a search of my own? It is unlikely that I will find the girl, as I am sure that you have done all that is possible to find her. However, as a reporter, I sometimes have to look for small clues and hints that will help me uncover the truth of a story."

"As you wish. We will all be grateful for any light you can shed on the mystery." She led me to the small room at the top of the house where the child had been accustomed to sleep.

"What is that door?" I asked, pointing to a small door let into the wall opposite the bed.

"It leads to the attics of the house." My hopes that this would prove to be the solution to the mystery were swiftly dashed, however. "It is always kept locked with this padlock here," she added.

I followed several similar false leads as I went through the various rooms in the house. In each case, either the clue had been followed up, and eliminated, or could be eliminated a priori on account of some circumstance such as the one I have just mentioned.

"I will take myself to the laboratories," I announced. "I am familiar enough with them not to require a guide, I think." And so I was, having been escorted through them several times by the Professor and his staff.

I searched the rooms, looking for anything that might provide a clue to the girl's disappearance. I was strongly of the impression, given that the toy had been discovered near them, that the laboratories would hold the key to this mystery. However, there was nothing that provided me with any inkling whatsoever as to her whereabouts.

At length I entered the room where stood the machine that had transported Lamartine and me into the Untime. I confess to experiencing a slight shiver as I beheld the complex mass of pipes and cables that comprised the apparatus, but was unable to determine to my own satisfaction whether I was shivering with fear or with anticipatory excitement.

A quick search revealed nothing of interest as regarded little Marie, but my curiosity regarding the control panel was piqued. Bear in mind that I had only witnessed Lamartine operating the controls, and had not seen the controls themselves in any detail, and also the fact that I suffer from a high degree of curiosity, both by trade and by nature. I lifted up the white cloth covering the panel, and beheld a mass of levers, dials and gauges, together with stopcocks and electrical switches.

In the middle of these was a small square of flowered white fabric, which I recognised as the handkerchief with which little Marie had ministered to my bruised shin.

"My God!" I exclaimed aloud.

"You may well use His name," came a voice from behind me. I turned. There in the doorway, his face black as thunder, stood Professor Lamartine!

Chapter XI

"What–what are you doing here?" I stammered.

"I think it is I who should be asking that question," the Professor said sternly. He held out his hand. "The handkerchief, if you please."

I gazed stupidly at the little white square of cloth that I held. "I know what it is," I told him.

"I am aware that you know," he replied in a voice as cold as ice. "The handkerchief, if you please," he repeated, and took a step towards me.

It was clear from the set of his face that he would brook no discussion, and I reluctantly handed the scrap of cambric to him. "Where is she?" I asked. "Is she alive?"

"I am certain that she is alive, and unharmed, though somewhat surprised, and almost certainly very cold," he answered me, a faint smile hovering about his lips.

I considered briefly what he might mean by this, but could only come to one conclusion. "You mean that you used that," and I pointed to the Untime apparatus, "to send her forward in time?"

"No, no," he smiled, though the expression was far from cheerful or pleasant. "I have not sent her forward in time at all."

"Then ...?"

"I merely sent her back three years in time."

"But . . ." My mind was a whirl. "What will happen to her? Three years from now – I mean from then—" My head was whirling. "And if she is caught in this trap where she is constantly sent back? But she cannot be, for she would have to be born?"

Lamartine chuckled unpleasantly as I sank onto a convenient chair. "You need have no fear regarding little Marie," he told me. "You know her as Mathilde's child, but Mathilde calls her thus only out of courtesy. Indeed, it is true that Mathilde discovered her outside in the garden, aged about two years old, some three years ago. No-one knew whence she had come, or anything of her background."

"And this is where you sent her?" I asked incredulously. "Back into the garden three years ago?"

"You are absolutely correct, my friend."

"But ..."

"You are going to ask me, are you not, whence she originally came? Who were her parents? You wish to ask me that sort of question?" He shrugged his shoulders and spread out his hands. "I have to tell you that I am unsure. Yes, even the great Professor Lamartine is unsure of the answer," he laughed, but without humour. "Of course, that is not to appear in your magazine, I need hardly add, along with any other matters connected with this incident."

"But this is monstrous!" I declared. "You have snatched away a young child's life, her future, as surely as if you had murdered her!"

"Did she ever have a life?" he retorted. "When was she ever born, we might even ask?"

I pondered this question. "When indeed? But where did she come from if she was never born?"

Lamartine shrugged once more. "I really have no idea. Is it of any importance? She will be well cared for by Mathilde when she is discovered. She will never know of the heartbreaks that come with age, or the pains of growing old. An enviable state, would you not agree?"

I could not understand this callousness that now seemed to have entered into the Professor's soul. Previously, he had been one of the kindest and most sympathetic of men, always ready to help and to share the joys and sorrows of others. This seeming indifference to Marie's fate was a new and disturbing element in his character. There was one further question, which I was burning to ask him, and come what may, I felt that I must know the answer to it.

"What," I asked Lamartine, "of your ambitions to rule the nation that you mentioned to me that evening following our journey together into the Untime? Have you abandoned this wild scheme?"

"On the contrary, my dear Gauthier. Little Marie is a part of my plans. I had to know what would happen when a sentient creature was sent back through the Untime."

I was horrified by his words, which implied an almost inhuman detachment from everyday feelings. "I shall inform the police!" I told him.

His answer to my words was to laugh in my face. "My dear Gauthier, you will not do such a thing, for two reasons. Firstly, the police will laugh at you. If you tell them that I have done away with little Marie, the first thing they will wish to establish is the *corpus delecti*. Without any body or proof of a crime, and without even this handkerchief in your possession," he waved the scrap of embroidered cloth, "there is no such evidence. They will laugh in your face when you tell your story. Or will you tell them that I have sent her back through the Untime? If you do that, I will have the kindness to come and visit you in the asylum where you will be locked away after they have listened to your story."

I considered this. "Very well. And the second reason?"

"The second reason, my friend, is here." He reached in his pocket, and pulled out a heavy revolver, which he pointed at me. "I do not intend to kill you – yet," he said calmly. "I merely show you this to remind you of its existence. And you yourself are well aware of how easy it is to travel through our space and time using the Untime. Should I ever discover that you are interfering with my plans, or informing others of my activities, you know that it is a trivial matter for me to make my way to wherever you may choose to hide, no matter where it may be, and kill you. I hope that this is clear to you?"

I nodded, dumbly. In truth, this new side of the Professor was one which frightened me not a little, and provided me with cause for serious concern.

"You will now return to the house," he continued, in the same calm, even tone, "and report that your search here for Marie has been unsuccessful. Naturally, you have not seen me, or any trace of Marie. I would then suggest that you return back to Paris immediately. In any event, it occurs to me now that I do not know why you are here. Perhaps you would care to enlighten me?"

"Your daughter requested me to come. Her telegram expressed concern at Marie's disappearance."

"Very well. So it was not idle curiosity on your part? Better than I had expected, I suppose. Now go." He gestured with the pistol towards the door, and I took the hint and moved towards the door of the laboratory building, my hand on the handle. "It is unlikely that you will see me again," he added. "Unless, that is, you decide to make my affairs public, or to interfere in any other way with my plans. I do not wish you to visit here again, except in the unlikely event of my extending an invitation to you. I hope I make myself clear?"

"Indeed you do. I will not wish you good luck with your ventures, but I do trust that you will come to a reconsideration of your plans."

"Get out!" he hissed at me through clenched teeth. "You are beginning to irritate me beyond measure, and I will not be responsible for the consequences if you continue in this vein. I will be watching to ensure that you return to Paris immediately. Do not even enter the house. If you have left any of your belongings there, such as a hat or stick, I will ensure that they are sent to you. Remember, I can be with you in an instant, anywhere, should you think of crossing me. Now go!"

I left hurriedly, and, not wishing to invoke Lamartine's wrath, skirted the house, and made my way onto the road leading to the station. I paused to mop my brow and reflect on what I had just experienced. Surely the Professor's wits had been turned by that extraordinary experience in the Untime, and it was my duty to inform the authorities so that he could be restrained and society protected against his wild fancies.

But then I considered that the Professor, even

if entertaining such lunacy, still possessed considerable intelligence and persuasive powers,
which he would certainly use to assure others
that it was he who was completely sane, and
convince them that it was I, rather than he,
who should be locked away from the rest of the
world. No, it would be useless, I concluded, for
me to consider such a course of action.

CHAPTER XII

For the next few days, I racked my brains, attempting to discover for myself a way in which Professor Lamartine could be brought to a point where reason could be brought to prevail over his mad fancies. There was not the slightest doubt in my mind that he was capable of using the Untime to track my movements and to pursue me with the intention of doing me harm, should I cross him and thwart his intentions.

Nor could I see a way of persuading the authorities that he posed a threat to our society. As he had rightly pointed out, any description of the Untime that I provided to the police would persuade them that it was I, not he, who was suffering from delusions. What, I asked myself, could be the solution?

I sent a message to Agathe, asking her if she had any details of how Marie had come to the Professor's household. She confirmed for me that Marie had originally been discovered by Mathilde some three years previously, as Lamartine had told me, and had appeared to be about two years old at that time. Although she had been found well-dressed in clothes of quality that indicated a certain class, her true identity remained a mystery.

I had told old Simon that Lamartine was out of the country, and that in his absence I would attempt to obtain material for my work from Professor Schneider at the Sorbonne. The savant and I were acquainted through my reporting of the proceedings of various scientific societies, and it had occurred to me that Schneider, whom I knew to be no friend of Lamartine, would provide a suitable ear into which I could pour my troubles.

Accordingly, I made an appointment to visit Schneider, and at the appointed day and hour, I knocked on his door.

"Enter," came the stentorian voice of Schneider. In contrast to the neat, almost fussy, appearance of Lamartine, Schneider was a big bear of a man, tall and thick-set, with a mop of wild curly black hair and a beard that recalled the wilds of Russia rather than a Parisian salon. "And what can I do for you, Gauthier? The last piece you wrote on our meeting was not too bad, I must say. Better than the average fare dished up by your colleagues. Whisky?" Schneider had acquired a taste for this appalling smoky spirit during a stay in Cambridge. To humour him, I managed to drink a little of the glass he poured for me without gagging.

"Professor Schneider," I said to him. "I must earnestly request you to keep secret what I am about to say, and not to repeat it to anyone, unless I ask you to do so."

Schneider threw back his head and laughed loudly. "You, a journalist, telling me I should hold my peace? Well, this is a change in the natural order of things, I must say! More whisky?" He poured some more of the vile liquid into my glass, and I was obliged to swallow some.

"I am perfectly serious, Professor," I told him. "My life is in danger if this news gets abroad."

"Oho! Is that so?" he asked. "I can see by your face that you are not joking about this matter. I apologise if I treated your words with somewhat less than the respect that they obviously deserve."

"Not only my life, but the future of France, or perhaps even the world, may hang in the balance."

"Serious words indeed, my friend. Tell me more."

I related to him the story of my adventure with Lamartine in the Untime, starting with the watch vanishing in a thunderclap, and then moving to the journey through the Untime undertaken by Lamartine and me, but without details of Lamartine's words or behaviour. I felt it unnecessary to describe the childish behaviour that Lamartine had exhibited during our visit to the Chamber of Deputies. Schneider followed my words with the utmost attention, writing a few notes on a pad of paper from time to time. At the end of my recital, he sat, his large head cupped in his hands, as he digested my words.

At length, he spoke. "Lamartine is correct when he claims that only a few can understand his Untime, as he calls it. Indeed, I have my doubts as to whether he himself possesses a full understanding of it and its potential. Describe to me once again your sensations during and after the experiment where you and he were in the apparatus. You have not yet informed me, though, why you feel your life is in danger."

"I will tell you more of that last anon," I said, and repeated the account of my feelings while in the Untime.

Again he sat in thought. "Now give me a more detailed description of the apparatus, if you would be so kind," he demanded.

"I can do better than that," I told him. "I possess a certain skill in sketching, and I have a trained memory for these things. I can produce a detailed drawing of the apparatus."

"Excellent," he said. "That will be of great value."

I set to work, and in a short time had produced a drawing which, to my mind, excellently conveyed the appearance of the mechanism in Lamartine's laboratory. I used another sheet to reproduce the appearance of the control panel as I had seen it when I discovered little Marie's handkerchief.

Schneider fairly snatched the paper from my hands and studied it, making inaudible comments to himself the while. "What was this?" he asked, pointing to a part of the apparatus.

"A tank for some gas or other. As you probably know, Lamartine had been investigating the properties of helium, and it may be that this is the fruit of those researches."

"Quite possibly," he murmured in an abstracted tone. "And these are Leyden jars?"

"That is how they appeared to me."

"Very well. I begin to gain some small understanding of the principles involved, thanks to these excellent sketches and your description. I have an idea that Lamartine's explanation of the events you experienced may be in error, but that is not a matter that easily submits itself to proof. Now," and here he turned to face me and looked me directly in the eye, "you told me just now that your life is in danger. Why do you say such a thing?"

I related how Lamartine had behaved in the legislature, and the contempt he had shown for the Deputies. I added how he seemed to have become obsessed, as I saw it, with the power that the Untime gave to those who entered it, how he had raved about the government of our country, and how he saw himself as the natural heir to political power. I added the threats that Lamartine had made towards me to ensure my silence on the matter, but ended my narrative at that day of the Untime, and what I had been told by his daughter about Lamartine's behaviour on the next day, considering that it was not yet time to describe to Schneider the disappearance of little Marie. Schneider heard me out in silence, gravely stroking his beard. When I paused, he spoke.

"You said yourself that you were fatigued and slept for an unprecedented length of time, did you not? Well then, it is obvious that whatever this Untime may ultimately prove to be, it has a profound effect on those who enter it. Is it not likely that such an experience will have widely differing effects on individuals? Consider the effects of alcohol, for example. Some men may drink a bottle, two bottles, or even more, and appear in total control of their faculties. Some will fall down, or even lose consciousness. Some may become maudlin and start to weep, while others will become pugnacious, and start a quarrel with the first man they encounter. Is it not likely, then, that this Untime will have sim- ilar effects on different men, which cannot be predicted in advance?"

"It is possible," I admitted.

"Have you noticed anything untoward in your- self, for example? In your own thoughts and actions?"

I considered this for a minute. "I suppose that

my dreams have become more vivid of late."

He looked at me gravely. "I cannot be certain at this stage," he said, "but I consider from all you have told me that the Untime will have an adverse effect on the health of those who experience it. Have you anything more to tell me about Lamartine?"

"Indeed I have," I replied, now convinced that Schneider treated the matter with appropriate seriousness. I proceeded to inform him of my call to Lamartine's house regarding the disappearance of the child, the discovery of the handkerchief in the laboratory, and the subsequent appearance of Lamartine and his threats uttered towards me. Schneider heard all this with an ever-increasing look of horror on his face.

Chapter XIII

"I CANNOT bring myself to believe this," he said at length. "Lamartine has always displayed a streak of – how shall I put it? – instability. But this passes all belief. I am glad you have found the courage to speak out to me. The police must be informed."

I gazed at him, horrified in my turn. "Have you not been attending to my words, Professor Schneider? Lamartine has threatened to attack any who attempt to stop him in his madness. I know from my own experience that his control of the Untime gives him the power to strike at any place and at any time."

"And of course, he would have the perfect

alibi," mused Schneider. "He could have dozens
of witnesses to provide that he was in Marseilles,
for example, just one minute after a crime was
committed in Paris."

"Or even at that same time," I added, "if he is
prepared to take the risk in going back in time."

"That is one matter that concerns me regarding the whole of Lamartine's theory. What he
claims is contrary to logic and to common
sense," said Schneider. "Let us take the little
girl, Marie, as an example. You were told that
she was discovered by the housekeeper, when
she was about two years old, and adopted into
the household?"

"That is correct."

"And three years later, when she is aged about
five, Lamartine claims to have sent her back
to that time. But a number of questions present themselves to me. Firstly, the obvious one,
which no doubt has occurred to you. Where did
she originate? Children do not spontaneously
appear from nowhere at the age of two. We cannot believe that she simply made her appearance into the world in that way, like the demon
king in a pantomime."

"It puzzles me also," I confessed.

"Not only that, but we are expected to believe

that when discovered, she was three years younger than when she started her journey through the Untime. We should assume, should we not, that she was clothed when Lamartine sent her on her journey?"

"One would sincerely hope that was the case."

"And what were the clothes discovered with the child when she was found by the housekeeper?"

"I was told that she was clothed, yes, and it was mentioned that they were of good quality. I am sure that I would have been informed had they had been ill-fitting. I begin to understand your point."

"And if the clothes were of the appropriate size for the two-year-old child, we somehow have to explain the metamorphosis of inanimate garments miraculously changing their form. It is possible, with some difficulty, to conceive of the notion of the ageing process being reversed in the case of a human body. It is even possible to conceive of a physical object, such as the timepiece that you mentioned, also reversing in time. But for an inanimate object to change its form in that way? No, my friend, we must look for some other explanation."

"You certainly make a good point," I agreed.

"Do you remember what you told me about Lamartine's analogy with the paper and the lines and so on? When he said to you that going back in time using the Untime would be like making a hole in the paper?"

"Of course."

"I believe he was right, though I do not believe that he had achieved a full understanding of the principles at the time he explained them to you. See here." He seized some paper and a pencil and drew rapidly. "What do we have here?" he said to me. "Where is the pencil point?"

"In the centre of the circle that you have just drawn."

"Indeed. And now?" He pushed the pencil through the surface of the paper.

"I do not know. It is no longer on the paper. Perhaps this is Lamartine's fifth dimension."

"Perhaps, and perhaps not." He lifted the edge of the paper, to reveal another sheet underneath. On this paper was drawn a square, within which rested the point of the pencil. "We are now in a different world, are we not?"

I gripped the edge of my chair. Schneider's explanation was even more dizzying that had been that of Lamartine. "I do not know what to say. The prospect is ... terrifying. You are saying that there may be a multiplicity of worlds?"

"Of entire universes," he corrected me. "And in all probability, not merely a multiplicity, but an infinity of them."

I was rocked to the core of my being by this concept. "It is unbelievable to me that this should be the case," I said. "Why, this would overthrow the foundations of science, were it proven to be true."

"It may be hard for you to believe," said Schneider, "and I do not make the claim that it is the truth. I merely put it forward as one possible explanation of the strange events that you are describing."

"There are others?"

"To be sure. There is, of course, the simple possibility that what you are describing to me is the product of an overheated imagination. No, no," as I started to protest. "I am not saying that this is in any way likely. Your manner and everything that you have described to me so far convince me that this is not the case. I merely put it forward as one explanation that might be advanced by others."

"And you have more explanations other than this fantastical one of the infinite universes?"

"Nothing that suggests itself more readily at

present. You are familiar with the work of Henri Poincaré?"

"I am familiar with the name, naturally."

"Maybe you are unaware of his work on clocks and time as they pass through the æther?"

"I have never heard of this."

"Well, perhaps that is not surprising. He has yet to publish the results of his work. I see that there may be some points in common between what I know of his achievements, and those of Lamartine, as you describe them. But my concern is that I do not believe that Lamartine has a full understanding of what he has unleashed, and I fear for the consequences that may result from what I can best describe as his inspired meddling."

"You believe that he may be creating problems to which he does not know the solution?"

"Exactly that. And it is not only he who is ignorant of the solution, I am sure, but the whole of the scientific world is also without a general comprehension of this discovery. Lamartine could unleash horrors and chaos beyond our imagination. I need hardly tell you that it is a terrible mistake to meddle with forces outside your understanding."

"Then he must be stopped."

"Indeed, regardless of any political ambitions that he may possess. In some ways, the political problems are of minor consequence compared to what he may unwittingly provoke."

"I hardly dare to consider the matters to which you refer."

"I am talking about a breach in the very fabric of our Universe itself. That is to say, the forces which hold it together, and which make us believe in the idea of cause preceding effect, and in our ability to make predictions according to scientific laws which we believe to be universal."

"And Lamartine might cause such a breach?"

Schneider threw up his hands. "He might. He might not. It is a risk that the world can scarcely afford to take, would you not agree? You may think I speak wildly here, and you dismiss my words as the result of a personal grudge against Lamartine. It is true that I dislike him as a person, and I have had occasion to find faults in his work in the past. However, I speak as a scientist here, not as a man with human frailties. Believe me, my dear Gauthier, Lamartine is juggling with bottles filled with nitroglycerine. It is not so much a matter of whether he will drop one as when he will drop it."

"So you will help me stop him?"

"Of course! Do you doubt me? We must ensure that his machine is destroyed, and that he is prevented from constructing another such apparatus ever again. I am with you in this absolutely. And, as I said to you earlier, it is essential that the police are informed of this. They can provide us with protection against any attacks that Lamartine may decide to launch against us."

I had not expected such a lively response to my account on the part of Schneider, and I embraced him warmly. "My friend!" I exclaimed. "Together we will save the world!"

Chapter XIV

SUCH sentiments were, of course, easier to express than to put into practice. It was certainly true that if Schneider were to inform the police that he suspected Lamartine of conducting dangerous experiments, there would be a greater chance that he would be believed than if I were to do the same. Nonetheless, Schneider expressed some doubts as to the wisdom of this course.

"In certain circles, it is well known that I have bones to pick with Lamartine. It might appear to be a case of professional jealousy were I to make the complaint."

"And who will believe a journalist?" I asked in

my turn.

In the end, we went together to see the Prefect of Police, M. Fournisseur, with whom Schneider had some acquaintance.

My new ally expressed his opinion, without providing details, that Lamartine's current experiments were hazardous, and posed a danger to the area around his house.

Fournisseur spread out his hands in a gesture of helplessness. "My dear Professor," he said to Schneider. "It is not for me to inform the local police in that town how they should run their affairs. They would send me away with a flea in my ear, and rightly so, were I to tell them their business."

"Then I will go further," said Schneider. "I will tell you that the experiments carried out by Lamartine are a powder keg. A powder keg that could place the whole of the country in jeopardy should action not be taken soon."

"Serious words, Professor," said the Prefect. "But they are words alone unless you can furnish me with some more details."

"I myself have witnessed some of the events of which Professor Schneider is speaking," I told him. "While I cannot pretend to anything approaching the erudition and comprehension that he displays, I can truthfully say that I am deeply concerned by the nature of the experiments, as well as by the state of Professor Lamartine's mind."

"Has he caused inconvenience to his neighbours?" asked Fournisseur.

"Why, yes," I answered. "Colonel Legrasse's household nearby made a complaint while I was visiting Professor Lamartine."

"In that case, that may be all that we need."

Professor Schneider, whose face had been turning a deep shade of red while he had been listening to this latest exchange, stood up, and crashed his massive fist down on the table in front of him.

"This is outrageous!" he exclaimed. "I am informing you of a matter that can destroy the whole nation, and you are concerned only with the feelings of Lamartine's neighbours. This is intolerable!"

"Calm yourself, my dear Professor," replied the Prefect. "You live in a world of mathematical certainties. I, on the other hand, must walk a delicate political tightrope in the performance of my profession. I will send one of my men to visit Lamartine, on the pretext that the neighbours have complained about the noise. They will inspect the apparatus that he is using for these mysterious experiments that you claim are so dangerous, and order its destruction if they determine that to be necessary."

Professor Schneider, who had by this time regained his seat, once again spoke. Although he was seated, his voice still boomed out. "Fournisseur, I will tell you now that from everything that Gauthier here has told me, your average policeman will have no chance of deducing the methods by which Lamartine's apparatus works, let alone discovering its functions. If it makes you happy to do so, then proceed with your plan, but I warn you now that it will be a waste of time."

"Then perhaps you would prefer to accompany my man on his journey?"

I was mentally beseeching Schneider to turn down the offer. If Lamartine knew of his visit, as he was sure to do, not only was Schneider's life in danger, but so was mine. Lamartine was well aware of my association with Schneider, and there would be no doubt in his mind that it was I who was the ultimate cause of Schneider's visit.

"I will go," Schneider said.

"No!" I burst out. "You cannot! It is certain

death for you, and for me, if you are to go!"

The Prefect looked at me strangely. "Has Professor Lamartine threatened you in any way?" he asked.

"He has done so, but in no way that I can explain simply. I simply wish to state that I fear for my life."

"This matter is becoming too deep for me, I fear."

"In that case, let me say merely that I feel it is unwise in the extreme for Professor Schneider or myself to come into contact with Professor Lamartine. I wish to state most categorically that I do not want my name, or that of Professor Schneider, in any way associated with this," I said with conviction. "It is most important that secrecy be preserved in this case."

The Prefect looked at me curiously. "I take it you have excellent reasons for saying all of this?"

"Indeed I do, but as I say, they are complex, and at this time I think you would find them to be incredible. I make this request most strongly, and I trust that you will take note of it."

"Very well. Professor?" he addressed Schneider.

"Very well, Gauthier," he said to me. "I would

welcome the chance to inspect the apparatus, but I take your point here. Do you, Fournisseur, send your man on his errand, but I fear it will prove a waste of time."

I now saw my chance to play my ace. "M. le Prefect, there is one other matter that I think will be of interest to your man. If he encounters Lamartine, as I am sure he must, he should make enquiries regarding an infant named Marie, who disappeared from the household about a week ago. She is or was the ward of the housekeeper, whom I know only as Mathilde."

The Prefect sat a little more upright in his chair. "Why did you not mention this earlier?" he asked. "This is the kind of matter in which we can offer our assistance, rather than investigating these fantasies that you claim we will not understand."

"I refrained from telling you earlier, Monsieur, for two reasons. Firstly, because the source of the knowledge of her disappearance might be traced to me, thereby putting me in some danger. Secondly, because I know for a fact that you will never solve the disappearance. There is no body to be discovered, and no trace of any crime at all. But I suggest most strongly that your man investigates little Marie, and asks Lamartine if he has any knowledge of her whereabouts, taking careful note of his reactions to the questions."

"You say that we will not solve the mystery of her disappearance. You seem very sure of this."

"I am as sure of your inability to solve this as I am of the reality of this table in front of me," I answered him. "This is no reflection on the capabilities of you or your men, but rather the nature of the disappearance itself."

The Prefect sighed. "I assume that this is all in connection with this mysterious experiment which is it beyond our power to understand?" he asked, with more than a hint of sarcasm in his voice, which I chose to ignore.

"Precisely so," I said. "If I were to tell you the truth of what I know, you would order me locked in a lunatic asylum."

The Prefect looked over at Schneider, and raised his eyebrows.

"M. Gauthier speaks the truth, as far as I am aware," he said. "There is danger to him, and also to myself, as he points out. I thank you, Gauthier, for your stance in this matter. It is not for myself, but for Gauthier's sake, that I now withdraw my offer to accompany your officer."

"Very well, then," the Prefect replied. "This is

one of the most extraordinary meetings of my life. You are telling me about crimes that it will be beyond my power to solve, and that you fear revenge from the perpetrators. I suppose that you will be demanding a police guard about your persons next?" He spoke mockingly, but I decided to take him at his word.

"That would be most welcome, M. le Prefect," I told him.

Fournisseur blinked in surprise. "I was not expecting that answer, as you may guess, but having made the offer, even if it was made partly in jest, I suppose I must honour it. Provide me with the details, and I will make the arrangements for you."

Chapter XV

We left the Prefecture, having arranged with Fournisseur that suitable police guards would be provided for both Schneider and me. It was galling not to be able to provide fuller details of the danger that we were in, but Schneider and I agreed that the truth as we understood it would be regarded as ridiculous by the authorities.

We had been informed that it would be a few days before the police guards would be made available to us, a circumstance that caused me a little concern. In that time while we were waiting for the official wheels to turn, however, a singular series of events occurred.

Old Simon, my editor, came to my desk at the office the day after Schneider and I had visited the Prefect.

"There has been a strange event reported near Vincennes," he informed me. "It would appear that a strange mechanism, which appears to be the apparatus for some sort of scientific experiment, has been discovered in an abandoned house in that area. Some builders who were making repairs to the property came across it. One of them was obviously hoping to make some money from the news and contacted a friend of mine who works for a daily newspaper, who in his turn passed it on to me. Perhaps you can make some sort of story out of it. Go and investigate, and if it seems interesting, maybe we can afford to send a photographer later."

And with that, I was sent on my way, having been provided with the address of the house, as well as of the firm of builders who claimed to have made the discovery. I decided to visit the house first, given that the mysterious machinery had been discovered there. On presentation of my card to one of the workmen, I was introduced to the foreman of the gang which had discovered this mysterious device, a villainous-looking rogue who gave his name solely as "Gérard", and who let me into the building. As I had been told, the house was abandoned, and everything was covered with dust.

"It's in here," said Gérard, opening a door and holding out his hand, obviously in expectation of a pourboire.

I gratified his cupidity, and entered the room alone. Gérard hovered by the doorway, watching my actions curiously. The daylight was filtered by the grimy shuttered windows, and it was difficult to distinguish the shapes inside the room, but as I examined them closer, my astonishment knew no bounds. It swiftly came to me that I was looking at a duplicate of the apparatus I had seen in Lamartine's laboratory. If my memory served me correctly, there were one or two minor differences between the apparatus in front of me, and that which I had seen earlier. As with the mechanism in Lamartine's house, the control panel was covered by a cloth. When I moved to examine the apparatus more closely, though, it was clear to me that it had not been used for some time, maybe even for a number of years, as the dust on it lay thick, and seemingly undisturbed. The square glass plate, similar to the one on which Lamartine and I had stood for our trip to the Untime, was opaque with dirt.

In a flash, it came to me what I had to do. "No-one is to enter this room until I return,"

I told Gérard, who regarded me with an air of amused perplexity. I dashed out into the street and hailed a passing cab to convey me to the Sorbonne, where I dismissed the driver, and fairly ran along the halls until I reached Professor Schneider's office, only to be informed that he was delivering a lecture.

"Where? Where?" I cried, and upon receiving directions, took myself at full tilt along the quiet corridors of the University to the lecture theatre, which I entered without ceremony. The students to whom Schneider was expounding his theories must have been taken aback by the sudden appearance of a wild-eyed man with his garments in a state of disarray, waving his stick, and demanding in a loud voice that their professor should accompany him immediately to an unknown destination.

To his great credit, Schneider patiently heard me out, and acquiesced immediately to my demands, dismissing his class.

"Now then, Gauthier, is there something amiss?" he said, in the tones of one humouring a dangerous lunatic.

"Nothing amiss, but it is essential that you come to Vincennes this instant," I told him. "There is the most extraordinary thing there that demands your attention. Do not bother yourself with a hat or overcoat, but come now."

Still giving me the impression that he considered me out of my senses, Schneider followed me to the street, where I hailed another cab to take us to Vincennes.

"Will you not tell me something of what all this is about?" Schneider asked me.

"All in good time," I answered him, forcing myself to remain outwardly calm, though my mind was churning through the possibilities connected with my discovery. Schneider visibly chafed at my reticence, but refrained from asking me further questions.

At length we reached the house in Vincennes, and Gérard regarded Schneider and me with a sceptical eye.

"I wasn't sure that you would be coming back," he said in a surly tone. "And if he's going to go in there," jerking a thumb at Professor Schneider, "it's going to cost you extra."

"Very well," I said, and dropped another few francs into the outstretched palm.

"Now, what do you make of this?" I asked Schneider, when we had entered the chamber.

"No-one has used this room for years, by the look of it," he answered, coughing as the dust caught his throat. "But what is this?" he asked, on catching sight of the apparatus. He gazed at it in silence for a few minutes, and then spoke. "This bears an uncanny resemblance to your drawing of Lamartine's contraption, does it not?"

"It is almost identical to the one I saw in his laboratory," I responded.

"But... but... he told you that it was a new discovery, and that he had only just perfected it, did he not?"

"That is so."

"And yet it is clear that this has not been seen or touched for at least a year. You agree?"

"Indubitably."

"Come, let us shed some light on this." He moved to the casement and flung open the shutters, allowing us to examine the mass of pipes and wires. "This is most interesting," he murmured to himself, as he moved between the Leyden jars and the electrical cables connecting them to the control panel. "Most interesting," he repeated, examining the vats and piping. It was a fascinating experience to watch the Professor at work. He appeared to be soaking up knowledge and understanding as readily as a sponge absorbs water. For a short period, his brow would furrow, and his face contort as he came to a fresh part of the mechanism. He would then use his large, but surprisingly skilful, fingers to turn, prod, tweak and otherwise manipulate the subject of his investigation. Suddenly he would release his breath in a long drawn-out sigh of satisfaction, and his expression would clear as an understanding of the apparatus came to him.

"Let us see, now," he would say to himself, pausing at one of the valves set into the mass of tubing. On turning the valve, a small amount of liquid might dribble into the palm of his hand, which he would then examine closely, perhaps sniffing at it, or even, on one occasion, tasting it. "Do not worry, Gauthier," he called to me on one of these occasions, as he caught sight of my astonished face. "There really is little or no danger attached to this."

At length he moved to the control panel and removed the cloth cover before using it to wipe the dust gently from the surface of the panel. He stood in silence examining the machinery before him for at least five minutes, and then called to me.

"Gauthier, you have your notebook and a pencil with you, I take it?"

"Naturally."

"Be so good as to draw these controls, taking careful note of the setting of each one."

I set to work, and though I did not understand the workings of the levers or the meaning of the dials and gauges that I was drawing, managed to produce a sketch which captured the control panel as we had found it.

"Can you tell me what has happened here?" I asked Schneider when I had finished. "What is the meaning of this apparatus? Who built it, and when?"

"Do you need to ask who built it?" Schneider asked me. "Obviously this is Lamartine's work. As to when it was built, I would say that it will be built very shortly, approximately six years ago."

CHAPTER XVI

SCHNEIDER'S words astonished me. "Your words make no sense. How can you use the future to describe an action that has happened in the past?" I asked. "What we have here stands before us already completed, and seemingly untouched for at least a year or more."

The Professor said nothing in reply, but merely smiled in a way that I found to be irritating in the extreme. I stood there, attempting to reconcile his words with the evidence before my eyes.

"I have it, I think!" I exclaimed, as light dawned in my mind. "You mean that at some point in the near future, Lamartine will use the machine at his laboratory to travel in the Untime to a few years before the present, will do whatever he has to do at that time, and, armed with the knowledge that he currently possesses, will construct this apparatus to return him to the time from which he originated!"

"Yes, that is what I believe," Schneider said to me. "Either he will depart our time in the near future, or it is conceivable that he has already done so."

"And do you believe he will return soon?" I asked.

"I think that it is most probable that Lamartine will return to a time very close to when he enters the Untime, so as not to alarm any by his absence from this world." Schneider had returned to an examination of the apparatus. "To whom does this house belong? Do you know? Does the workman who admitted us?"

"I can ask," I replied, but it seemed that Gérard had no more idea than we, having been employed simply as the foreman of a gang of workmen who had been employed to put right a house in a poor state of repair.

"Listen, my man," said Schneider, who had interrupted his study of the apparatus and joined the labourer and me outside the room. "When is this work due to be finished?"

"Two weeks from today," said the other.

"How much will it take for it to be three weeks?" Schneider asked him.

"I don't understand what you mean."

"I require the undisturbed use of this house for one week, starting from today. That means that you and your men will stay away from this house for one week. How much money do you require for this to happen?"

I was astounded by this extraordinary request, but Gérard seemed to take it in his stride. "Well, there's three of us as well as myself, and we'd want our wages for that time, monsieur," (I noticed that his speech had become slightly more deferential given the possibility of more money coming his way) "and then there's got to be something else on top of that for the trouble. Someone's got to explain it to the boss, after all."

"How much?" asked Schneider.

Gérard named a sum which I personally considered to be outrageous, but it appeared to satisfy Schneider.

"When do you want us to leave?" asked the workman.

"Immediately," answered the Professor, and withdrew his purse from his pocket before counting out the specified sum into Gérard's hand. "Now go, all of you, and I warn you that I do not want to see any of you again before this time next week. You may leave your tools here. It may be that we will require them. The sum I have given you is easily enough to cover the cost of any damage that we may cause to them, and I am in no mood for further bargaining." He glared ferociously at the smaller man as he said these words.

"I understand, monsieur," replied the workman, and took his leave of us.

"What do you mean by this?" I asked, when the sounds from below had ceased, informing us that the workmen had departed.

"I believe, that thanks to your having located this apparatus, I can discover the principles by which Lamartine has achieved his results. It is clear that some of these tanks and vats will need to be refilled with the gases and liquids that they originally contained, but that is merely a matter of a day or so, with the assistance of the University laboratories."

"And then?" I asked.

"And then, my dear Gauthier, I intend to take myself into the Untime, as did you and Lamartine."

I was appalled at his words. "You cannot, should not, do this," I told him. "You said yourself that a journey into the Untime could cause some sort of damage. Are you prepared to risk your life, your sanity, your intelligence, your very mind, simply to satisfy your curiosity?"

"Indeed I am," he said to me. "I believe my intellect to be strong enough to survive the Untime, whatever it may have done to Lamartine."

"I still consider it to be a foolhardy and unnecessary risk," I said to him. "After all, Lamartine designed the machine and was familiar with its workings and with its principles of operation. With the greatest respect, Professor Schneider, and I mean no insult here, you are approaching this matter from a position of relative ignorance – relative, that is, to a man who has presumably spent many years of study investigating the matter," I added hurriedly, as I saw Schneider's face change at my words.

However, Schneider stood his ground. "I have several advantages over Lamartine. Firstly, I have the benefit of your account, and your experience. I know with certainty that this machine is capable of doing what it is intended to do, which is considerably more than Lamartine did when he commenced its construction.

Secondly, I have the benefit of a greater knowledge of the work of Poincaré on the subject. Lamartine quarrelled violently with him some years back – indeed, there was talk of their fighting a duel – and I am sure that there has been no communication between them since then. Lastly, I consider my intellect to be stronger, and my constitution more resilient, than that of Lamartine, or even of you, intelligent and healthy as you may be. I have faith that I will survive the experience, and return from this Untime in full health, wiser and with more knowledge than when I started. Now, may I count on your assistance?"

I was not fully persuaded by Schneider's air of confidence, but I had to admit to myself that his words made a certain kind of sense. "I am reasonably certain that I can persuade my editor to allow me the time to assist you."

"Very well," said he. "Let us clean the apparatus first. This will help us to determine what we need in order to put it into full working order."

We stripped off our coats and rolled up our sleeves, but it was soon obvious that we would need more in the way of cleaning materials than the few rags we discovered in the room. However, following an extensive search of the house, we discovered a cupboard stocked with the cloths and polishes that Schneider deemed necessary to place the apparatus in a state where it could be examined and operated.

"I had never imagined myself as a charwoman," I said to Schneider after the first thirty minutes of hard work. My hands were black, and so was my face, if the state of Schneider's countenance was any guide. However, the apparatus was starting to appear much cleaner than before, and it was possible for me to recognise the brass and other materials that had composed the machinery at Lamartine's laboratory. We worked solidly for another two hours or so before Schneider called a halt to our labours.

"Excellent," he said, and wiped his already dirty forehead with a greasy hand, thereby depositing more grime on his face. "We have made excellent progress, but I fear we will not be welcome at the better dining establishments. I suggest that we visit a Turkish bath in order to repair the damage done to our appearances, and resume our tasks tomorrow, which would be better performed in more appropriate apparel."

"Very well," I said. "That sounds like an excellent plan."

Following our sojourn in the bath, I took my

leave of Schneider. Although he seemed to be interested purely in the scientific and technical aspects of the machinery that we had discovered, I had another object in view; one which was not in the scientific realm, but which nonetheless promised to supply some answers to the mystery of the machinery in the deserted house.

My card identifying me as a writer for my magazine opened doors in the neighbourhood of Vincennes that would otherwise have remained closed to me, and I was able to obtain the information I sought. It came as little surprise to me, although it confounded common-sense.

Chapter XVII

I REALISED that some risk, both to me and to Agathe, was incurred by my communicating with her, but it seemed to me to be imperative that I verified the truth of the answer to my question, which I already suspected. Accordingly, I dispatched a telegram to her, signed only with my initials, and inviting her to meet me at "the usual place", by which I meant the restaurant where we had met previously, and the meaning of which I hoped she would understand. Though I knew that these precautions would not deceive her father for longer than a minute, I had hopes that they would at least prevent any servants from informing him of the meaning of my message, should they chance to see it, and be subsequently questioned by him.

At the appointed time I was waiting at the restaurant, and to my intense relief I espied Agathe making her way through the crowd towards me. I stood up and greeted her warmly.

"Does anyone know you are here?" were my first words.

"How mysterious you make it all sound," she smiled at me. "No, no-one knows. I simply told the servants I was going out for the evening, but did not mention my destination or my companion."

"And I trust that you have the telegram with you?"

"Why no. Is there a reason why I should have brought it."

I sighed inwardly. "No, there is no reason," I told her, trusting that she would be unaware of my disquiet and concern that Lamartine might discover it and follow her trail.

"Why have you invited me here?" she asked me.

"Of course, I enjoy your company, and if I may be so bold as to say so, I enjoy gazing into your beautiful eyes," I said, as light-heartedly as I could manage. She smiled in reply. "However, there is another reason. Perhaps you can tell me something about your father. I know little of him other than what he has told me, and almost nothing of his life before I met him just over one year ago. Where was he, for example, six years ago?"

She furrowed her brow prettily as she searched for the answer. "Six years ago, I remember that he went to Brazil, and then to Argentina. He was offered some sort of place at some of the universities there. He stayed there for several years. A little over three years, as I recall."

"And tell me, Agathe." I leaned forward in my excitement. "Tell me, was he absent from your house when little Marie was found? When Mathilde came across her?"

My pretty companion smiled. "You seem to have an obsession with little Marie and her discovery. She is still missing, though," and her face turned serious. "It is most mysterious. I have no idea where she has gone, and the police are baffled. In answer to your question, yes, he was away at that time."

"The police are now involved?"

"Yes, an agent called the other day to say that there had been some complaints regarding the explosions in the Professor's laboratory. While he was talking to me, Mathilde burst in and proceeded to tell him about Marie's disappearance."

"What was your father's reaction to this?"

"He is still away from the house."

"And the police are investigating?"

"It is strange," she mused. "When the agent was informed of Marie's disappearance, he did not seem as surprised or concerned about it as I might have expected, given the circumstances. But yes, he dispatched a few more agents who made a search, but they found nothing, and we have been assured that the local gendarmerie is now aware and will be looking out for her."

"That is all to the good, I suppose. But let us return to the Professor. He was away in South America for all that time, you say?"

"That is correct."

"And did you or your mother ever go out to visit him during that time?"

She shook her head. "No. The Professor told is that the conditions there were too dangerous for us to visit, especially for a girl of my age, and even though I begged him to let me visit, he continued to send refusals in his letters."

I was now confident that I had most pieces of the puzzle, and I quizzed Agathe some more regarding her father's state of mind on the occasions when she had last seen him a few days earlier.

"As I told you before, he appeared to be obsessed with politics on the day after you visited and there was a loud explosion, but the next day he said nothing about it. He did seem to be distracted by little Marie, though." She paused in thought and then looked at me strangely. "I believe that you know what has happened to her. It is something terrible, is it not? Can you tell me?"

"I will tell you everything, my darling." The endearment fell naturally from my lips, and though it was the first time I had ever addressed her in this way, it seemed to be natural for me to do so. To my astonishment, she smiled back at me, with a look of what appeared to be encouragement at my words. This gave me the confidence to go on with what I felt I must tell her. "Agathe, it is your father who has stolen Marie," I said to her.

A look of disbelief, mingled with horror, stole over her face, as the import of these words crept over her. "But why would he ever do such a thing?" she asked.

"It is all in the name of science," I said to her. "Your father is undoubtedly one of the scientific geniuses of the age, but in this instance, he is involved in an affair holding great danger for anyone connected with it." As briefly and as simply as I could, I described to her the disappearance of the watch that had caused the thunderclap, and the principles that the Professor had explained to me. It was clear that Agathe Lamartine was a true daughter of her father. She followed my words and my explanation, at times interjecting some comment or question that showed that she was in full understanding of my words.

"There is more," I told her, and proceeded to give her an account of the journey that her father and I had undertaken together to the Untime. As best I could, I described the almost ineffable nature of the Untime, and the feeling of power that I experienced over Time and space. As I described her father's words and behaviour during our sojourn in the Untime when we visited the Chamber of Deputies, and also on our return from that mysterious dimension, I could see her face cloud over with dismay.

"I cannot believe that Father would act and speak in such a way," she exclaimed. The fact that she referred to him as "Father", rather than her usual appellation of "the Professor" indicated to me the depth of emotion to which my words stirred her.

"Believe me, Agathe, this is true," I assured her. "Remember his strange obsession with politics the next day, and his changed behaviour."

"Indeed so. You think that this Untime was the cause of the change in his character?"

"I am sure of it," I told her.

"But what has all of this to do with Marie?" she asked. "Surely he would not treat that darling little infant as he did a watch? Oh, tell me that this is not so, please."

"I cannot do that," I said, simply, and she gazed at me in horror.

"Then where— when— what has happened to the child?" she cried, in such a tone that the diners at other tables turned to look at us.

"Please, my dear, be quiet," I begged her, once again seizing her hand in mine, an action which did not seem to displease her. I told her of my discovery of her father in the laboratory on the day when I had visited to help search for the missing child. When I came to the part of my narrative where I described her father threatening me with a revolver, she drew in her breath sharply and put released her hand from mine, before putting both hands to her cheeks.

"It is an incredible tale that you are telling me, Jules," she said to me, using my Christian name for the first time in my memory, as I continued with my tale. "But I do not believe that you are inventing this story."

"There is still more that I must tell you," I said to her. "I have been making enquiries. During the time that you believed that your father was in South America, your father wrote to you regularly?"

"Oh yes, indeed he did. But why do you say 'believed'?" she asked, curiously. "He had a strange arrangement, though. All the letters he sent to us passed through his university department, where he still held a position, and came to us in envelopes with French stamps, posted from Paris."

"Really?" I said. "That must have been a sad disappointment."

"It was, indeed," she said. "And I was surprised how little about Brazil and Argentina he had to tell us in his letters. I was looking forward to reading about those places, but the letters were chiefly trivial enquiries about our health and so on."

"And when you replied, where did you address the letters?"

"To the university department, and they would forward them to him in America."

"Agathe," I said to her, placing my hands on the table, and leaning forward, "Several trustworthy persons have sworn to me that they saw him in Paris during the time that you believed him to be out of the country."

Chapter XVIII

S HE shrank back, as suddenly as if I had made a move to strike her, and then sat silently in thought for a few seconds. "These people who swore to you that they had seen him, what manner of people were they?"

"Of the lower classes," I told her. "One old woman who told me that she had been your father's housekeeper in a house in Vincennes. The details she provided were most circumstantial. There was also an old coal-heaver who described a man who could only be your father who lived there for a few years."

"I suppose I must believe you are sincere when you tell me all of these things," she said.

"But it seems so hard to believe such a thing about one's own father."

"I can only give you the facts as I see them," I replied. "They may admit of another interpretation, but I find it hard to construct any other."

"And Marie?" she asked.

"I told you just now, did I not, of your father's words to me."

"Poor little Marie." She sat in silent thought for a while, and burst out with, "If I understand what you are saying, we will never see little Marie again."

"I am afraid you are correct, as far as I can tell," I told her gravely.

"But what can we do? Poor Father, I fear for his sanity and his happiness."

As it happened, this was a long way from being my major concern, but I held my peace on the matter. "I have enlisted the assistance of Professor Schneider," I said to her.

"That great hulking bear of a man!" she exclaimed indignantly. "Why, if you only knew how he hates my father!"

"I believe he is sufficiently in control of his emotions for that not to play a major part in influencing his actions. He has confessed the enmity between himself and your father to me, but he makes no attempt to dissemble, or to conceal this. I sincerely believe that he is guided by other motives in his wish to stop your father." I told her some more of Schneider's fears that the Untime might lead to the destruction of our Universe as we currently understand it, and told her of the machinery we had discovered in the abandoned house in Vincennes.

"Do you have an explanation for this?" she said.

"Indeed I do. I believe that your father has already gone back to that house in Vincennes a few years before this. I have been to see the letting agents today, and I discovered that a man, very much resembling your father in appearance, was the last tenant of that house. The lease expired only recently, even though there has been no-one living there for some time. In the past, he will use the knowledge he now possesses to build himself a machine that will return him to the future – his future, that is. This time in which we live now, or rather, a short time from now."

"And all this business has occurred, or will occur – I hardly know how I should express this – while he was supposedly in South America?"

"I believe so. By going into the past, one raises

the question of the possibility that one is in two places at one time. This, of course, could lead to paradoxical situations where one might easily meet oneself. Imagine meeting yourself, and causing an injury to yourself. Would oneself, the later version of oneself, that is, feel the effects of that injury?" I laughed lightly, but she considered the matter with all seriousness.

"Or," she ruminated, "perhaps if one travels into the past, the person that one was at that time, that is to say the earlier self, disappears from that time? In that way, it would be impossible to meet oneself, or..." She considered her own words for a short while. "But that cannot be, can it? "

"I do not know. I can ask Professor Schneider when I see him tomorrow. Indeed, I wish that you would come tomorrow and meet him, and see for yourself what we have discovered in the house at Vincennes."

"I am beginning to understand what you are saying. While my father was in the past – the past relative to our time now, I mean – it was impossible for him to also exist at the time to which he was travelling from now. It was therefore necessary for him to disappear from view, as far as we were concerned, at the least, and the easiest way for him to do that was to pretend to take an extended trip abroad."

My head was spinning with the complexity of the ideas that were passing between us. "It is perfectly possible that you are correct there. You must certainly meet Professor Schneider and tell him what you know, and also what you feel may be the truth. I told you truthfully that he has no love for your father, but I do believe that he has a respect for his theories and for his discoveries. He would listen to his daughter – you – and your suggestions and ideas with more respect than he would give to mine, I am sure."

"Then I will visit you tomorrow. The address?"

I gave her the address of the house, but warned her, "I do not think it would be wise to write this down. Should your father somehow return and come across it, he will no doubt recognise it, and ask you for its meaning. Rather, you should commit it to memory." I asked her to repeat the address until I was confident that she had it by heart. "And you will come?" I asked. I fear that my voice betrayed my anxiety, for she turned and bestowed on me a sweet smile.

"You should have no concern regarding that. You have persuaded me that there is cause for concern, and yet..." Her voice tailed off.

"What is it, Agathe?" I asked anxiously.

"It is nothing really. This whole affair seems too incredible – almost impossible – for me to consider seriously. Are you quite sure that your experience in this machine has not turned your own wits?"

I laughed. "I have the evidence of the letting agents as well as that of those whom I have questioned," I pointed out to her. "There is also the evidence of the machinery in the abandoned house, which is identical to that I have seen in your father's laboratory. This is not simply a fancy in my head, believe me, Agathe."

"Poor father!" she said, sighing in a manner which I found to be most fetching. "I knew that he was under some strain, but I had no idea that he was suffering in this way."

It was touching to observe the degree of filial devotion the Professor aroused in his daughter, but I could hardly be expected to display sympathy for a man who had threatened me with a loaded revolver and promised to hunt me down should I fail to obey his commands.

"In any event," I said, "he is not showing himself at your house, even if he is, as I believe, concealing himself in his laboratories?"

"That is correct. He informed us a few days

ago that he would be away from the house on business. Of course, you may well be correct, and he is living in the laboratory at present."

"Then, Agathe, I must ask you to help us before you pay your visit tomorrow. I wish you to return to the house and search his study for any papers or anything that might appear to have any relevance to this business of the Untime, and then bring those papers to me?"

She bit her lip as she turned these words over in her mind. "His study is usually locked," she told me, "but if you really consider it necessary, I could probably find a way to enter it. However, from what you say, most of his notes will be in his laboratory, and if you feel that he is there, and in no mood to deal with others, it would be foolish in the extreme for me to attempt to enter."

"I would not dream of placing you in danger," I assured her. "I simply ask you to do what you can."

"I have only known you a short time, Jules," (again my Christian name!) "but I know you to be an honest and level-headed man. You know that I am devoted to my father, but as a result of what you have just told me, I will help you, and through you, will aid him!"

In a fever of admiration and of affection – nay, love! – for this remarkable woman, I snatched up her hand and pressed it to my lips, covering it with ardent kisses. She smiled at me, and suffered her hand to remain in mine a little longer before withdrawing it. At that moment, despite the danger that we faced, I believe I was the happiest man on this earth.

CHAPTER XIX

THE next day saw me at the Vincennes house, once more engaged in the cleaning of the apparatus that promised to lead us to the Untime. I had attired myself somewhat more appropriately for the occasion, and I no longer cursed so frequently as the dirt and dust from the machine transferred itself to my garments.

Schneider, too, had adopted more informal dress, and he too was working with a will, polishing brass rods, adjusting pipes and fittings, and constantly making notes on what he discovered as he worked.

It was, perhaps, the middle of the morning (I had left my watch at my apartment, fearing for its safety) when we perceived a knock at the door.

"I paid that man Gérard enough money to stay away, did I not?" explained Schneider in a state of some irritation. "Will you see who is knocking, and send them away, Gauthier? I am in the middle of some complex measurements here and do not wish to be interrupted."

I wiped my oily hands on a rag, and set off down the stairs. On opening the door, I beheld Agathe. It was not entirely a surprise to me, given that I had requested her presence, but I was not prepared for her to arrive so early.

"You appear fatigued," I told her. "I was not expecting you to come here at this early hour."

She smiled in reply as she took in my dishevelled and unkempt appearance. "Why, M. Gauthier," she laughed. "Have you taken up a new profession? Does whatever you are doing to put you in that condition really pay you better than writing for that magazine?"

"By no means," I said. "As I told you yesterday, Professor Schneider and I are busy cleaning and preparing the machinery that was discovered here, which corresponds to that which I saw in your father's laboratory."

"Show me!" she commanded, her eyes

gleaming.

"It is dirty. I fear for your fine clothes." As I said these words, I was suddenly aware that her garments were not of the quality with which I usually associated her.

At this, she laughed outright. "My dear Jules, your concerns should be for me, rather than for my clothes, should they not? See," and with this, she spun around, showing that her garments were indeed those of a servant used to performing the most menial of domestic tasks. "Lead me. I am ready for all the dirt and grime that you can summon."

I had no option but to lead the way up the stairs, and take her to the room where Professor Schneider was still hard at work. He started when he saw Agathe.

"My dear Gauthier," he said to me. "I am aware that you dislike this work, but there is no call whatsoever for you to shirk it, and to pass it over to a common maid, who is almost certainly likely to cause some catastrophe in her ignorance as she attempts to clean this delicate mechanism."

I was mortified by his failure to recognise Agathe as a young lady of breeding, and looked over to her to see how she would react to this gaffe. To my surprise, she was smiling quietly, and showed no inclination to correct his mistake, clearly waiting for my intervention.

"Professor Schneider," I began hesitantly, "I fear that you are unaware of this young lady's identity." He looked up, and regarded me, and then Agathe, with some interest. "May I introduce Mademoiselle Agathe Lamartine, the daughter of Professor Lamartine?"

Confusion spread over the Professor's bear-like face as he realised the implications of my words. "My dear young lady... Mademoiselle... I am so sorry... your dress..."

"There is nothing for which you need apologise," she told him. "I am fully aware that my dress could cause confusion if it were the only criterion by which I am judged."

"Thank you, Mademoiselle. But," as a thought seemed to strike him, "may I ask what you are doing here? How did you come to know of this place? Who sent you here? What is your purpose in being here?" His voice rose in pitch and intensity with each question.

I decided that these were questions best answered by me. "She is here at my invitation, Professor. I trust Mademoiselle Lamartine absolutely. We met last night, and I told her about her father, and about this discovery here." Here Schneider let out a most undignified snort. "I asked her to search in her father's study for any papers relating to the Untime."

"And has she brought them? Have you?" he accused, turning on her.

"Indeed I have, Professor Schneider," she answered meekly, bringing a folded sheaf of papers from her bosom, and passing them to me. The warmth of her body was still on the papers as they rested in my hand, and despite myself, I trembled at the indirect intimacy. I had no doubt that her perfume also still remained on them, but I was not about to put this to the test in front of others, but merely handed the papers in my turn to Schneider, who took them, placed his pince-nez on his nose, and riffled through them.

"Where did you find these?" he enquired sharply of Agathe, looking up.

"They were in a drawer in the desk in his study," she answered him.

"Was the drawer locked?"

She turned red and stammered. "Yes. Yes, it was. I had a spare key with which I opened the lock."

"Is this relevant?" I asked Schneider.

"Indeed it is. Professor Lamartine is well aware of what you know, Gauthier, and it is not impossible that he might leave some papers containing false information in a prominent position hoping that they might be discovered, and thereby put the discoverer on a false trail. If, however, these papers were in a locked drawer, this possibility becomes less likely." He returned to the papers, and studied them intently. "It is excellent stuff as far as it goes," he told us, "but it does not go far enough, I fear. Some vital conclusions are missing."

"Perhaps these would help?" suggested Agathe, proffering another set of papers. I had not seen from where she had produced these, but Schneider did not seem to be concerned with their immediate provenance, merely taking the papers with a brusque word of thanks.

"Where were these discovered, then?" he asked.

"In his laboratory," she said. Schneider smiled a strange smile that I was unable to comprehend.

I drew in my breath. "I warned you, did I not, Agathe, that you should never go there."

"I took every precaution. I went to the laboratory. There was no sign of him there." Once again, Schneider gave what can only be described as a snort at these words. "I took these papers from his desk in the laboratory," she added. "The Professor, my father, that is, had given me a key to the laboratory, in case I ever took a fancy to perform my own experiments," she added by way of explanation.

"Your experiments?" I exclaimed. This was the first I had ever heard of Agathe's interest in such things.

"Why are you so surprised that the child of a scientist should follow her father?"

"Nothing, except that you..." my voice tailed off.

"...that I am a woman? Well, why should a woman not engage herself in the sciences? There is a woman from Poland who has recently married a Frenchman, Pierre Curie, and is making great progress in her field, discovering new elements, I am told. Why should I not do the same?"

I regarded Agathe with a new respect. I had never before encountered such a person, and her words astounded me.

Schneider, however, appeared to take the news in his stride. "And I take it that your father was not in his laboratory?"

"Obviously not, or I would not have these

papers," she replied. "Indeed, there has been no sign of him anywhere for several days. He informed us that he had gone to Brest to hold discussions with the naval officers there, and these were of such a secret nature that we were not to attempt to communicate with him."

Schneider gave another of his inscrutable smiles. "And when you entered the laboratory, you saw the machine there, similar to this one here, that Gauthier here has described to me?" he asked.

"Indeed so, and it is almost identical, as far as I can tell on this first inspection," she said.

Schneider made a grunting sound, and resumed his perusal of the papers.

"There is an error here," he said, looking up. "One that could lead your father, Mademoiselle, into more dangerous paths than those of which he is currently aware?"

"What might that be?"

"I believe, after reading these notes, that Professor Lamartine is under the impression that he can use the Untime to go back in time and change history."

"But that would surely be a good thing? If the wrongs and evils of the past could be corrected?"

"It would indeed, if it were possible," replied

Schneider. "But sadly, it is impossible." He shook his head.

Chapter XX

"**B**ut if we can go back in time, we can have an effect on what happens there, can we not?" I asked.

"You cannot change history," Schneider said to us. "To admit such a thing was possible would be to admit that many different histories exist."

"Why do they not?" I asked him. "For example, if I were to return to 1792 and rescue the King from the guillotine?"

"You could not do such a thing," he replied to me, shaking his head. "Something would prevent you from doing so."

"What would prevent me?"

"I cannot tell you exactly what it would be that

would prevent you, but circumstances would prevail in such a way that you would be unable to accomplish your goal. You would be prevented somehow. Maybe you would break your leg on the way to the Tuileries for your rescue attempt, or you would be stopped by a guard. It is impossible to say exactly how events would transpire. The history you know, and that you will always know, is that on September 21, 1792, Louis XVI of France was executed by the guillotine. Nothing you can do in the Untime will change that fact.

"However," he continued, speaking as if he were delivering a lecture to his students at the Sorbonne, "if we accept the possibility of a number of universes, such as I described earlier, then it might be that in a different universe, we would now be living in the reign of Louis XX, whose family had reigned in an unbroken line for the past hundred years."

"I cannot believe this," said Agathe. "I refuse to believe in your multiple universes." She seized a pen and began to scribble mathematical equations on a sheet of paper that lay to hand. I was completely unable to comprehend their meaning, and watched dumbfounded as the symbols continued to appear on the page as Agathe wrote, seemingly totally engrossed in her calculations. At length, she put down the pen, and passed the paper to Schneider, who took it and glanced at it casually. His eyes were still fixed on it as he laid it aside on the table, but suddenly his manner changed.

He picked up the paper once more, and scanned it, obviously giving it his full attention, running his finger down the line of equations. When he had reached the bottom of the paper, his finger returned to the top, and he repeated the operation, at a slower pace. His lips moved silently as he traced the mathematics, and the process took a good three or four minutes.

At length he laid the paper aside once again, and sat in silence for a few minutes more. Eventually, he spoke.

"My sincere congratulations, Mademoiselle," he said, in a tone which was unlike his usual rough accents. "You are undoubtedly your father's daughter, and I would venture to suggest that your mental prowess exceeds his." He scribbled a couple of lines at the bottom of the paper, and passed it back to her.

She took the proffered paper, and scanned the additions, shaking her head. "No, no," she murmured, using the pen to amend his writing before returning the paper to him.

He scanned it once more, muttering to himself, and then looked up at her, gazing into her eyes. "My hat is off to you," he declared. He sketched the motion of doffing an imaginary cap with an exaggerated motion, and Agathe flushed.

"You mean, sir, that my little effort—"

"'Little effort' be damned!" thundered Schneider in his customary tones, clearly temporarily oblivious of the fact that he was addressing a member of the fair sex. "Your 'little effort' has completely overturned my theory in a matter of minutes. I cannot recall when I have seen such an argument so clearly and concisely expressed. I would ask one favour of you, Mademoiselle."

"What is that?"

"That you do not publish this work and my feeble attempts at criticism. It would make me a laughing stock throughout the world. Have no fear, though. I am not one of those who takes the work of others and passes it off as their own. I would simply ask you to keep this in the private eye for some time. May I beseech you to do this?"

"Of course, Professor," my Agathe replied, a merry twinkle in her eye, "if this really means so much to you."

"It does indeed mean much to me, and I thank you sincerely for your generosity of spirit in this matter," he answered her.

"Does this theory of Mlle. Lamartine disprove your thesis that we cannot change the past?" I asked. I was well aware that the mathematical reasoning that had just passed between the two was as incomprehensible to me as the workings of a steam-engine would be to an orang-utan, but I wished to have some explanation regarding its significance.

"By no means," he said. "By no means. It strengthens my conviction that we have one past and one past only. It does, however, somewhat work against my previous idea regarding a multiplicity of universes. Indeed, it completely invalidates it." He spoke with a rueful smile, which he turned on Agathe. "I promise you that there is a position for you to teach at the Sorbonne, should you ever desire it. I swear to you that, should you decide to take that course, I will do all in my power to smooth your path."

"Thank you, sir," she replied, with an admirable modesty of demeanour.

However, the task before us was not to engage in flights of philosophical fancy, but consisted merely of the mundane cleaning of the apparatus before us.

Such an occupation, though demanding physically at times, made few demands on my mental faculties, and I was therefore able to ponder on the exchange that had just taken place between my two companions. I was unable, naturally, to appreciate the finer points of the mathematics that my Agathe (as I now, perhaps somewhat prematurely, mentally referred to her) had placed before Schneider, but I was now able to understand, to my relief, that both she and Schneider considered our universe to be the only one in existence. More immediately as far as my heart was concerned, however, was the thought that the girl with whom I found myself in love (for this was not a conscious decision on my part) was the equal, if not the superior, of one of the foremost savants in France, at least in the field of theoretical mathematics. The prospect of an alliance with such a powerful intellect would give any man pause for thought, I told myself, and I vainly tried to disabuse myself of the idea that there was any mutual attraction between us.

This attempt was not assisted by the smiles and words of encouragement that came my way from Agathe at regular intervals as we worked together polishing the brass-work and glass of the apparatus, and cleaning the wooden bars of the framework. While we were doing this, Professor Schneider was engaged in tightening valves and re-filling the tanks and reservoirs that held the mysterious liquids and gasses which he had brought from his laboratory.

A thought struck me, and I attracted Schneider's attention. "We are cleaning this apparatus, are we not, and placing it in working order?"

"Of course, you fool," he exclaimed testily. "What else?"

"For what reason?"

"Surely it is obvious to you?" He smiled, but the expression on his face was not a pleasant one.

"So that Professor Lamartine can return here using it?"

"For Heaven's sake, man," protested Schneider, and the tone of his voice was angry. "You do not believe that Lamartine needs this to come back here? You told me yourself that in this Untime, you could roam at will through time and space?"

"I did."

"We have no idea when or where he will

choose to come back to us. I think we may be certain that it will be soon. But where?" He spread his hands in an expressive gesture. "It could be anywhere in this world. I would be extremely surprised if it were in this house."

"But, then...?"

Agathe interrupted me. "What Professor Schneider means, Jules, is that if we cannot find my father in the normal time and space that we inhabit, then the Untime is where we must search for him."

"But you cannot do that, my dear, and Professor Schneider cannot..." My voice trailed off as I realised my two companions were looking at me.

Chapter XXI

"YOU wish me to go into the Untime to discover his whereabouts?" I stammered.

"I would have thought that was obvious," replied Schneider in a somewhat sarcastic tone.

In a little gentler voice, my Agathe added, "Jules, you must understand that neither Professor Schneider nor I has ever been into this Untime. It was strange, you say?"

"Monstrously so," I answered her, surprising myself with my choice of word.

"But you, my dear, are the only man other than my father to have experienced this strange state. If either Professor Schneider or I should enter it—"

"God forbid, Agathe, that you should expose yourself to the Untime!"

"And you said yourself, did you not, Gauthier, that I was unsuitable to enter the Untime?" Schneider reminded me. To my horror, I confessed that this was so. "In that case," Schneider went on, smiling the sweet smile of a devil, "you are the only one of our little company who is suited to take this voyage."

"Do you suppose that I can locate your father in the Untime?" I asked Agathe.

"From what you have told me, that is exactly what you did on the past occasion."

"And then what am I expected to do once he has been found?"

"You must stop him returning," said Schneider. "At least, you must stop him returning with his ideas about ruling our world."

"Do you think I can persuade him?" I was doubtful of my ability to do any such thing at the best of times, let alone in the Untime. "You must remember that we are talking of a man who had threatened me with a revolver and had sworn to hunt me down and kill me if I crossed his path."

"If you cannot persuade him, you must stop him and prevent him from causing any mischief," Schneider told me. I could hear Agathe catch her breath.

"You mean that Jules must kill my father?"

Schneider nodded his great bear-like head. "But only as a last resort. Consider, Mademoiselle. You have proved to me that you have a sound head on your shoulders. Should your father be unaware of the consequences of the equations that you produced so admirably earlier, what is the conclusion?"

I could see her turning the matter over in her mind, and suddenly visibly stop short and turn pale. "It would be the end of the world," she whispered hoarsely. "If not the end of the Universe as we know it."

"And what is one man's life against that?" Schneider demanded of her. "Even when that one man is your father?"

Agathe bit her trembling lip. "You are correct, *maître*, but you cannot expect me to dance with joy when I hear you say this."

"Be brave, my dear," I told her, placing a hand lightly on her shoulder. However, she shrugged off my hand with a twist of her body, and walked away from Schneider and me to the other side of the room, by the window.

"It is hard for me to accept in my heart what

you say, Professor," she said to Schneider, "though my head acknowledges the truth of your words. Poor father. Poor Jules," she added, looking at me, and then broke into sobs. "No, do not touch me," she said, as I moved to comfort her. I looked over at Schneider, who merely raised his eyebrows and glanced at the apparatus that we had been cleaning.

I took the hint, picking up one of the rags we used for polishing the brass rods, and left Agathe to her weeping, though it nearly broke my heart to see her in that state of distress.

After a few minutes, her sobs stopped. "I am going out for a few minutes," she informed us. "I am sure you two men will have plenty to discuss." And, with a toss of her curls, she was gone.

"Women!" exclaimed Schneider. "Even the best of them, such as she, seem to be incapable of rational thought at times of crisis."

"I hardly think you are being fair to Mademoiselle Lamartine," I retorted. "You have just informed her that a young man for whom she has displayed some partiality is to take the life of her beloved father. May I turn the tables on you, Professor, and ask you exactly what would be your reaction under similar circumstances?"

"Impertinence!" he replied gruffly. "I shall not dignify such an enquiry with an answer." With that, he turned once more to the mechanism, and made several seemingly unnecessary adjustments to one of the numberless valves and stopcocks.

Not a word passed between us for some fifteen minutes, during which time we worked diligently at the restoration of the apparatus. The door opened, and Agathe entered the room.

"I have considered what you said, Professor," she addressed Schneider. "Of course you are right in saying that my father must be stopped from his meddling, and that the best way of achieving this is to meet him in the Untime. However, I am in complete disagreement as to both the means and the agency by which this shall be accomplished."

Schneider laid down the tools with which he had been working, and regarded her gravely. "Pray continue," he invited her.

"First, I think it is only natural on my part for me to express the wish that my father's life be spared, if this is at all possible. If persuasion, rather than force, can be used, I would find this to be infinitely preferable."

Schneider nodded. "I quite understand, Mademoiselle."

"And so," she continued, "I feel that it would not be wise to undertake to send M. Gauthier here to undertake the mission. Jules, you told me that my father threatened you, did you not?"

"Yes, that is correct."

"Do either of you think that he would be persuaded by M. Gauthier, charming and clever with words though he may be, rather than his own flesh and blood – myself?" she declaimed.

"You make an excellent point, Mademoiselle," replied Schneider.

He seemed poised to say more, but before he could utter a sound, I leaped into the discussion. "Agathe!" I exclaimed with all the vigour of which I was capable, "you shall not enter the Untime! It cannot be!"

She laid a calming hand on my sleeve. "Why not, my dear Jules?" she asked, with a smile that would have melted the heart of a marble statue.

"It is an absurd idea," I answered, angrily. "You have no conception of the Untime, other than as a series of equations on a piece of paper. You would become completely disorientated were you to enter the Untime. And your constitution, Agathe. Consider your health and the risk, not only to your body, but to your mind. Why, Professor Schneider here has declared to me that entering the Untime can cause severe damage to one's mental faculties. Is that not so, Professor?"

To my horror, the wretch refused to support me in this assertion. "It is true, Gauthier, that I may have made a remark to that effect in the past. However, on reflection and further calculation, I have come to revise my opinion on the matter. It is now my opinion that no harm will result to Mademoiselle Lamartine from a trip to the Untime."

I could cheerfully have put my hands around the Professor's throat and throttled him on the spot, had it not been for the presence of Agathe, which stayed my hand. It was she who broke the silence.

"I do confess that I feel more than a little nervous at the prospect of entering the Untime, and therefore I was going to suggest, before he so gallantly intervened on my behalf, that M. Gauthier accompanied me. That is to say, that the two of us enter the Untime together."

At these words, I felt a weight was lifted from my mind. It would be I, Jules Gauthier, who would be the protector of this remarkable woman whom I loved, and it would be I who would be her guide through the mysteries of those strange dimensions revealed by her father. My heart lifted as I considered the prospect, and I clasped her hand and lifted it to my lips.

"Together, my darling," I exclaimed in my passion. "We will conquer the Untime together!"

Chapter XXII

NOTWITHSTANDING this determination, it was clear that more work needed to be done before Agathe and I could enter the Untime. Schneider reminded us both that there were many chemicals and liquids which were still necessary for the machinery to function properly, and he also gave it as his opinion that we had little time to spare before Lamartine reappeared in our time once more. This was a signal to us to work hard on the reconstruction of the apparatus, and we applied ourselves to the task to such good effect that Schneider pronounced the machine to be in working order the very day after the conversation recorded above.

"You must test it," I told him. "Take a watch or some such and send it forward in time by an hour or so." I offered my own timepiece for the purpose.

"I suppose that is a wise precaution," he admitted, taking the watch. "I feel I have sufficient knowledge of the way in which the controls work."

He placed the watch in the centre of the glass plate and bent to the control panel.

"When Professor Lamartine performed this experiment in front of me," I reminded him, "we required dark goggles, and stopped our ears with cotton-wool. Remember that this operation will produce a considerable flash and noise. We would also do well to cover the windows, so that we do not attract the attention of the neighbours."

"Very well," he said. "Do we have any such goggles here? I have seen none."

"Nor I," I replied.

It was Agathe who discovered two sets of goggles in a bureau drawer, with the lenses constructed from smoked glass. I was more than happy to allow her and Schneider to be the witnesses of the disappearance, my eyes and ears having suffered from such an event in the past. However, I gave both Agathe and Schneider due warning, which they took under advisement, and we proceeded to hang the heavy drapes over the windows once more, as they had been when I first entered the room several days previously. I watched my beloved and Schneider fill their ears with some balls of the cotton waste, taken from the supply that we had acquired for wiping down the machine, and adjust the goggles over their heads. I waved a farewell with my hand, and stepped down the stairs and into the street.

After I had been waiting for about a minute, a loud report issued from the house. A horse pulling a carriage shied, and it was necessary for the driver to calm him, but otherwise there was no other reaction that I could observe, from the neighbours or from any passer-by. I re-entered the house and mounted the stairs to find Agathe collapsed in a chair, with Professor Schneider standing over her, fanning her face with a sheet of paper. A glance at the apparatus was enough to show me that the watch had vanished.

"The poor girl was overcome by the noise and the flash," he told me. "To be frank with you, it took me by surprise, even though you had warned us of the intensity of the event. I have removed her goggles, as you can see, but her eyes remain closed."

I poured a glass of mineral water from the bottles with which the Professor and I had provided ourselves, and held it to her lips. With her eyes still closed, she accepted a few sips of water, and then opened her eyes and looked me in the eye.

"How are you, my dear?" I asked her, but received no reply other than a look of incomprehension. "She has been deafened by the violence of the explosion!" I cried, but happily it transpired that I was mistaken in my assumption. My Agathe smiled sweetly at me, and raised her hands to her ears, whence she drew the balls of cotton waste that had plugged them.

"Now what was it you were saying to me just now, Jules?" she asked, with that sweet but impudent smile on her face.

"I was asking if you were well," I laughed. "But it appears that my enquiry is a little superfluous.

"Thank you, but I am now quite well and recovered. However, the noise of the explosion was more than I was expecting, and I am afraid I must have lost my senses."

"Are you sure that you will be able to travel to

the Untime and survive its rigours?" I asked her.

"I can only tell you that I will do my utmost." The look on her face was one of determination, and was enough to convince me of her intent.

"How long until the watch re-appears?" I asked the Professor.

"I set the time for approximately thirty minutes from now," he informed me. "Mademoiselle Lamartine assisted me in this, and though we are not completely familiar with the workings of the mechanism, I can express with reasonable confidence that the setting is tolerably accurate. We have now another," he pulled a large watch from his pocket, "twenty-three minutes to wait. I suggest that we spend the time in settling what objects you should take with you into the Untime."

I laughed in his face. "My dear Professor Schneider," I told him. "In the Untime, one is totally unconscious of one's body. There is no way in which any physical object would be of any use there. The only thing that I might recommend," I added, remembering my own experience, "would be a small bottle of eau-de-vie or something similar. There is something in the Untime that saps the heat from one's body on returning to our dimensions."

"That may well be so," said Schneider. "However, it would seem prudent to be prepared for any eventuality when you leave the Untime, at whatever time or place you may find yourself."

Again, I laughed. "The place may be the North Pole or the middle of the Sahara desert. And the time? That may be the present day, or it may be the Middle Ages or the Classical Age of the Greeks. Or it may be a time in the future, when the whole world is ruled by electrical devices, and humanity is no more than a redundant cog in the world's machinery."

"What a poetic turn of phrase you have, to be sure," smiled Agathe. "But then, I suppose that is your trade."

"My point, all poetry aside," I went on, "is that to be sure of being prepared for any eventuality, one would need to carry a vast trunk, crammed with every contrivance known to man."

"At least let me persuade you to take this on your travels," answered the Professor, reaching inside his coat and withdrawing a large, heavy revolver, at the sight of which Agathe let out a little involuntary shriek of fear.

"You would want Jules here to use this against my father?" she exclaimed.

"I sincerely hope that it will prove unnecessary," he answered her. "However, I believe it behoves him and you to be well prepared for any eventuality. If what I have been told, and what my own calculations tell me are correct, then there is no knowing what you may encounter in the Untime."

"You are beginning to give me even more cause for alarm," said Agathe. "To what sort of things are you referring?"

"Given the infinite nature of Space, and the eternal nature of Time, it could be anything? From the monstrous lizards that roamed the Earth in ancient times, to such creatures as may inhabit the most distant planets in our Universe, and of which we can have no conception as to their nature."

I laughed. "In that case, my dear Professor Schneider," I retorted, returning the weapon to him, "I hardly think that such a crude physical weapon such as a revolver will be of any assistance to us in our travels. In any event, suppose that we do leave the Untime to enter the frozen wastes of Siberia or the steaming jungles of the Amazon, whether in our own time, or at any time in the past or the future, we will have no way of returning to the Untime, and hence to Paris. What must be done, must be done in the Untime, and there is therefore no need for us to carry such a weapon. Furthermore, did I not mention to you earlier, if I am not mistaken, that Professor Lamartine and I were careful to remove all metal from our persons before entering the Untime? I hardly wish to risk entering it carrying that monstrosity," and I indicated the pistol.

Schneider appeared to be a little discomfited by my refusal, but accepted my argument, albeit with what appeared to be bad grace.

"In that case, since you seem determined to set off unprepared and defenceless, I would suggest that you start as soon as the watch reappears, which will be in approximately three minutes from now."

Almost as he finished speaking, the watch appeared on the glass plate, and I went to pick it up, noting the time. "Indeed, it is at the same time as when it left us," I said.

"Although the machinery appears to be slightly imperfectly adjusted," said Schneider, "as can be seen from the early appearance of the watch, this should make no difference to animate sentient beings such as yourself and Mademoiselle Lamartine. It is time for you to take your places.

As Gauthier has told us, youi should remove all
metal from your persons."

CHAPTER XXIII

HAVING divested myself of all metal objects, and Agathe having done the same, she and I took our place on the glass plate which stood at the centre of the machinery.

"Hold my hand, Jules," she said softly to me. "I do not consider myself a coward, but I need the reassurance of your presence."

I took her small, cool, dry hand in mine, uncomfortably aware of the fact that my own palm was moist with anxiety.

Although I had undergone this experience in the past, I still felt considerable trepidation as I watched Professor Schneider approach the control panel. After all, I reasoned, he was not

the inventor of the machine, and his understanding of the principles governing it, though
far in advance of my own, was far from perfect,
as was shown by the way in which the watch
had returned to us somewhat earlier than we
had expected.

As before, there was an uncomfortable feeling that my body had disappeared. The choking
sensation and the heat that I had experienced
on the previous occasion were also very much
in evidence, and I experienced considerable discomfort once again, but as before, this
passed quite quickly. I was intensely aware of
the presence of Agathe beside me, but the pres-
sure of her hand in mine had disappeared, as
indeed had her hand itself, and mine.

Though I had no head to turn, it seemed,
nonetheless I could direct my attention in a
particular direction, and though all that I could
perceive was the same pale green glow that
had accompanied me on my previous visit to
the Untime, I was very much aware of Agathe's
presence. This was in contrast to the previous
occasion, when I had not been aware of the
presence of her father without a conscious
effort on my part to detect it.

Although, as I say, nothing was visible, Agathe

still seemed to me as an invisible luminous presence. I realise that what I have just set down is a contradiction in terms, and that you will write me down as a madman for these words, but it is the closest that I can come to explaining myself here.

I remembered the method by which I had been able to communicate with Professor Lamartine previously, and adjusted my mind in an attempt to make contact with Agathe. Almost immediately, her unheard words filled my head. You must realise that when we were communicating with each other in the Untime in this way, although no words were audible, it was still very possible to distinguish tone of voice and so on, and on this occasion, it was in a much clearer fashion than had been the case with Agathe's father and myself previously.

I had occasion to speak confidentially at a later date with an English savant specialising in psychic matters, and he gave it as his considered belief that the affection that was present between Agathe and myself was the cause of this improved link between our souls in the Untime.

"It is magnificent!" she exclaimed. Certainly, there seemed to be no trepidation in her voice, and there was a confidence there that, quite frankly, I envied. "It is extraordinary, Jules," she continued. "I can see nothing but this pale mist that surrounds me, but at the same time, I am fully conscious of your presence, and of your voice inside me. How exciting this all is!"

I could not help but admire her spirit and her attitude. I had been fully prepared to act as her guide and support, should she fall prey to the terrors of the Untime, but it now appeared to me that I might well be the one supported, given her seemingly indomitable nature.

"I am beginning to understand," she went on, "the megalomania that afflicted my dear father."

"I hope that this is not going to affect you also," I replied.

There was the delicious sound of a chuckle inside my mind. "My dear Jules, I sincerely trust that you do not believe me to be subject to these same temptations."

"By no means," I assured her.

"Very well, then. I have the strong impression that a single step will take us anywhere in the Universe, simply by willing it to be so. Is that your understanding?"

"That is what I believe."

"Very good, then. My study of my father's

papers, and my own mathematical calculations also, have persuaded me of this. I have always entertained a fancy to see a kangaroo in its natural habitat. Shall we take a brief stroll together to Australia, my dear Jules?" There was something between delight and mockery in the way that her words resounded, which I found entrancing.

"With all my heart," I responded, in the same vein, and together we took the two steps that brought us to the edge of the Australian desert. Naturally, we did not leave the Untime, for we would have had no way of re-entering, but it was possible for us to observe the arid landscape, albeit through a faint green haze. In the distance, it was possible to discern some of the marsupials about which Agathe had expressed her interest. Not ten metres in front of us was a family of the Aboriginal inhabitants of the place, consisting of a mother, a father, and two small children, one of whom was being carried on his mother's back. Although his back was turned to us, the little mite seemed aware of our presence, and turned his head towards us, looking straight into my eyes, though I assumed that we were invisible to the little fellow, since there was no recognition in his face, rather there was simply a fixed fascination. His mother became aware of his attention, and turned to face us. Soon the whole family was staring fixedly in our direction, but apparently without being able to see us.

Without warning, the father of the family seized his long wooden spear and hurled it directly at me. If I had been physically present, it would, I judged, have struck me in the chest, but in the Untime, it merely passed insensibly straight through me.

I sensed a gasp from Agathe. "Are you hurt?" I heard.

"Not at all," I sent back to her. "There was no feeling at all."

"I think it is time for us to go," her words echoed in my head.

We took ourselves back into the middle of the Untime, where the pale green mist enveloped us once more.

"Do you think," Agathe asked me, " that we are appearing as ghosts or spirits to those people?"

"I am not sure that we are actually appearing," I answered her, "but it seems to me that the general reaction is that which some people describe when they describe seeing a ghost. Where would you like to go next, my dear?"

"It is not where I would like to go next, but when. Can we step backward and forward in time as easily as we did through space just now? Please do reassure me of this, as I have no wish to be trapped in some time where there is no escape."

"I know from experience that it is possible to travel forward in time," I told her. I see no reason why it should not be as easy to travel backward, provided always that we stay within the Untime, and do not leave the green that surrounds us."

"Green?" came her question. "But it is pink, surely? You are not colour-blind, are you?"

I was able to assure her categorically that I did not suffer from that condition, having recently taken a test as part of the research for an article I was writing on the subject. "But what time would you like to visit?" I asked.

Her answer astonished me. "I would like to visit Ancient Egypt at the time of Cleopatra. Her story has always fascinated me, that she was able to entrance and seduce the most powerful men in the world at that time, and that, it is said, without being beautiful."

"I hope that you are not intending to make her your model," I laughed.

"Indeed not. Humour my womanly fantasy, if you would, though, my dear Jules."

Again, I lack the words to describe how we navigated our way through the centuries to the court of Cleopatra, as she entertained the great Roman general Marcus Antonius. We remained within our coloured mists, apparently out of sight behind a pillar in the throne room.

Chapter XXIV

Ⱨ ERE, as an aside, I wish to set down one of the strangest parts of our adventure in the Untime, which has little or no bearing on the story that I am relating, but it seems to me on reflection that it would be remiss of me not to report it to you. I have explained previously that Time and space were fluid in the Untime, and that moving around in these dimensions was a trivial affair, no matter what the distance or time involved. However, there was yet another dimension, if so it may be termed, of which I was not aware when we entered the Untime, and whose existence I still find it hard to credit, even after I have experienced it at first hand.

If my words and my description here seem a little incoherent, please forgive me. I am, to my knowledge, the only man, and one of only two people in this world to have undergone this experience, and it was so extraordinary that mere words have failed me in attempting to describe it and its effect on me.

This dimension is the one of gender. Incredible as it may seem, in the Untime, it was possible for me to change gender at will, and I became aware of this very shortly after I entered the Untime with Agathe, before we made our journey to Australia. I have a suspicion, which, of course, it is impossible for me to verify or disprove, that it was the presence of Agathe in the Untime with me which provided me with this awareness, and possibly also facilitated the process of change. Of course, my first visit to the Untime was made in the company of Professor Lamartine, another man, and one to whom I felt no emotional attachment, but it is possible that I am making assumptions here that cannot be justified.

Of course, in the Untime, one is bodiless, and it was not possible for me to know whether such a change in my gender was mental only, or whether it would be reflected in my physical appearance should I choose to leave the Untime. I confess that I was most unwilling to make the experiment, quite apart from the difficulty of returning to the Untime should I leave it, and therefore am unable to inform you of the probable result in this regard, should you by some chance in the future find yourself able to visit the Untime, and wish to undertake this change.

While we were finding our feet in the Untime, so to speak, Agathe and I were able to communicate with each other, as I mentioned, and I was able to inform her, phrasing the matter as delicately as possible, of what I had discovered, and what I had achieved. She showed her mettle and her qualities as an explorer of the unknown, and immediately decided for herself that she wished to experiment with this new dimension. Like me, she was unwilling to take herself out of the Untime in her changed state, but was happy to explore the feelings and emotions of a different gender.

As far as the purely mental side of changing gender is concerned, I am able to report that the experience was unlike anything else I have experienced. For those who claim that the differences between men and women are merely those that relate to bodily appearance, I can only reply that you have no conception of the true state of things. My thoughts in my female self took on a new resonance and depth that were unique in my experience. I found myself in tune with the universe on a different level from that I had previously experienced. My sympathy and empathy with all things appeared to be enhanced, and I found myself more deeply engaged with everything around me. It was easier for me to relate to matters outside myself, insofar as I was able to consider them while I was in the Untime, and I gained a different kind of understanding to that which I was accustomed.

At the same time, various aspects of my personality that I had not previously regarded as being exclusively masculine disappeared from my perspective. The barriers that my mind had thrown up over the years to protect me against the slings and arrows of fortune seemed to be weaker, and I felt more vulnerable to those aspects of the world that seemed to oppress me or to be out of tune with my interests. I began to understand some of the feelings in women that men classify as emotional fragility. Even so, if I am to be frank, I enjoyed the sensations that these female sensations produced in me.

I felt a little less happy, though, at the loss of my masculine armour. I cannot honestly say that I found the experience of this loss to be altogether pleasant, as some of those characteristics by which I usually define and differentiate myself from others had also disappeared, or so it seemed to me, since they were so bound up with the masculine image which I present to the world. As with so many aspects of the Untime, it is almost impossible to express the whole of the experience and the feelings that it aroused in mere words, but this changing of my gender is one that I will never forget, and which I am immensely grateful to have undergone, though I know that I will never enter the Untime again. However, while I was undergoing this experience, though so many of the sensations were pleasant, on an intellectual plane, I found the concept to be jarring and unpleasing. I was glad to return to my normal self, and to leave the female version of my character behind, though if I am to be honest, I would have to say that there are times when I wish I could return to it.

After our adventure in the Untime, on comparing notes with Agathe, I discovered that she had experienced much the same feelings as had I, but in reverse. She, too, had shed some aspects of her character which may be described as feminine, and had gained other, masculine character traits. Like me, she felt the loss of some of the characteristics of her original gender, but considered others to be a gain.

Incidentally, we both noted a strange phenomenon. As I have mentioned, I believed the mist with which we surrounded in the Untime as being green, while Agathe reported its colour as being pink. When I took on the female gender, it seemed to me that the colour of the mist changed to pink, and then reverted to green when I re-assumed the male gender. For Agathe, the situation was reversed – the mist changed from pink to green and then back to pink. Proof, if there be any who still doubt it, that men and women do indeed perceive the world in different ways.

After discussing the whole of the matter at length (which we were only to do following our marriage, however) we admitted to each other that we were both happy to revert to our original genders within the Untime, a process which happily proved to be as easy as the initial change, but both of us might welcome the chance, should it be offered, to repeat the process at some time in the future – provided always that it was reversible.

This extraordinary experience, which, dare I say it, is almost certainly unique, has changed the life that Agathe and I live together. Each of us now possesses an understanding of each other which is denied to many couples who are not so fortunate as to have acquired such comprehension that comes with a change in gender, however temporary such a change may have been. If half the world were to gain the understanding of the other half that both Agathe and I encountered, I venture to suggest that the world would be a better and a happier place.

Chapter XXV

WHEN we were standing in what appeared to be Cleopatra's throne room, though servants, almost certainly slaves, were very much in evidence, there was no sign of the Queen, or of her famous paramour. We could distinguish the sound of trumpets and of drums beating a measured cadence, which grew louder, as slaves bearing golden symbols of royalty entered, followed by two litters borne on the shoulders of enormous Nubian slaves.

These litters were placed on the ground, as the trumpets blared a final discordant note, and two maidservants opened the curtains of the first one. Out of the litter stepped a scantily-dressed woman, somewhat short and dumpy in appearance, with a heavily painted face and black hair that was patently a wig. As the assembled crowd fell to its knees and bowed their heads, I realised that this somewhat unprepossessing woman making her way to the throne must be the famous Cleopatra herself. It was not clear to me at first sight how such a character could ever have obtained the reputation of a great seductress. There was, nothing that I could discern, with the eye of a lover of Agathe, that could compare in any way with the charms of my beloved.

"Well, what do you think?" Agathe's words came to me.

"I am astounded that her reputation that has come down to us is what it is," I answered. However, as I observed Cleopatra, I became aware of a seductive aura that surrounded her movements and her person, and I was less sure of the words that I had just spoken. "Let us now see what the famous Mark Antony has to show us."

As if on cue, the curtains of the second litter parted, and a muscular masculine arm, wearing many golden armbands, appeared in the gap. The arm was followed by the body of a man who must, in his prime, have been a perfect Hercules, but now appeared as a pitiful wreck. It was clear to my eye that he was suffering from the effects of overindulgence in the recent past, and that he was having difficulty making his way out of the litter. Two slaves approached him, and offered their shoulders as support, but he brushed them aside with massive sweeps of his arm, swaying slightly on his feet as he did so.

He lifted his head, and I saw his face for the first time. It was one of a man who was born to nobility and power, and who was used to command. That much was clear, but at the same time, it was also painfully obvious that this was a man who had been ruined, either at his own hands, or at those of others, who had exploited his weaknesses to bring him to this present shameful condition.

He spoke in a language which was unknown to me, and a slave approached him, running, and bearing a jewelled goblet in one hand and a jug in another. Kneeling before Marcus Antonius (for this was indeed that tragic ruined figure), he poured dark wine into the goblet, which Antonius then seized and drained in one mighty draught, before holding it out to be refilled.

In the meantime, Cleopatra sat watching on her throne, a half-smile of cynical amusement on her face. She spoke a few words in what appeared to be the same tongue that Antonius had used earlier, and her face changed to a welcoming expression. As if mesmerised, Antonius started to lurch toward her, and this time he did not refuse the proffered assistance of the slaves.

Even so, as he reached the bottom step of the dais on which stood the throne, his foot slipped, and he fell heavily to the ground. As he reached for the waiting arms of the slaves, struggling to his feet, his face froze, and he turned his gaze, with an expression of terror upon his face, in the direction of Agathe and myself. He extended his left fist towards us with the index and little fingers extended, in a gesture that I recalled was intended by the ancient Romans to ward off evil, and slowly took hesitant steps in our direction, before bellowing something incomprehensible to the room at large.

Immediately there was a rustling and a commotion and all in the room reacted. Some produced jewelled amulets from within their garments, and some repeated in our direction the gesture that Antonius had made towards us. However, it did not seem that any of those had seen us, though some certainly appeared to be conscious of our presence.

The Queen gave an order, and a slave bowed low and ran from the chamber, while the court fluttered and fidgeted in an ecstasy of terror. Cleopatra herself seemed unmoved by the events around her, and sat calmly, even regally, on her throne as she surveyed the scene.

Marcus Antonius, for his part, was plainly in the grip of an almost paralysing fear. As had been the case with the Australian aboriginals, he plainly sensed our presence, but was unable to confirm it. It may well be that he regarded his perception of us as one of the effects of his love of wine, or some such, but in any event, our presence was obviously unwelcome to him.

Faint, almost inaudible, mutterings filled the throne room for the space of a few minutes. The near-silence was broken by the return of the slave who had been dispatched earlier.

He preceded an impressive personage, dressed in what appeared to be priestly robes, and followed by a number of slaves carrying mysterious impedimenta. He bowed low to Cleopatra, who addressed him in brusque tones, obviously commands.

At once, the slaves laid out their burdens,

consisting of a low table and various gilded objects that they placed upon it. The priest faced the table, and pointed his staff in a direction that was nowhere near where we were located and started to chant, in a language different to that used by Cleopatra and Antonius.

The action seemed to raise Antonius to a rage. Seizing the unfortunate priest roughly by the shoulders, he spun the wretched man round to face us with such force that he nearly fell to the ground, and pointed accurately in our direction.

The priest, somewhat discomfited by this, raised his staff again, and continued his chanting. It was clear to me that he, unlike Antonius, had no perception of our presence, and was merely going through a form of words. Even so, I felt a strange, uncomfortable tingling sensation (though how this was possible in my incorporeal state, I cannot properly explain) and on communicating with Agathe, I learned that she was also experiencing the same feelings.

In the meantime, Antonius continued to glare at us with his bloodshot eyes, sipping continually from the goblet which he still held, and which was being constantly refilled by the slave standing by his elbow.

After about five minutes of chanting, the priest lowered his staff, and turned to face Antonius, who spoke to him in an angry tone, pointing once more in our direction. The priest resumed his chanting, and took two steps closer to us. The unpleasant tingling sensation became stronger, and I began to feel that it would be wise for us to move from the place.

On letting Agathe know my feelings on the matter, I was not completely surprised to find her in agreement.

"In any event," she communicated to me, "although these tourist excursions to different times and places are fascinating, they are not the reason why we are here. We must act to find my father, and to persuade him away from his dreams of world domination."

"Of course," I agreed, and with one step, we were back in the mists of the Untime, well away from Cleopatra and her court.

"I suppose," remarked Agathe, "that we have just been exorcised as ghosts or spirits." Her laughter sounded inside my head.

"I suppose that is so," I agreed. "I wonder if our appearance and banishment is recorded in any historical documents? Is your curiosity now satisfied with regard to Cleopatra, by the way?"

"Indeed it is. It is not for me to say, but I began to perceive why a certain type of man would find her attractive. Did you find her to your liking, Jules?"

I did not wish to answer this question, but instead suggested that we visit the future.

"Can we really see what life will be like in two hundred years?" she said.

"Come, my dear," I said, and we stepped forward to the year 2096.

Chapter XXVI

ALTHOUGH we were enclosed by the faint green mist once more, the overwhelming impression of the future was one of greyness. We had moved ourselves in space to the Arc de Triomphe at the top of the Champs Elysées. The Arc itself stood above us, as imposing and as magnificent as always, but the expected view of Haussmann's grand avenues was missing.

Instead, we beheld soulless slabs of grey stone or concrete, towering to dizzying heights, and pierced by small windows, which could hardly have afforded any illumination to the inhabitants of these barracks.

It was natural for me to suppose that there would be fewer horses in this France of the future, but there were none at all in evidence. Instead, we were surrounded by a swirling stream of small vehicles, proceeding almost silently, but at a terrifying speed, propelled by their own mechanisms, perhaps using electricity, or perhaps steam, but it was impossible to tell from their appearance.

There were relatively few pedestrians, and those who were visible hurried along the pavements by the side of the road, dressed in brightly coloured clothing in a style that can only be described as immodest, with seemingly naked limbs very much in evidence. These garments formed the only splash of colour in the scene. The distant horizon was invisible behind a grey haze, and the sky was a leaden colour, unbroken by any shape of clouds, let alone a patch of blue sky.

"What has happened?" asked Agathe. "This must be Paris, but what a Paris it has become. It seems like a Hell on earth. Let us leave here and go to a more congenial spot, and discover what is happening elsewhere at this time."

I suggested Zermatt, a pleasant Swiss mountain resort where those who indulged in such things skated and skied on the snow. We soon found ourselves on a pleasant Alpine meadow, where to our relief, the blue sky was visible in places through the overcast.

I was enjoying the prospect, when Agathe interrupted my thoughts.

"Jules!" she exclaimed. "Where is the snow?"

"Why, it is—" and there I stopped. We had travelled to Zermatt in November, a time when the lower slopes of the Alps, not to mention the peaks, should be covered with snow. Instead, the area where we were standing, which should have been covered in a white blanket, was covered by a profusion of Alpine flowers. Not only that, but the peaks that towered above us were bare of snow.

"Are you sure we are in the right place, and that this is indeed November?" Agathe asked me, and her voice tailed off, as she knew she could answer the question for herself through the omniscience provided by the Untime. "What has happened, though? What could possibly have made this change?"

As we stood pondering the matter, an animal came into view at some distance from us, which I soon discerned to be a camel. This extraordinary (for the area) sight was followed by another such beast, and another, and I was soon treated to the spectacle of a caravan of camels progressing along a valley in the Alps. Their handlers, who walked beside the beasts, were equally unlikely inhabitants of the mountains, resembling as they did Bedouins in dress and appearance.

"What in the name of goodness is happening here?" I asked.

"Let us return to Egypt, but the Egypt of this time, not that of Cleopatra," she said. "If the Egyptians are now living in Switzerland, who is living in Egypt?"

We took ourselves to the land of the Pyramids, and were further stunned by our discoveries there. The mighty Sphinx, which admittedly I had only seen in illustrations and photographs, was almost completely covered by sand. There was no sign of any human existence near the Pyramids, which must have been likewise half-buried in the drifts, since they were nowhere near the size that I had been led to believe.

"Let us look at the Nile," suggested Agathe, and we went to the river – or rather what had been the mighty waterway, now reduced to a mere trickle, not a metre wide, between what had presumably been the banks of the river, but the outlines of which were now, like all else, obscured by the sand. The city of Cairo, when we explored further, was a ghost city, likewise covered by sand, with only the tops of the doors on the ground floors of the buildings visible above the drifting dunes. The deserted minarets of the mosques towered above us, silent witnesses to – what?

The sight was impressive and frightening. I did not know what was stranger and more repellent to me; the grey machine-like appearance of my beloved Paris, or this strange silent ruin of a great city, inhabited only by a few jackals, which we glimpsed in the distance, skulking between the buildings like silent ghosts.

Beside me, Agathe shuddered. "What has happened to our world, Jules?" she asked, and there was a tremor in her words. "What has caused this catastrophe?"

"I have no idea," I told her, and shuddered in my turn. "Let us go back into the Untime."

We turned away back into the formless green mist, when I suddenly became aware of another consciousness in the Untime. This was something inhuman, and one which produced an almost paralysing terror.

Chapter XXVII

ALTHOUGH we were without bodies, it seemed to me that Agathe clung to me as she and I simultaneously sensed the presence of this Other in the Untime.

"What is it?" were her words to me.

I was unable to answer this. My sensations were those of emotions, not of words, as they were with Agathe and had been with her father. The overriding impression that I gained from this Other was one of raw anger and hostility, which overwhelmed me, almost to the point of my losing consciousness. I could feel Agathe's mind beside me weakening under the onslaught, and I desperately fought to stay alert, for her sake.

"What are you? Who are you?" I thought in the direction of the Other. I had no way of knowing whether my words would be understood, or whether the Other was capable of replying, but I sent out the message time and time again, with all the intensity I could muster.

The reply came, but it was a reply of images, not of words, and I reeled from the shock. The picture that presented itself in my mind was one of a nightmare creature. It is a vision that haunts me still on the nights that I find myself unable to sleep, and I know that Agathe, too, still suffers from its memory, though she fell into a mental coma almost immediately after the Other revealed itself to us. I would say that she fainted, but the phrase would have little or no meaning when applied to our incorporeal state.

How can I begin to describe the horror that appeared before my mind's eye? It was a nightmare vision of innumerable tentacles and feelers, covered with a skin that appeared hideously wrinkled and coated with slime, writhing and squirming in a manner that was at once both obscene and fascinating. Behind this seething forest of glistening flesh shone a mass of dark eyes, similar to the eyes of a spider, as seen through a high-powered lens or microscope.

There was a mouth, too, framed by a massive hooked beak, which opened and closed, revealing in its black depths rows of serrated teeth, flecked with some nameless ichor that appeared to smoke and steam, and a long black serpent's tongue that constantly flicked back and forth, as though it had a mind and an existence of its own, independent of the horrific entity to which it was attached.

Two pairs of enormous bat-like wings soared above this monstrosity, beating slowly, though it was impossible to discern in what sort of atmosphere this creature had its being, and how it flew.

But, over and above the physical experience of this thing, the whole excited a kind of horror and disgust such as I have never experienced in the past, and never want to encounter again. This feeling was visceral in nature, and it was impossible for me to persuade myself that the vision before me was merely in my mind, so strongly did it impress itself upon me.

Given the bizarre and horrifying nature of its features, it was impossible to interpret any kind of facial expression, but the anger and rage that I had first discerned as emanating from it were, if anything, stronger than before.

"What do you want?" I sent out to the Other, but even as I did so, I knew the answer. This horror wanted us! Its meat and drink were the souls of those who braved the Untime, whether they be human beings, or creatures from other worlds whose form and being is unknown to us.

I laughed bitterly to myself at the thought of the revolver that Professor Schneider had offered to us before our departure into the Untime. What use would such an instrument possibly be against a monster of this kind? Even assuming that it had a bodily physical existence, even the heaviest revolver would be of little more use than a child's peashooter when deployed against its massive form.

I now had to consider how I was to escape this thing's terrible intentions. I had to assume that it was as easy for it to travel through the Untime to any point in space or time as it was for me to do the same. If I were to leave the Untime, I would be faced with the problem of returning to the same place and time that I left. Space would be easy – I could, for example, place myself in the middle of the Sahara desert, or even the unexplored interior of the great Antarctic continent, and hope that the beast would follow me there. Once out of the Untime, I would surely perish, either in the maw of this thing, or else of heat and thirst induced by the desert, or cold, should I choose the Antarctic. I would die, however, with the satisfaction of knowing that the beast would be incapable of surviving the harsh climate to which I had transported myself.

But... and there is always a but! I was in the Untime with Agathe, whose mind was currently closed to me, though I knew with certainty that she was still alive. If I were to take her with me to the desert or the frozen icy wastes, she would likewise die with me, which was a truly unimaginable prospect, and it was impossible for me to even consider leaving her alone in the Untime in her present condition.

Nor could I consider a temporal move through the Untime. Either to the past or the present, the monster could surely follow me as quickly and with the same facility as I myself moved. How would I return to my own time once I left the Untime? And, once again, Agathe's condition made it impossible for me to consider such a course of action.

The only practicable exit from the Untime was the house in Vincennes at the time when we had left it. That was likewise impossible

for me to consider seriously, given that the
monster would follow me out of the Untime
into the world. Was I, even posthumously (as I
surely would perish), to be known as the man
who unleashed such a horror on the fair city of
Paris? No, no, and a thousand times no!

My decision was made. I must stay in the
Untime, and fight the horror with the only
weapon at my disposal – my mind! Though I
had little or no idea how I would achieve this,
it came to me that my opponent, though large
and of a fearsome aspect, possessed little in the
way of mental faculties, and it was possible for
me to defeat it with relatively little effort on my
part.

Once again, I am using words in an attempt
to describe a state and actions which were
essentially non-verbal. If I sometimes use physical terms and expressions, I would ask you to
remember that all this, though taking place in
the mental realm alone, often had the same
effect as physical sensations, including blows
and attacks, with the resultant feelings of pain
and agony. If my writing seems absurd to you as
a result of this seeming contradiction, I crave
your indulgence.

There was one other curious aspect to the

monster, which alternately attracted and repelled me. How, I hear you ask, could I feel attraction to such a loathsome entity? The answer is through the power of scent.

I have never experienced the sense of smell in a dream, but the sensations I received from the Other in the Untime were almost overpowering. By turns, the monster emanated the sweetest scent imaginable; almost impossible to describe accurately, but the closest I can come is that my memory has it as the sweet odour of vanilla, mixed with that of roses. The smell was irresistibly seductive, and I found myself being drawn towards the monster without any conscious volition on my part, even while I shuddered at the horror of its source.

Alternating with this scent was a foul sewer stench, which initially I could perceive only fleetingly, but the more I gazed on the monster, the more prolonged the periods of this nauseating smell became, and the vanilla and roses dwindled away and became less and less frequent, until at length the only smell perceptible from the Other was that of filth and decay. All the attraction I had felt previously disappeared.

As I confronted the monster, it seemed to me to be necessary to give my opponent a name.

By naming one's fears, one is able to confront
them and engage with them at a more intimate
and deeper level than if they are simply nameless horrors. I therefore dubbed the monster
"Dagon", and immediately I had done this, I felt
a surge of power over my enemy.

Dagon attacked me with all the power of its
mind, and I reeled under the shock. The closest
thing to which I can compare it is as if I were
being roasted by a jet of intense flame. But I
knew what to do as if I had practiced for this
eventuality. Immediately my mind conjured
up a wall of ice, against which the flame licked
harmlessly, and I could sense Dagon's snarling
as its attack was foiled.

For several rounds, Dagon launched its weapons against me, and I was able to respond.
Once it tried an attack against the still insensible Agathe, but I beat it back easily, since I was
under no immediate threat and could use all
my energy against it. Still, though, I was unable
to take the offensive in the struggle.

As I beat off the attacks, I became aware of
another presence close at hand. At first I
thought it was Agathe regaining consciousness, but a sardonic chuckle soon corrected my
misapprehension.

"So you could not keep away, eh, Gauthier?" came the words of Professor Lamartine.

Chapter XXVIII

To say I was surprised to hear his voice is something of an understatement. However, on reflection, I remembered that we had entered the Untime in search of this very man, and it should have been no surprise at all to me to encounter him.

"I perceive you have met Moloch," he said to me.

"I call it Dagon," I replied. I repelled another attack, this one taking the form of a hail of pebbles, against which I erected a shield from which they rebounded harmlessly.

"Moloch, Dagon, Beelzebub. Can you doubt that he and his kind are the origin of the old pagan gods?"

"No doubt in my mind whatsoever," I answered, warding off another shower of stones. I was beginning to be irritated that Lamartine was not assisting me in defending his daughter. However, as soon as I had formulated the thought, I remembered that in the Untime, thoughts are not private.

"What? My Agathe is with you?" came the response. "How dare you bring her into this wilderness? And how did you get here anyway?"

"It was impossible to stop her. We came through the machine in the Vincennes house." Another attack by Dagon, this time in the form of a spray of acid. I quickly coated Agathe and myself with an alkaline solution, including Lamartine for good measure, and the acid hissed and bubbled in a futile manner against this defence. I explained Agathe's situation and her current condition and the dilemma in which I found myself to Lamartine.

"Well, maybe you are not as stupid as I believed you to be. But now, if you will excuse me, I will take Agathe with me and I will return to that house in Vincennes. You may amuse yourself with our friend here." He laughed unpleasantly.

"If that is what you want to do," I said, "pray go

ahead. Professor Schneider will be waiting for you there, together with a number of gentlemen from the Gendarmerie, who will be delighted to make your acquaintance in connection with the disappearance of little Marie." I added the gendarmes on the spur of the moment, and it appeared that my invention had an effect on him.

"Schneider, that pompous buffoon? I spit on him. But the gendarmes, ah, that is a different matter. Then I will go elsewhere with Agathe. As you know, anywhere in space and time is possible for one in the Untime."

"First, though, you will have to take Agathe from me," I retorted.

"Why, detaching Agathe from your company should prove a simple matter," he sneered. As he spoke, Dagon shifted its attention from me to the unsuspecting Lamartine, and cast a shower of fiery scorpion-like creatures at him, many of which appeared to strike him, and he winced at their impact.

"It seems to me," I said, being unable to refrain from gloating a little at the discomfiture of my enemy, "that it is you who may have to provide amusement for our friend, while Agathe and I leave the Untime together. Believe me, if you return out of the Untime to our own time, you will find many hands raised against you."

"No!" he fairly shrieked. "You cannot do this to me! We are bound by our common humanity. We, the representatives of homo sapiens, must stand together against this hellish monster."

This was a very different tune that he was singing now from the one he had sung only minutes earlier, and I did not hesitate to remind him of the fact, as I used my powers, which were gaining in strength with every one of Dagon's attacks, to deflect a wave of burning oil that threatened to engulf the three of us.

"Very well," he huffed. "I give you my word. You and Agathe will be able to leave the Untime together. I suppose I am correct in assuming that there is some kind of understanding between the two of you?"

The old devil! How could he possibly have known? But I answered as truthfully as I could. "Yes, I love her, and I believe she loves me."

"Then you may have a father's blessing, if that is what you desire. Now let us defeat this beast."

"May I make a suggestion, Professor?" I asked, as a hundred whips, grasped by a hundred tentacles, lashed down upon us, and I quickly raised up a shield to protect us. The attacks were becoming indiscriminate now, not aimed at any one of us, but seemingly expressions of furious anger and rage, directed at our little group as a whole.

"By all means," he gasped.

"I feel confident enough to launch attacks of my own against Dagon, provided that you can hold off the attacks he launches against us. I do not have the strength to defend and attack at the same time."

"I will do my best," said Lamartine, whose confidence and bluster seemed to have evaporated since Dagon's attacks had started to include him as a target.

"Let us work together, then," I told him. Together we beat off a number of assaults from Dagon, of different kinds each time, and Lamartine's defences appeared to be growing in strength and effectiveness at each attack. Though my defences were undeniably stronger, the Professor brought a touch of ingenuity and sophistication to his efforts, which more than compensated for the relative weakness of the defence itself.

"Very well," I said to him after the fifth such attack. "Are you ready to hold off the assault alone, while I go on the attack?"

"I am ready," he said, his voice steady.

I timed my moves carefully. Dagon flashed a mass of flaming swords at us, and Lamartine threw up a corresponding mass of adamantine shields against which the swords clanged harmlessly and the flames extinguished themselves. While this was going on, I conjured up a huge crossbow, similar to the ones used in medieval times in the sieges of castles, and aimed a barbed dart in the general direction of the dark shining eyes visible through the forest of tentacles.

A second or so after the bolt had been loosed, an ear-splitting inhuman scream split the Untime, and the tentacles which had been holding the swords recoiled as if stung.

"Bravo, Gauthier!" exclaimed the Professor. "A few more of those, and we shall have disposed of this thing."

"It will be ready for something similar next time," I reminded him. "I must change tactics."

We waited for the next assault, but Dagon seemed disinclined to initiate hostilities this time. "It was hurt worse by the dart than I imagined," I said.

"Alternatively," responded Lamartine, "it is intelligent enough to know that it cannot defend itself and launch an attack at the same time. It is waiting for us to attack so that it can defend itself, and having successfully done so, then launch its own attack."

This line of thought seemed plausible to me. "What do you propose that we do?" I asked him.

"Why, attack, of course," he said. "I will be ready, should it launch a counter-attack against us."

I prepared my attack, which consisted of fire-balls, and sent the blazing projectiles on their way. Again, the fearsome scream, and a hail of arrows, but rather than the indiscriminate attacks that Dagon had been making, these were now all directed solely at the Professor. His defences were becoming weaker, and I made a move to assist him.

"No! Go back!" he shouted to me. "Don't you see? The thing is attempting to pick us off one by one, so that it may feast at leisure. Go now, and take Agathe with you. Go! Go, you fool, and save my daughter!" he screamed, as an arrow pierced his arm.

"I cannot leave you now," I said, but even as I spoke, I realised the futility of my words, and the correctness of the Professor's analysis of the situation.

"You must leave," he repeated. "Our enemy cannot leave the Untime unless one of us accompanies him. You go now with Agathe, and leave me here to die. You tell me there is no future for me in Paris. Very well, then. Let my last moments at least serve one whom I love." So saying, he turned to the monster Dagon, and flung a dart of his own into the mass of tentacles.

Again a shriek from Dagon, but there was no respite in the storm of arrows that flew towards the Professor.

I took hold of Agathe, who was still insensible, and took the steps towards the house in Vincennes. Before we stepped out of the Untime, I glanced back. The Professor was lying, still, his body riddled by arrows, and Dagon was moving ever closer to his body, the dark beak snapping in seeming anticipation of the coming feast.

I shuddered, and took another step, which carried me into Vincennes.

Chapter XXIX

IT is hard for me to put the events following our return from the Untime into order. Schneider informed me later that when I and Agathe appeared, he assumed that we were corpses. As before, my body was apparently extremely cold, as was that of Agathe, and I had collapsed insensible.

However, on arranging our supposed cadavers in more seemly postures than the ones into which we had fallen, he detected a faint pulse in my wrist, and after holding a mirror up to Agathe's nostrils, detected signs of life in her, also.

According to Schneider, both Agathe and I

were unconscious for the best part of twelve hours after our return, during which time, he did not dare to leave the room, let alone the house. However, at length I opened my eyes and looked around me.

On observing that I was awake, Schneider hastened to my side, and gave me some brandy and water, which restored my strength a little.

"How is she?" were my first words, when I had swallowed a little of the elixir.

"She is still unconscious," he told me. "But she is breathing steadily, and there appears to be no physical damage."

"Thank God!" I breathed, and fell back. Slowly, as I returned to full consciousness, our experiences in the Untime came back to me in all their horror.

"Lamartine?" I croaked. "He is not here?"

Schneider shook his head. "No, naturally he is not here," he said, as if humouring an infant. "I was hoping you would be able to inform me of his whereabouts, That, after all, was the reason for you entering the Untime."

Briefly, for I did not wish Agathe to hear all that I had to say about her father, I informed Schneider of what had passed in the Untime, omitting the details of the change in gender, which I had no wish to discuss with anyone at that time. He was fascinated by my account of our visit to Australia, and to Cleopatra's court, but he sucked his teeth when I told him of Dagon, and the battle that had been waged.

"This is one of the matters that I feared Lamartine did not understand well enough," he said. "Heaven knows that this planet with its modest three dimensions holds enough dangers in the form of predatory fauna. We might well expect the Untime to contain monsters beyond our imagination, and who knows what the result might be should they decide to make their home with us?

"Lamartine has perished defending the one he loved," he added. "I can see for myself, Gauthier, that you also love his daughter. I am sure that you had the courage to die for her. Do you have the courage to live for her?"

"Why, what can you mean?" I asked.

"As I mentioned at one time, there is a possibility that one's mental faculties will be permanently impaired as the result of a stay in the Untime. Do you have the courage to stay with her and to maintain her if it transpires that she is in that state, to the end of your days?"

The prospect that he held before me filled

me with horror, and it must have showed in my eyes, for Schneider, watching me, nodded slowly. However, a single glance at the prostrate form stretched out on the chaise longue was enough . "Of course I will do anything for her," I replied with some heat. "Can you doubt me?"

"No, I cannot say that I would," replied Schneider, "having seen for myself what manner of man you are. But wait..." As he spoke, Agathe's eyelids fluttered, and her hand stole to her brow.

I waited with trepidation to see whether my dear Agathe was indeed the same person who had entered the Untime, or whether she was, as I prayed she was not, impaired and damaged by her sojourn in those mysterious dimensions.

I need not have worried. She opened her eyes, and looked at me. "Jules?" she said in faint tones. "And Professor Schneider? You need not fear for my mental state. I am perfectly in command of all my faculties, even if my physical state is somewhat weak at present."

Schneider and I regarded each other with horror that she had apparently been listening to our conversation. I looked at her enquiringly.

"I was not unconscious at any time," she said to me. "When that monster approached us, my mind was still alert and remained so all the time, though I was unable to communicate, and it soon became obvious that even my unconscious thoughts were not perceptible to those near me. I was conscious of the way in which you so bravely protected me, though, dear Jules, and the way that you and my father fought together to save me, and how my father sacrificed himself—" At this point, her eyes filled with tears, and Schneider, embarrassed, went to her side and offered her his handkerchief, with which she wiped her eyes.

"You need have no worries or regrets, Jules," she assured me. "Naturally, I mourn my father, and am sad that he and you quarrelled in the Untime,

but—" Once again, she shook with sobs, but this time I was by her side, and I held her hand and pressed it gently.

"It will pass," she said. "Time will repair what the Untime destroyed."

And so it transpired.

Immediately after Agathe's and my return from the Untime, Professor Schneider was able to inform the world, in an interview that I persuaded old Simon to print in the magazine, that Professor Lamartine had perished in an accident connected with his diving-apparatus at the naval dockyards. For reasons of national security, details were not to be revealed, and his body was unfortunately never recovered. Though this news caused some alarm among the public, and demands for an enquiry into the matter, the affair was never followed up.

Little Marie was never seen again. To the best of my knowledge, the gendarmerie still have her listed as missing. The poor little tot is, as far as I can understand these things, perpetually in the past, in an endless loop in which she ages three years, and then is violently hurled back into the past.

You may express some wonder as to what happened to the apparatus which we used to enter the Untime, both at Lamartine's laboratory and at the Vincennes house. When Agathe and I had fully recovered from the physical effects of the Untime, which took about one month, she and I met Professor Schneider, to discuss what should be done with Lamartine's inventions. Schneider had persuaded the owner of the Vincennes property to let it to him, without any further work being done to it, so we had no concerns about the machinery being tampered with or misused. There was also the machinery at the Lamartine laboratories to be considered.

Though both Agathe and I had experience of the Untime, and we could both could perceive its value as a tool to be used for historical research, and also of its convenience as regards instant travel, we both decided, with Schneider's reluctant agreement, that the risks involved in maintaining these links to the Untime were too great, and the possibilities for abuse by unscrupulous parties were too tempting.

Accordingly, Schneider and I personally dismantled both sets of apparatus, and sold the parts as scrap metal. Agathe went through her father's writings, and extracted any which appeared to be concerned with the Untime, which we then burned. Though Agathe was stricken with grief at the death of her father, she came to the realisation, after looking through the papers that she discovered in the laboratory, that his great mind had for some time been slipping away from the paths of reason. Though he was capable enough in so many ways, his thoughts and energies when outside the scientific sphere appeared to be more than a little irrational.

Professor Schneider, to whom she showed the papers on which she based her discovery, concurred. To him, it seemed that over-exposure to the quicksilver which was employed in the Untime apparatus could well have caused Lamartine's mind to become unhinged, to put it bluntly, and gave me his confidential opinion that if the degeneration of his faculties had continued, there would have been no alternative but to place the distinguished professor into the care of an asylum for the insane.

As tactfully as I was able, I conveyed these opinions to Agathe, who was aghast at the news, and fell into a fresh paroxysm of grief from which it took her some considerable time to recover.

During this period of grief, she and I talked at length about our experiences in the Untime, and it was clear to both of us that the bond that had been forged between us there was one that would never be broken. I proposed marriage to this remarkable woman, and to my everlasting joy, she accepted me without reservation. The thought of a future happy life together with me, I may say with all due modesty, was one of those factors that brought Agathe from the shadow of grief back to the land of the living.

Six months after our return from the Untime, Agathe and I were married, and Professor

Schneider acted as our best man.

True to his word, Schneider found Agathe a place at the University, where she conducts research into matters beyond my poor understanding, and has won herself a name among those who are conversant in these matters.

But whatever else she may be, she remains my faithful and loving companion, with whom I can never forget that we once shared the excitement and the perils of the Untime.

THE UNTIME REVISITED

Epigraph

"Time is. Time was. Time is past."
Words attributed to the brazen head supposedly
constructed by Friars Roger Bacon and Bungay.

CHAPTER I

IN my previous account of my journey through the Untime, you will recall that we determined to destroy the apparatus of Professor Rémy Lamartine that had enabled us to journey instantaneously through time and space. This decision was arrived at after some considerable thought and debate on the part of Professor Schneider, my wife (at that time my fiancée) Agathe, and myself.

There were good reasons advanced for retaining the apparatus in working order, these chiefly being the opportunities for instantaneous and easy travel anywhere in the Universe. In addition, the Untime presented those engaged in the study of the past with an unparalleled chance to witness historical events with their own eyes, thereby settling for ever those matters of historical debate that so vex those in the field.

Against these undoubted advantages, we had to set many other factors, any one of which, in my view, would justify the closing of all future doors to the Untime.

First was that of the difficulty of constructing the machinery. When I first encountered the apparatus constructed by Professor Lamartine, I was struck by its complexity, and further acquaintance with the machinery failed to render its workings less mysterious or more simple in my eyes. Even Professor Schneider, who understood the matter better than I could ever hope to do, and Agathe, who in my opinion had an even clearer understanding than that of Schneider himself (though Schneider, naturally, did not share my view of the matter), confessed themselves puzzled, if not outright baffled, by the way in which the principles of the Untime had been exploited by Professor Lamartine in his machinery to explore these mysterious dimensions. The difficulty and expense of manufacturing other such machines combined to make us disbelieve in the possibility of repeating Lamartine's success.

Next on the list of our reasons for destruction was another danger, little understood, but whose effects were well noted by both Schneider and myself; that is to say, the danger of damage to one's mental faculties. Though it could well be argued that Lamartine's derangement was at least in part the result of poisoning by quicksilver, it was undeniable that his experiences in the Untime had served to disorder his wits still further. As for myself, I was well aware that my sleeping and my dreams had been affected by my visits to the Untime, but it would appear, from the reactions of those around me, that my mental state had been materially unaffected (naturally, I was unable to judge this for myself). As far as Agathe, my beloved, was concerned, as far as I was able to judge, she was composed of stronger mental stuff than either Schneider or myself. I had no fears for the state of her mind.

There were also problems with the Untime which could impose an adverse effect on the fabric of our society. As Schneider and I had decided when Lamartine was seemingly determined to kill me, any criminal familiar with the Untime could establish an alibi with little or no trouble.

Many other factors entered into our calculations, one of which was the existence in the Untime of terrifying monsters, not of our world, and hideous beyond the wildest imaginings of a lunatic. Agathe and I had encountered one of these horrors, which had claimed the life of Professor Lamartine. This being, as potent and appalling as it was, might be, according to Schneider, merely a minnow among sharks in this unknown and unrealised menagerie of the unknown.

Finally, and this is what persuaded us all, more than any other single factor, there was the knowledge that the very principles by which the Untime was governed were little understood. Though both Agathe and Schneider had been able to reconstruct much of the theoretical edifice on which Lamartine had constructed his experiments, firm proof for these theories was lacking.

"Furthermore," Schneider told me, "we will continue to lack such understanding and proof without practical experiments and experience by adventurers within the Untime. Such experience will lead to understanding, but a terrible risk is involved." The risk to which he referred

was more terrible than any that I have so far
mentioned. Indeed, Schneider and my Agathe
both gave it as their opinion that a misunder-
standing of the principles involved in the explo-
ration of the Untime might involve the end of
the Universe as we currently understand it.

Bearing all these in mind, we accordingly
destroyed the apparatus in Vincennes as well
as that in Lamartine's laboratory at his home.
Agathe collected and burned all the papers
that related to his work on the Untime, and
we mutually swore ourselves to secrecy on the
matter.

The memory of the Untime, particularly that
last journey I took in that mysterious dimension with Agathe, when we visited Australia, the
ancient past, and the distant future, nonetheless stayed with me. Not only the memory of
what we had witnessed, but also the memory
of my sensations within the Untime, remained
indelibly imprinted on my memory.

CHAPTER II

IT was therefore with more than a little surprise when, somewhat more than two years after the events described in my previous chronicle, and somewhat a little more than a year after my marriage to Agathe, that I received a visit from Professor Schneider. Though Schneider and I had remained on friendly terms, and indeed, he had managed to procure Agathe a place on the faculty at the Sorbonne, it was the first time that he had visited our humble dwelling.

Upon my entry into the matrimonial field, I had moved from my somewhat Bohemian rooms in the Fifth arrondissement on the Left Bank, to a somewhat more bourgeois location in the Seventeenth, as befitted my new status as a married man. Our apartment was on the second floor, and was pleasantly close to the Parc Monceau. Though the area and the apartment itself were somewhat foreign to my previous tastes, I had to admit that marriage had worked its civilising effect on my previous bachelor *modus vivendi*. It was rare, indeed unknown, for Schneider to cross the river for a purely social matter, and the look on his face also informed me that the reason for his visit could hardly be a trivial one.

I welcomed him to our house, and escorted him to the chamber where we were accustomed to receive visitors. The maid (and yes! we had risen to the status of employing a maid – a far cry, you may say, from the Jules Gauthier of previous days) brought us coffee and pastries.

"Married life would appear to have its benefits," remarked Schneider, taking an éclair from the plate before him with obvious anticipation. "A blessed state that I have been fortunate enough to escape," he smiled. "Although it must be admitted that your charming wife is one of the few women with whom I can imagine the state to be indeed blessed."

"I am happy to hear that."

"Why, her opinions on many matters verge

on the first-rate." (I hid a smile at this) "The other day, she showed me some calculations which utterly repudiated the work of Lejeune on the composition of matter. Work, I may tell you, on which he has spent the past ten years." He chuckled, somewhat unpleasantly. "She has almost the intellectual capacity of a man, but then, given her parentage, I should not be surprised. Lamartine, for all his faults, had a head on his shoulders, after all." He took a bite of his pastry.

"But you did not come here to congratulate me on my choice of marital partner," I smiled. I was, however, inwardly delighted that Schneider should speak of my wife in such glowing terms. I myself, being an almost complete ignoramus in the field in which she and Schneider laboured, was unable to judge her worth in these matters.

"No, I did not," Schneider answered me. He finished his coffee, and looked about the room. I recognised this sign, and hastened to pour him a small glass of cognac, which he accepted with thanks. I was aware that he preferred the foul spirit drunk in the north of Britain, but I refused to keep any of the vile liquid in our apartment.

"Gauthier," he informed me, "a problem has

been brought to my attention. It is one where maybe you can shed some light on the mystery."

"You intrigue me," I answered. "How can I, a mere journalist, shed light where a professor of the Sorbonne confesses himself baffled?"

"By reason of your experience," he informed me. "Listen to what I have to tell you. My colleague, Doctor Henri Menton, is very taken with the ideas of some Jewish Viennese quack, whom he met here in Paris at Charcot's lectures, which involves patients recounting their dreams to him. Pah!" I verily believe that if he had not been in our drawing-room, he would have spat. "He may as well cut open an ox and examine its entrails as attempt to make some sort of diagnosis based on what his patients dream. Ridiculous!"

"I do not altogether agree," I told him. "Sometimes it seems to me that beneath our consciousness, in what we might call a sub-conscious part of our mind, what we have been thinking in the day makes itself apparent to us in the night time. In a garbled form, admittedly, but at the same time, it may be a genuine reflection of our inner selves."

Schneider positively glared at me. "Have you read the writings of this man Freud?" I shook my head. "Because you are telling me all that Menton tells me that this charlatan is doing. Which makes you as big a fool as he, and I am now in two minds as to whether to tell you of these developments." Though I resented being called a fool, I was well enough acquainted with Professor Schneider and his views to realise that this epithet was applied by him on a regular basis to a good nine-tenths of the world's population, and therefore bit my tongue to choke off the retort that sprang to my mind. Schneider paused, and continued. "It is only because you are the only man to have experienced these things and lived that I bother."

"What things?"

For answer, Schneider asked me to describe the hideous monster that we had encountered in the Untime, and which had been responsible for the death of Agathe's father, Professor Lamartine.

This being was possessed of a loathsome and terrifying appearance, having some of the properties of a cephalopod, with a mass of writhing tentacles, and a skin which repelled by its texture and general colour. In order to cut it down to size in my mind, I had dubbed the thing "Dagon", and indeed, it seemed that this, or beings very similar to it, formed the basis for ancient beliefs in idols and demons. It had been clear to me that this thing feasted on the souls of those other beings that it found in the Untime. Whether it was indeed native to the Untime (should such a thing be possible) or whether it had strayed from another planet or star millions of miles away, I had no idea.

At one time, I had believed that my only escape from it would be by returning to an inhospitable part of this Earth, and letting it perish there. Naturally, my life would likewise have ended at that point, but that was of no consequence to me at that time. However, the life of my beloved Agathe, who was with me in the Untime, was of more importance, and I therefore stayed and battled the monster, with Professor Lamartine as my unlikely ally. In the end, he succumbed to its deadly attack, allowing his daughter and me to escape.

Schneider listened to my description in silence. At the end of my recital, he silently held out his empty brandy glass, which I refilled.

"You have just provided me," he said, after having taken a generous sip of my best brandy, "with a description that is almost identical to that related to me by Menton."

"Why? Has he dreamed of this thing?"

"No, no, of course not. Several of his patients have reported seeing this in their dreams, however."

"Several?" I enquired.

"Indeed. Were it just one dreamer, we could ascribe it to imagination and coincidence. Apparently, though, Menton reports that more than half a dozen of his patients have reported the same dream – nightmare, rather. What they are all describing is identical to what you have just told me."

"But they have not entered the Untime!"

"Correct. Unless we regard our dreaming selves as having entered the Untime. Personally, I believe that since we are able to describe the Untime in terms of mathematical equations—"

"You may well be able to do so," I said, smiling, "and so may my wife, but I am totally incapable of such a thing, as you are well aware."

"Very well," he amended. Shall we rather say that some of us may be able to describe the Untime mathematically? I do not regard dreams as being in the realm of mathematics. Therefore, I say that the idea of entering the Untime in dreams is as ridiculous as the fantasies of the Viennese charlatan, Freud."

"But yet they are perceiving one of the denizens of the Untime? Then the beast is entering our world from the Untime. Maybe it has no physical existence as we understand it, but instead enters our minds?"

"When you speak of minds in this way," scoffed Schneider, "I begin to wonder whether you have lost your own."

"I merely made a suggestion," I retorted, somewhat nettled. "I am beginning to wonder why you have taken the trouble to inform me of this matter, since you appear to regard my views on the subject as irrelevant."

"Very well," he said. "Though I do not share your belief as to the incorporeal nature of this thing, it does seem to me that there is some sort of leak that connects the Untime to our place and time. Should this thing, whatever it may be, or even worse, should its cousins, who may prove to be even less to our liking, decide that they will invade our world, we are in danger."

It was my turn to scoff. "Surely we are not frightened of dreams?" I asked.

"I would disregard all of this," Schneider said sombrely, "if dreams were all that had occurred."

"What has happened?" I asked. I could feel a chill going through me.

"Menton has told me of the histories of his patients. In three of the six cases of which he has informed me, the patient came to him and related his or her dream. Menton recorded the event, and scheduled an appointment with these patients for the next week. When the patients failed to keep the appointment, Menton made enquiries."

"They had died?"

Schneider shook his head. "Worse than that. In each of these three cases, they were alive, but only in their bodies. The patients had become empty husks of human beings, drooling idiots, incapable of speech or seemingly of rational thought. Their minds, in a word, had been stolen."

Chapter III

A FEELING of horror swept over me as I heard his words. "You cannot believe that the monster which appeared to them in their dreams – their nightmares, rather – has taken their souls?"

"I prefer not to believe in the superstition of 'a soul'," Schneider replied, somewhat stiffly. "If you wish to talk of souls, I would suggest that you consult a priest. However, it would appear that the intellectual faculties of these unfortunates have been eliminated. I would like you to accompany me to meet Menton, and interview him regarding the symptoms of his patients. If he is willing, perhaps it may be possible to meet these sufferers."

"Let us assume that we can establish the fact that these dreams are indeed coming from the Untime. That the monsters in the dreams of these poor people are those that I encountered? What then?"

Schneider shifted his bulk uneasily in his chair. "If that is the case," he answered, with each word delivered in a solemn manner, "you must return to the Untime and defeat this threat."

To say I was astounded by his words would be an understatement. "But—" I began. Schneider held up a bear-like paw to stop me.

"Enough," he growled. "We will cross these bridges that you are about to mention when we come to them. If we come to them," he added.

We continued our conversation, determining those times when it would be convenient for me to visit Doctor Menton. At length, Schneider heaved himself to his feet.

"I will let you know, Gauthier," he said on departing, "when it will be convenient for Menton to see you and to acquaint you further with the details."

When he had left, I confess that my mind was in some turmoil. My last venture into the

Untime had caused a severe upset to my peace of mind. Now there was a possibility that I was to re-enter that mysterious, attractive, and terrifying landscape. And, if what Schneider said was true, I was not to avoid the horrors that lurked there, but was actively to seek them out with a view to their destruction. Imagine for yourself how I felt when I reflected upon this.

I was still sunk in the depths of reflection when my Agathe returned from giving her lecture at the Sorbonne.

Though I strove to maintain a cheery appearance, I was not sufficiently practiced in deception to convince Agathe that all was well. She sat beside me, and with true wifely concern enquired of me what might be the cause of my distress.

I informed her of what Schneider had told me, and she recoiled with a gasp of horror.

"My dear Jules," she exclaimed. "Can it be that the barrier between our world, and that of the Untime is broken?"

"You would have a better understanding of the answer to that question than would I," I replied. "You know well that my understanding is limited to the explanations intended for infants that have been extended to me by you and Schneider."

"If we consider the Untime to be a set of immeasurable dimensions, even of whose precise number we remain unsure," she said, "then there is every possibility, if Professor Schneider's theories are correct, that they will remain closed off from our understanding without some mechanical bridge to them, such as that devised by my father."

I seized on her unspoken words, rather than the spoken ones. Such is the nature of journalism. "But, my dear," I said, "it would appear that you have a different view of the matter than does Schneider?"

She sighed. "You are correct. I have not mentioned to him, for fear he would dismiss it as a mere female fancy, and I would lose his esteem. Promise me, Jules, that you will not do the same if I tell you of my opinion on the matter."

"How can I make such a promise," I asked, smiling, "when I have no idea what it is that I will hear from you? What I will promise you, however, is that I will listen to what you have to say with an open mind, and attempt to receive it without prejudice."

"Very well, then," she said, and turned to face me, looking me squarely in the eye. "My father believed, and Schneider likewise believes, that the Untime is merely a set of physical properties. Properties that are unlike any others that we have encountered in the past, and which are chiefly, by their very nature, unknowable. To that end, my father expended a great deal of time and effort, not to mention money, on the construction of the apparatus that he and we used to enter the Untime."

"This is very true," I agreed.

"However, it is my firm belief that the Untime contains a large component which is not that of matter that is subject to physical measurement, or describable in terms of physical properties."

"What else can there be other than such physical measurements or properties?" I asked, perplexed.

"Why, the power of our minds – our spirits – our souls," she said.

"I can understand why you have not mentioned this to Schneider," I said, laughing. "Forgive me, my dear, I am not laughing at you, but at the memory of my earlier conversation with the Professor." I explained Schneider's reaction to my mention of souls, and she joined in my laughter. "But," I continued, "this is surely at odds with your work at the Sorbonne, and does not match the strict logical nature of your work there, does it?"

"And it is for precisely that reason that I am reluctant to share it with the world," she said. "You know that next month I have been invited to address the Royal Society in London on the subject of electrical charges within atoms. If I were to be known as proposing something so outré as the Untime's connection with our mental faculties, why, you can imagine for yourself how my reputation might suffer. Even the Untime itself would prove to be such an outlandish concept that I might never again be taken seriously, were I to so much as mention it."

"I am sure you have your reasons for your statement," I said. "You should remember, though, that I saw with my own eyes a watch disappear and reappear when I was with your father, and you yourself witnessed something similar with Professor Schneider, did you not? Pocket watches are not in possession of souls."

"Of course, what you say is true," she admitted. "But let us consider some of the most noteworthy features of the Untime. For example, we were able to move about freely in time and in space, simply by willing it to be so, were we not?"

"Indeed we were," I answered her. I recalled how we were able to visit the outback country of Australia, and the Egypt of Cleopatra's day, simply by willing it to be so.

"Also," she went on, "there was a distinct feeling of incorporeality when we were in the Untime. For example, the spear thrown at you by that Australian native appeared to pass straight through you. And at the same time, while we were in the Untime, we were in some ways perceptible to those in the normal time. You mentioned yourself the experiences of my father and you in the Chamber of Deputies. The savages in Australia, and Marcus Antonius himself in Egypt, were aware of our presence."

"Could that not be explained by mathematical science?" I asked. "Not that I wish you to attempt to prove that to me," I added hurriedly, having learned early in my marriage that my dear wife was only too willing to explain such matters to her dolt of a husband, who was left standing in the metaphorical dust by her words.

"Certainly it could be explained to some degree using mathematical methods," she conceded. "However, you should be aware that were I to do so, it would require various constructs and assumptions which have yet to be proven mathematically, though they are generally assumed to be true."

"Very well, then. And do you have more to support your ideas?"

"Why, yes. The very monster that we encountered is surely enough to convince me. As you know, at that time I was incapable of communication with you or with my father, but I was aware of the events around me.

"You fought, my brave Jules, alongside my poor father, a most desperate and gallant battle against that creature of Hell – and I do not use that name lightly, believe me. Fire, acid, blazing missiles, and defences against all of these played their part, did they not?"

"They did indeed," I answered her.

"But you may assume, though I confess that we have no definite proof of this, that these had no physical presence, though the monster itself certainly would appear to have such. These weapons and defences would seem to have been creations that emanated only from your mind, and the mind of the monster. Even though they were capable of injury to you, and even death, as we saw in the tragic case of my father, they had no physical reality.

"And lastly," she continued, "there is the strange example of our being able to change gender." She blushed slightly at the indelicacy of the incident.

This is a matter to which I alluded in my previous account. In addition to the dimensions of time and of space, the Untime appeared to open up to us the dimension of gender, in which we were able to move to a gender other than the one in which we were born. Such a move was at the same time exhilarating and frightening, and was one whose memory will remain with me for the rest of my days. I may add that Agathe experienced similar feelings in this regard.

"That change," she went on, "was purely a mental one, as far as we are able to judge, was it not?"

"Yes, it was."

"And remember also, she said, that the communications between us while we were in the Untime were mental, not verbal."

"Very true."

"So," my wife concluded, with a triumphant air, "so many of the matters related to the Untime are non-material. Though it is true that the watches and timepieces supposedly travelled through the Untime, a conscious mind was needed to set the process in motion, and it is my opinion that the apparatus that my father constructed was merely a trigger, or if you like, an amplification apparatus for the power of our minds, which activated the Untime."

"This seems to be somewhat far-fetched," I said.

"Not at all," she retorted, a little crossly, I felt. "Consider the monster that you met. What did you name it?"

"Dagon," I replied, "after the Mesopotamian idol."

"And my father named it Moloch, did he not, after the hideous idol of the Canaanites. Both of you, do you not see, perceived it as one of the hideous old gods of the past; those gods which are now seen as demons and devils. The Untime, Jules, is the origin of these... these things. Hence, I say that it is Hell – the Hell from which all our demons and devils are spawned."

"And you are saying, then, that the ancients had a way of entering the Untime?"

She frowned, charmingly. "It may be so," she said. "But I think that it is more likely that the denizens of the Untime discovered a way to enter our world than the other way around. It may be that certain rituals weakened the barrier between those performing them and the Untime."

"And you think that this is happening now, with these patients of Doctor Menton?"

"I think it is quite possible," she replied. "There is one thing that you may ask of Menton, or his patients, if you are lucky enough to meet them."

"Or unlucky enough," I retorted. "I confess that the idea of meeting these poor wretches is not one that fills me with anticipation. What is it that you feel I should be asking?"

"Why, it is whether they believe that they have been in contact with ghosts or the spirits of the departed."

"Aha!" I exclaimed. "When I was with your father in the Chamber of Deputies, it seemed that at least one of the Deputies there saw us as some sort of ghost."

"As did those Australian natives, and Marcus Antonius at Cleopatra's court," she said. "It is my opinion that these people who see ghosts are also those who act as windows into our world for the inhabitants of the Untime."

"So those entities which have been reported in the past as being ghosts, demons, and the like, are all products of the Untime, you say?"

"I think it to be more than likely."

"And that these monsters are able, in some way which may not be entirely physical, to enter our world, or at least the minds of people in our world, and have an effect on them?"

She nodded.

My mind was in a whirl. The existence of the Untime as a scientific concept had been staggering enough to me. I was, however, prepared to accept the idea as a scientific premise. What Agathe was proposing to me, however, was scarcely credible or amenable to reasoned thought. However, on reflection, I had to admit that her words provided more than a little explanation of what we had observed.

"Very well, then," I said. "Though it may appear absurd to others, I will ask Menton about ghosts and spirits."

Chapter IV

IT transpired that only a few days passed before Doctor Menton was to see one of his patients at a time which was also convenient for me and Schneider to pay a visit.

Accordingly, I met the Professor at his office in the Sorbonne, and we made our way together to the consulting-room of Doctor Menton.

The Doctor was a small man with a fussy manner, almost completely bald, and with a well-waxed moustache that stood up in points from the side of his head. Dressed with impeccable taste, he betrayed a certain eccentricity of habit by the display of a sprig of parsley in his buttonhole. He followed my gaze and noted my surprise.

"Why yes," he explained. "I find it most health-ful, and the smell is a refreshment to me when I make the rounds of the wards in the hospitals."

Schneider said nothing to this, but gave vent to an eloquent sniff. "When is your patient due?" he asked Menton.

"She is due in five and three-quarter minutes," replied Menton, pulling out his watch. "As far as Mlle. Clarice Duplessis" (I shall refer to her by this pseudonym in this account) "is concerned, you two are doctors who are interested in her case. Please do not disabuse her of this. Her nerves are in a delicate state, and she would hardly welcome strangers who are unconnected with the medical profession. I need hardly add that I would likewise be most displeased and would request you to leave immediately should you disabuse her of this idea."

We gave our assurances, and Menton appeared to be satisfied.

Within the appointed time, there was a knock on the door, and Mlle. Duplessis was admitted. She was a woman of a certain age, and a most unprepossessing appearance. She appeared to be somewhat distraught, and her face bore a somewhat haggard look as she removed her mantle and bonnet.

Menton did not introduce Schneider and me, but merely mentioned us to his patient as doctors who were taking an interest in her case. He then proceeded to proceed with what passed for treatment at his hands. To my astonishment, Menton did not invite her to sit, but rather asked her to lie on a couch in one corner of the room. She obediently did so, and he seated himself at the head of the couch, where his face and body appeared to be outside her field of vision.

He then proceeded to mesmerise her. Although I had seen mesmerism in the music halls, I had never witnessed it in a setting such as this. Menton used none of the shining objects or pendulums that I had seen on the stage, but the power of his voice alone seemed to be sufficient to send the woman into some sort of trance state.

To my astonishment, once she was seemingly asleep, Menton began asking her questions on the most indelicate range of subjects, the nature of which I will not begin to spell out here. Suffice it to say that both Schneider (if his reaction was any guide) and I were both taken aback that a man, though he be a doctor, should make such queries of a woman.

However, Mlle. Duplessis seemed to be unencumbered by modesty, possibly as a result of the mesmerism, and replied frankly and with embarrassing honesty to Menton's interrogation. At length, the questioning along these lines stopped, and Menton asked her to describe the dream involving the monster that she had mentioned on the previous occasion.

The following is a digest of her words to Menton. You must imagine them as being spoken in a series of disjointed fits and starts, and composed of half-sentences, rather than the complete phrases I have written here.

"Two nights ago, I was walking in my dream along a pleasant grassy glade in a wood, but I had the sense that something large and terrifying was coming towards me. As I turned a corner, the sky turned black, and the grass withered under my feet. Though I heard nothing, my mind was filled with sudden fear, as if I had heard the roar of a lion or some other savage beast. I looked up and saw a beast that was hideous, and which filled me with the utmost trepidation."

Here Menton asked her to describe the beast as accurately as possible.

"It was," she told him, "immense. It was covered with a slimy wrinkled skin that writhed and wriggled in a repulsive fashion. The black eyes were scarcely visible through a forest of tendrils or tentacles that likewise writhed in a disgustingly suggestive and repellent way. There was a black mouth, and a tongue that flickered in and out, and smoke or some such issued from it."

This was certainly a being of the same type that I had beheld in the Untime, if indeed it was not the identical monster. When pressed for more details by Menton, Mlle. Duplessis reported the same phenomenon that I had observed; that is to say, the emission of a powerfully attractive odour, alternating with a foul stench, with the stench gradually replacing the pleasant scent.

"I was just about to enter the creature's mouth," she told Menton, "when I awoke suddenly, screaming in terror. Hélène, my maid, who was already awake, burst into my room, convinced that I was being murdered or worse by ruffians. I was in a state of complete distress, and I was unable to compose myself for the rest of the day." She appeared to be ready to sink back into this state that she had just described, and Menton wordlessly handed her a glass containing some liquid, which she drained at a gulp, and which appeared to calm her a little. "A little laudanum," he explained to us afterwards.

It appeared that there was no more to say regarding the appearance of the monster, and Menton nodded to us, raising his eyebrows, as if to ask us whether we wished to make any further enquiries of our own.

I took my cue, and asked Mlle. Duplessis, "Mademoiselle, may I ask if you have ever seen a ghost?"

The reply was startling. "Of course I have. But of a complete certainty. I see them all around me."

Menton shrugged, but made a note in a notebook by his side.

His patient continued. "There is hardly a day that passes when I do not see such a thing."

"May I ask how you know that these are ghosts?" I enquired, cautiously.

"Pah! What else can they be? They come and go without a sound. They appear in locked rooms. They walk through walls. Furthermore, Hélène has never seen them, even when in the same room as me. I have always been psychic, though. Even as a child, I was able to foretell death and to see the black dog that stalks the night."

Schneider shrugged dismissively, clearly incredulous at this report. However, I felt it to be in some way a confirmation of what I had experienced in the Untime as a "ghost", both in the company of Agathe and in that of her father.

Menton, for his part, seemed to take these words of his patient in his stride, and merely continued to write in his notebook. He shot an interrogative glance at me, but I shook my head, having heard what I wanted to know.

The session with the patient came to an end, and Mlle. Duplessis left the room.

"Most interesting," Menton said to me. "You seem to have opened a new avenue in this study of the psyche. I had never thought of questioning my patients on such an arcane aspect of the world. I shall definitely communicate this to Dr. Freud when I next write to him. Many thanks."

It was with some amusement that I heard this, since in the first place, Menton had no idea of the true intention behind my question, and in the second, the idea was not mine, but that of my wife. However, I had no intention of educating him on either point.

I did, however, enquire as to whether it would be possible to visit one of his former patients who was now confined in the asylum, having lost their wits after reporting the dream of the monster. Though Menton was unable to give a firm answer on this point, he did inform us that he considered such a visit to be a possibility, and promised to contact me directly should permission for such to be given by the relevant authorities.

As we walked along the street after having quitted Menton's offices, Schneider turned to me. "Why in the name of the D_____ did you ask such a question about ghosts?" he growled.

I was hard put to give any reasonable answer, but simply referred him to the events that I had encountered, where those in our world appeared to be aware of my presence in the Untime.

"So you feel that there may be some connection there? What the credulous see as 'ghosts' and spirits may in fact be travellers in the Untime? Possible, but unlikely, I feel."

I forbore from informing him of Agathe's hypothesis, assuming, as did she, that he would dismiss it as mere speculation. However, when I returned home, I was quick to inform her of the fact that there was some corroboration for her theory.

"I knew it," she said, clapping her hands in an

ecstasy of delight. "It is clear to me that there are more than mere physical dimensions to the Untime."

"That is a cause for serious concern," I told her. "We had previously considered that your father's apparatus was necessary to cross the barrier between the Untime and our world."

"Not so," she corrected me. "It was necessary for us to enter the Untime, was it not? We needed no such apparatus to leave it."

I considered what this might mean. "Your opinion is, then, that the monsters in the Untime could break into our world at any moment?"

"Indeed, that is what I believe. Indeed, they may already have entered, through the minds of those unfortunates who are being treated by this friend of Schneider. But as to whether they can assume a physical form or not, I have no idea. It is possible, I suppose, that they are still in the Untime, though only on the periphery, as were we when we took our little trip through time and space. It may be that they are concerned that they will be unable to re-enter the Untime."

"But why would they be making a visit at this time? Menton told me that he had never previously encountered such visions in his patients, and now, he talks of it as a positive epidemic, if dreams may be so described."

Agathe looked away, and could not meet my eye. "My dear Jules," she said at length. "I fear that my father is responsible for this danger to our world. When he opened the portal between our world and the Untime, I have little doubt that the existence of our world became more widely known to the inhabitants of those dimensions."

"You believe these monsters to be natives of the Untime, then?"

She shook her head. "I cannot tell you. However, from what we know, they appear to be singularly well-adapted to an existence there, do they not? I think it is more than likely that they originated on some other world than ours, possibly circling a distant star, but discovered a method at some distant time in the past of entering the Untime, which is probably completely different from that which my father discovered, and of continuing their existence there. Indeed, the beings may well have abandoned their physical existence completely, and may exist only as these mental apparitions."

I found it difficult to comprehend her thinking on this, but simply asked her if it would be possible to enter the Untime without her father's apparatus.

She considered the matter for a minute or so, and then turned to me, smiling. "I believe that it might be so. Of course, some of the principles of my father's apparatus would apply, but I do believe that it would be possible to make the attempt. The method I have in mind would be considerably less involved and costly than that my father employed."

"I am sure that Schneider will be relieved to hear that," I told her.

"Surely he does not wish you to enter the Untime again?" she exclaimed, with a little gasp of horror.

"Who better?" I answered, as confidently as I could manage. However, this show of bravado on my part masked a real fear that another encounter with the monstrous horror, or worse, could result in the loss of my life, or worse, of my reason.

"Then if you go, I must accompany you," she said.

I attempted to dissuade her from this resolve. Though I had no doubts as to her willingness to face the Untime, and her resolve, I knew from experience that on the last occasion, when I had faced Dagon, she had been incapacitated by an unreasoning terror. I scarcely considered it to be in her interests, or my own, for that matter, for her to venture into the Untime once more. As gently as I could, I endeavoured to justify my reasoning to her, but she would have none of it.

"I am now sure," she told me, "that I am capable of withstanding the strain of the Untime with you."

My face must have displayed my unbelief, for she seemed almost angry in her repetition of her claim. "I will not," she assured me, "fall prey to that weakness again, I can assure you."

Having learned on previous occasions that argument with Agathe was something best avoided, I refrained from further comments, and contented myself with asking her how she believed we could enter the Untime without the apparatus her father had prepared.

"For the exact details," she told me, "we may require the help of Professor Schneider. That will mean the exposition of my theory to him, and that is a prospect that frightens me more than anything we may encounter in the Untime."

"Very well," I said to her. "Rest assured that I will give you my full support in this."

At that moment, the maid entered, bearing a

note from Doctor Menton which had just been delivered.

"Will there be an answer?" she asked.

I scanned the message. "It is Menton inviting me to the asylum tomorrow morning to see one of his patients who had previously dreamed of the monster."

"Then I am coming with you. I wish to see this phenomenon for myself," Agathe declared. "Louise," she addressed the maid. "You may tell Doctor Menton to expect two visitors tomorrow."

When Louise had departed, I turned to Agathe with some concern. "Does not this proposed visit to the lunatics not cause you some worry?" I asked.

For answer, laughed. "My dear Jules," she assured me. "I spend much of my time at the Sorbonne where, believe me, the professors seem at times to be as little in command of their wits as those poor souls in the asylum."

Chapter V

WE set off for the Pitié-Salpêtrière, where Menton had arranged to meet us. He was waiting at the gate of the hospital, and seemed somewhat unsettled when he beheld Agathe by my side.

"I am not sure that this will be a suitable experience for you, my dear Mademoiselle—" he began before I could perform the introduction.

"Doctor Menton," I interrupted him. "May I present my wife, Agathe Gauthier. Agathe, this is Doctor Menton, of whom I believe you have heard Professor Schneider speak."

Menton was covered with confusion, as I had intended, I confess, and bent low over Agathe's hand, presumably to hide his confusion and embarrassment. "My dear Gauthier," he said to me, "I had no idea... But even so, I have my doubts as to the propriety of allowing your wife. Some of those housed here are—" he coughed, interrupting himself, "—shall we say, of a certain indelicacy in their nature."

It was Agathe who answered. "I believe that I have already heard and seen most of what these unfortunates may say or exhibit. If you are concerned about their language, or the nature of their talk, please be aware that my father, the late Professor Lamartine, employed many workmen on his scientific projects, and as a young girl, I often expanded my vocabulary and my general knowledge of the world from these teachers." She flashed a dazzling smile at Menton, who appeared nonplussed. "Furthermore," she went on, "should any of these wish to exhibit parts of their body which are usually left covered, I am, after all, a married woman. Such sights, even if I had not visited the Louvre and seen the sculptures and works of art there, are hardly unfamiliar to me."

"A most advanced young woman," I heard Menton mutter to himself almost inaudibly.

"She is a colleague of yours at the Sorbonne,"

I informed him, not without a certain malicious pleasure at his further discomfiture.

"Really?" he replied, and led the way to the ward where his patient was confined without offering any further comments. I am ashamed to say that I winked at Agathe as we trailed in the Doctor's wake, and she returned my sign. Of such small intimacies are happy marriages composed.

The patient, an elderly woman by the name of Berthe Jabotte (again I am employing a pseudonym), was sitting in her bed, in a small windowless room where she was the only patient. All trace of intelligence appeared to have fled from her countenance. One might even say that all trace of humanity had vanished. She regarded us with a blank stare, in which there was no flicker of recognition.

"There seems to be almost no perception of the outside world," said Menton. To illustrate his point, he snapped his fingers next to the poor woman's ear, and waved his hands rapidly to and fro before her eyes. There was not even the faintest flicker to signify that these had been noted by her. "She is a poor thing, but of interest from the scientific point of view." He thereupon proceeded to slap the wretched creature, tolerably hard, upon the cheek, several times, but provoked no reaction. "As you can see, the nervous reactions are almost extinct."

Agathe was watching, an expression of distaste on her face. "Doctor," she asked Menton, "do you have a match about your person?"

"Why, yes," he replied, retrieving a box from his pocket and passing it to her.

Menton and I watched with interest as Agathe turned away from Mme. Jabotte and struck a match, suddenly turning and presenting the flame directly before the eyes of the madwoman. The reaction was sudden and terrifying.

Mme. Jabotte, who up to that time had seemed placid and passive, suddenly jerked into a state of rigidity, her eyes opened wide, and let out a deafening shriek, alien and inhuman in its nature, and yet, despite its strangeness, horribly familiar to me, though I was unable to describe why it should be so.

Both Menton and I instinctively backed away, but Agathe stood her ground, and extinguished the flame. As if she had also blown out the life in the lunatic, Mme. Jabotte's body slumped back onto the bed, her eyes closed, and she appeared lifeless. Menton seized her wrist and felt her pulse.

"Her heart appears to have suffered a considerable strain," he said angrily to Agathe. "You may have weakened it permanently," he accused her. "Were you aware that this would occur?"

"I was not certain of it," she replied calmly. "I suspected that there might be some reaction, though, but I confess that it was many times more violent than I had expected."

"You are no alienist, and possess no medical training," said Menton. "How could you come to believe that such a reaction would occur?"

"If I were to tell you, you would not believe me," Agathe smiled. "Accordingly, I think we have seen enough. Jules, you will escort me." She offered me her arm, which I took, and Menton, with bad grace, accompanied us, leaving the unfortunate Mme. Jabotte in the care of the attendant who had led us to the room.

Menton was clearly in a foul temper, occasioned by the disturbance to his patient, and I could tell that if we required his cooperation in the future, some powerful act of diplomacy would have to be performed.

We bade him a stiff farewell, and returned to our apartment. Though I was bursting with curiosity to ask Agathe the meaning of Mme. Jabotte's sudden outburst and the strange cry she had uttered, she maintained a silence on the subject, preferring, it seems, to discuss the menu for the night's meal, and the wisdom or otherwise of new covers for the armchairs.

At length we reached our home, and Agathe faced me, a look of deep concern on her face. "Jules," she told me, "there is little time to waste. The monsters from the Untime are coming to our world faster and in greater numbers that we imagined, I fear."

"Why do you say that?" I asked her. "And what was the meaning of the match?"

"When I struck the match, and looked into that poor woman's eyes, my dear, I could perceive the Untime, and a monster that was the twin of Dagon that you battled. When I gazed at her face, it was as if I was looking through a window into that realm of horrors."

"And the flame?"

"That match was true light, not the pseudo-light of the Untime. I believed that these creatures of the Untime hate and fear light, such as fire and flame, let alone the bright light of the sun. They are creatures of darkness and the night."

I now knew the origin of my memory of the scream uttered by the lunatic. It was the same unearthly hideous sound as that uttered by Dagon when my weapons had wounded it. A shiver ran down my back.

"In the Middle Ages," Agathe said to me, "that poor woman would have been described as being possessed by demons or devils. It seems to me that there are people for whom the barrier between our world and the Untime is weaker than for the rest of us. These are seen as mad or possessed, and in extreme cases, such as the one we just witnessed, the sufferer's soul has been sucked out by the horrors of the Untime."

"And you fear that the barrier is becoming weaker?"

"I am sure of it," she told me. "Why else would there be this near-epidemic of dreams of Dagon and his cohorts? Surely this is not a normal state of affairs?"

"Indeed it is not," I answered her, "but your father took a considerable time, did he not, in the design and construction of the apparatus that allowed travel to the Untime? If we are to defeat these monsters, we must visit them, and battle them on their own ground? Or do you consider it preferable to fight them here in our world?"

"I believe that my father took an overly

complex approach to the problem," she answered. "Though he understood many of the basic theoretical principles of the Untime, he nonetheless failed to grasp some of the practical aspects of it."

"I look forward to hearing you explain this to Schneider," I said. "The man seems obsessed with machinery and apparatus, and will hardly give a sympathetic ear to your explanations of a mental explanation for the Untime."

"I am well aware of that," she said, "and for that reason, I wish you to make the explanation. I fancy it will be received better from a man than from a woman, though I am at a loss as to why any intelligent person should think in that way."

"Then you will have to explain your reasoning to me," I told her.

I will not weary you with all the details that she provided to me in order to convince Schneider of the truth of her theories. In truth, it would be difficult, if not impossible, for me to recall them now. The mathematical principles on which her premises were erected were far beyond my understanding at that time, and I certainly cannot reproduce them after some years have passed. However, she pronounced herself satisfied with her student, and accordingly, I presented myself to Schneider with Agathe's thoughts on the nature of the Untime, which, to my embarrassment, I was forced to pass off as my own.

Hesitatingly, I explained to him that maybe Lamartine's original apparatus which we had destroyed was over-complex, and that the entrance to the Untime was possibly simpler than we imagined.

I had taken the precaution of writing out some of the mathematical equations with which Agathe had perplexed me, and showed them to Schneider. It was useless for me to pretend that these were my work, as was shown when Schneider asked me a question about one of the axioms, about which I had not the faintest understanding.

He looked at me with a piercing eye. "Why did your wife not come to me herself with these ideas?" he asked in a stern voice. "Surely it would be better for her to explain these things in person?"

I told him of her worries regarding the sex of the person explaining the theories. Schneider stroked his beard, considering.

"She has a valid point," he conceded. "Almost

certainly I would not be well-disposed towards the idea of a woman propounding such an idea. On the other hand," and he paused, "I know for myself that she is capable of bold and imaginative thinking, and I should therefore not be prejudiced against her ideas simply because they come from a woman. Tell me again what she saw in that madwoman's eyes."

I dutifully related what I had been told by Agathe, and Schneider listened with attention.

"Of course, I did not see this monster," he said, "and I have only your word for the way in which the Untime appeared to you, but I will take her word on this. If Menton was surprised by this," and he chuckled, and once again his laughter was not altogether pleasant, I fear to say, "then she may well be correct."

I was delighted, naturally, that the Professor was more sympathetic and more open to the ideas put forward that we had assumed he would be, and returned to my wife with a written invitation from Schneider to explain her theories to him in person. Being Schneider, he had added a little twist to the tail in the form of a sentence explaining that I was clearly incapable of understanding or explaining the mechanism by which the Untime could be entered.

Though true, this was a somewhat unwelcome sentiment for me to hear.

Even so, when Agathe called on Schneider to present her ideas and theories, I accompanied her on her visit, and listened as she outlined a simpler approach to the idea of entering the Untime, which eliminated many of the tubes and pipes that formed a part of her father's apparatus. Even Schneider, whom I would have expected to be familiar with the subject, appeared to be taken aback by the rapidity with which she expounded her ideas and the novel structure that she proposed for the machine with which she proposed that we re-enter the Untime.

For my part, I was astounded by the detail with which she remembered not only the principles of her father's apparatus, but also the details of its construction.

"I believe," she said, "that my father had been too preoccupied with his study of the so-called 'noble gases' to ignore them completely, but the cooling of the coils that he accomplished with enormous difficulty can be easily accomplished with an ample supply of cool water. Ice would be more effective, naturally, but would add a complication we can ill afford."

"Ah," said Schneider, "your use of the word 'afford' brings up a very practical point. Who will be paying for this venture? I fear that the University will be unable to meet the expenses of this project."

"Surely," said I, "this is a matter that touches upon national security, not to mention the fate of our world. Could not the government be persuaded into providing the funding here?"

Schneider there back his head and laughed heartily. "My dear Gauthier," he said. "Though you are a journalist, you would seem to have a particularly obtuse nature when it comes to understanding our lords and masters. Who, do you suppose, will go to the Place Beauvau, and explain to Monsieur the Minister that monsters from a mysterious dimension are about to invade our land and take away the souls of our citizens? Why, you might as well take yourself straight to the asylum and ask to be measured for a straitjacket." He shrugged. "If you wish to make the attempt, I promise you that I will use every effort to have you certified as sane, though I confess I would personally have my doubts, were I to attempt this. The short answer to your question," he concluded, "is no."

"Then we will have to meet all the expenses

out of our own pockets," Agathe said. "Happily, I still have a considerable sum from my father's estate which should cover the cost of producing the new apparatus."

"But can you do it?" I asked incredulously. "How can you recall the complex arrangement of the apparatus and hope to reproduce it?"

"We can work from first principles, my dear Jules," replied Agathe, with an air of some superiority. "Even though we destroyed my father's papers, I can recall the essentials clearly, and derive the remainder from them."

"You will need to resign your post at the magazine," Schneider said to me. "Your assistance will be needed during the construction of the apparatus, and it will be inconvenient if you are working at those times."

"Have you considered how I will live?" I asked. "I do not work for no pay, you realise, and if I am to resign my position, I will have no income."

"There is my salary as a lecturer here at the Sorbonne," smiled Agathe, "which is not inconsiderable. Furthermore, I am entitled to employ a laboratory assistant, and this is a post which has yet to be filled."

It struck me that I was to be subordinate in my work to my wife, a situation that seemed to me to be against the natural order of things, and I was about to protest at this, but I was waved to silence by Agathe. "I will explain later," she said.

"Very well then," said Schneider. "I will use my influence with the authorities to secure a room in the University where we may conduct our researches undisturbed. Time is of the essence here, and we must make best use of this precious resource. Mme. Gauthier, I wish you to make a list of the materials that you consider will be required to construct the new apparatus. I will secure the room."

"And I?" I asked.

"You will hand in your notice, and start work as assistant to Madame Gauthier as soon as possible."

Chapter VI

YOU may be sure that such a change in my life was not one which I was willing to undertake lightly. However, when I considered the alternative, which was the desecration and possible destruction of our world by the monsters of the Untime, it became clear to me that I had little or no choice in the matter.

Old Simon, my editor, naturally wished to know why I no longer wished to work at the magazine. I told him some story about overwork and nervous strain, at which he laughed heartily.

"My dear Gauthier," he chuckled. "Overwork has never, as far as I am aware, been a serious problem in your case. However, for the sake of argument, let us assume that it is so. I must confess that your work for us has on the whole been of a relatively high standard." (Old Simon was far from generous with his praise, and such an expression was as close to fulsome appreciation as he ever approached.) "If, therefore, you should ever decide that you wish to re-join us, rest assured that your application will not automatically be rejected." I knew my editor well enough to realise that this could be interpreted as meaning that my position would be made available to me in the future, should I so desire.

I therefore thanked old Simon, and performed the melancholy task of emptying my desk before quitting the office, unsure as to whether I would ever re-enter it.

On my return home, I discovered Agathe surrounded by papers, seemingly engaged in calculations. Without looking up, she started to speak.

"Where would one buy a glass plate a metre on a side, and five centimetres thick?" she asked me.

"I take it this is the glass plate on which one stands to enter the Untime?" I replied. "I confess that I have no idea where one might locate such a thing."

"Then," she answered me, her eyes twinkling, "your first task as my laboratory assistant is to discover such a place where we can obtain it, and to let me know how much it will cost."

"Now?" I asked.

"Yes. No. Wait for a few minutes. I may have other items on the list with which you will be able to assist me. Some can come from University stores, but others will have to be purchased, and I have very little idea where to find such items."

I therefore sat in silence while she scribbled away, and at length presented me with a list of materials that she deemed necessary for the construction of the portal to the Untime.

"I am sorry to treat you in this fashion," she smiled, and bent forward to bestow a kiss on my cheek. "However, as Schneider has said, it is necessary that you do this as soon as possible. I trust it will not take you too long to discover where we may obtain these things easily and without undue delay."

The list contained many esoteric items, for some of which the names alone were familiar to me. However, I had a plan in mind which would allow me to locate the suppliers of these things.

On quitting the apartment, I made my way to the suburban house where Professor Lamartine's widow still resided, and behind which the laboratories, now abandoned, still occupied the former stable block. I paid my respects to my mother-in-law, who welcomed me warmly and asked for news of her daughter, pressing me to share her lunch, but I explained that I wished to view some papers of her late husband in the laboratory, and it was imperative that I return to Paris as soon as I had sone so.

I entered the laboratory, the tables and benches of which were now, sadly, covered with a thin layer of dust, all research having ceased, and the assistants dismissed upon the death of the Professor. However, it was in Lamartine's own office that I sought the answer to the riddles that had been posed to me by my wife.

Ignoring the cabinets in which Lamartine's scientific notes had been stored, I searched instead through the files containing the records of his financial transactions. There, I discovered the orders and the bills for the materials that had been used in the construction of his apparatus to enter the Untime, the overwhelming majority of which were identical to those comprising the list given to me by Agathe.

I copied down the names and addresses of those merchants who had provided the components for the mechanism, together with the sums paid by Professor Lamartine for them, and found to my relief that there remained only two or three items on Agathe's list where I was unsure of the source. Bidding my farewell to Mme. Lamartine, and promising her that Agathe and I would soon pay her a visit, I returned to Paris, and made my way to the University, where I was swiftly enrolled on the staff, signing the appropriate papers, and initiated into some of the mysteries of my new office.

On consulting the catalogues of some of the suppliers of laboratory apparatus, I discovered that several of these firms supplied materials very similar to the few for which I was still searching. I therefore paid visits to these establishments, and was able to ascertain that these items would be made available, and received estimates of the prices that we might expect to pay for them.

I returned to our apartment in some triumph, bearing my notes with me. Agathe appeared surprised to see me.

"I trust you will take some refreshment before

you set out on your quest again," she said to me. "I trust that you will be able to discover the answers soon."

"I have already completed the task," I told her, with not a little pride in my voice, and I proceeded to tell her of the methods I had employed.

"You have done very well," she said. "I was expecting this work to take at least two days. How is Mama, by the way?"

I reassured her as to the health of her mother, and was then, following Agathe's perusal of my notes, given instructions by her to place orders for all the items there, as well as to requisition other items from the stores of the University.

The next days were passed in receiving and assembling the items that had been ordered. Schneider, as promised, had secured a large room in an annexe of the University, in a secluded corner of the building where onlookers and curious intruders would be unlikely to visit.

He had also, to my relief, secured the services of two burly workmen, whose task it was to lift and put in place the heavier items of the apparatus, following the plans and directions supplied by my wife. The more delicate tasks of the assembly were left to me, and I was forced to acquire skills which I had previously assumed were those only of the labouring classes. I flatter myself that as a result of this work I acquired not a little skill with regard to plumbing, and the soldering of pipes, which has occasionally been of use to me in later life.

The work of assembling the apparatus took about a week, but a few days after starting the work, I was alarmed by a development in my mind.

I awoke in the middle of the night, having been jerked awake by the vision of Dagon, or one of its brethren, so real as to be almost palpable. The alternating scent and stench that I had encountered in the Untime were as discernible in my dream as they had been then, and my feelings of terror were as petrifying and as soul-chilling.

I have no recollection of doing so, but Agathe told me that I awoke her with a piercing scream.

I do, however, recall sitting up in bed, my hair streaming with the cold water from the carafe which Agathe had emptied over my head in a successful attempt to bring me to full consciousness. Her arms around me brought me back to the land of everyday, and I accepted the towel that she passed to me.

"What is the matter, my dear?" she asked, and listened with horror as I recounted my dream.

"What if you are to lose your mind?" she enquired, speaking the thought that I had hardly dared articulate to myself. She was almost on the verge of hysteria, and her genuine concern for me was obvious. "Those patients of Menton, who sit there in the asylum like empty husks of themselves. How could I ever live were you to enter that state, my dear Jules?" She fell to weeping, and I, for my part, had little to say. How could I keep myself from the attacks of the monsters of the Untime?

When I had been in the Untime itself, it had been possible, even if not easy, for me to direct my thoughts, and to implement defences and counter-attacks against the monster. In the dream, however, I was powerless and impotent against anything that the monster could bring to bear upon me. I explained this to Agathe, who tearfully nodded in sympathy.

"What you are describing sounds similar to the state in which I found myself in the Untime. I was conscious of the monster, and conscious of the harm it could do me, but I found myself powerless to resist, or indeed to do anything to resist it," she told me. This did nothing, as you may imagine, to reassure me. If her father and I had not beaten off Dagon, her father at the expense of his own life, there is no doubt that she would have perished within the Untime, and her soul, if not her life, would have been sucked out of her.

If I had had any doubts in the past as to the possible mental nature of the Untime, these had now vanished. That night, I dared not go back to sleep, but rose and dressed, and vainly attempted to read a book until the day broke, and the terrors of the night had vanished. My dear Agathe, though I implored her to return to bed, likewise sat beside me, though her eyes closed and I believe that she succeeded in sleeping a little.

Following breakfast, I made my way, fatigued by the lack of sleep the previous night, and troubled by a slight headache, to the University, where only one of my assistants was present.

"Where is Jean-Paul?" I asked him.

"His wife called on me, just as I was setting off here," he told me. "She said that he had had a bad dream last night, and he still had a head-ache. And it's not from drink, as you might be thinking, monsieur. I've known Jean-Paul these

past twenty years, and the only time I saw him
with a drop too much inside him was at his
daughter's wedding some five years ago. One or
two glasses of red, and no more for him."

"And you, Louis?"

"Well, monsieur, I confess that I had perhaps
one glass more than was good for me last night,
but I also was troubled by a dream."

I was immediately troubled by this news.

"What kind of dream?" I asked Louis, fearful
as to what his response might be.

His answer, when it came, confirmed my worst
imaginings. He had seen and experienced the
same monster as had I, and as had, no doubt,
had Jean-Paul. His description corresponded
exactly to what I had seen in my sleep, and like
me, he had found it impossible to sleep. He
did, however, deny that he was suffering from
a headache.

Were the monsters of the Untime about to
attack us all? And if so, what defences could we
mount against them before we could confront
them on their own ground, that is to say, in the
Untime itself?

I made a sudden decision. "Do not stay in
this room," I told Louis. "Take yourself to the
café across the street from the side gate of the

University, and await me there. Here, take this money and buy yourself a coffee. I strongly advise against alcohol. Go, man," I urged him. "You will be paid for your time, do not fear, as will Jean-Paul." He left, and I departed the room, locking the door behind me, and went in search of Agathe in her office.

I explained to my wife what had occurred, and she looked at me with a thrill of horror evident in her face.

"I have made the apparatus too powerful," she told me.

"In what way?" I asked.

"The principle of my apparatus, as opposed to that of my father, was to ensure that there was an easy passage between the Untime and the minds of those operating it. The passage was to be facilitated by the crystal columns and electrum plates that you installed yesterday."

I began to see the hideous possibility that she was opening before my eyes. "You believe that the apparatus may serve as a conduit, not only to allow us to enter the Untime, but for the denizens of the Untime to visit our minds?"

"Precisely," she answered me. "The fact that all three of you working on the apparatus have suffered in this way, immediately following the installation of the columns and plates, can be no coincidence."

"Then let us remove them until we are certain that all else is ready for us to enter the Untime."

"Indeed, that is what we must do. Come." She rose, and led the way down the interminable corridors of the Sorbonne towards the workshop where the apparatus was being constructed. At the door, she grasped the handle, and paused.

"I have locked the door," I informed her.

"Hush!" she commanded me. "Listen."

I dutifully strained my ears, and could make out a faint shriek from the locked and empty room. It was the sound of the monsters of the Untime!

Chapter VII

LOOKED at Agathe with a mounting sense of terror. "What are we to do?" I asked. "Are the monsters visiting us?"

"It would appear so," she said. "Where is your workman?"

"I sent him to the café," I told her. "I saw him depart with my own eyes. At least he will be safe."

"I must fetch Schneider," she declared. "You must stay here, Jules, and you must not desert your post. It goes without saying that no-one is to be allowed into the room until I return with Schneider."

I assented, though the idea of standing guard

outside this room which might well be filled with nameless horrors was not one which appealed to me.

She departed, and I stood outside the door, waiting. Despite my attempts to exclude them from my consciousness, the sounds within the room became ever louder and more clear to me. I was unable to shut them out of my mind, and although at one point I plugged my ears with my fingers, it seemed to make little or no difference to the intensity of the screams and bellowing roars that came to me.

As a result of the previous night's experiences, I was fatigued, and my tiredness grew greater as I stood and waited for what seemed like an eternity. At one point my eyelids drooped, and I could see before my closed eyes the hideous shape of Dagon, smoking teeth bared behind the pulsating mass of tentacles. I jerked myself awake, and even slapped myself hard on the cheek in a vain attempt to maintain my wakeful state.

Again, a wave of fatigue swept over me, and I could feel my knees buckling before I snapped awake once more, and forced myself to stay alert. The sound of the monsters had changed by now. No longer screams and roars, the sounds that came through the door were now obscene chuckles and gurgling liquid sounds, such sounds that I had never heard before, and, may it please God, I will never hear again.

At length, Agathe reappeared, but alone. "Schneider is not to be found," she told me, distraught. "I had forgotten that today he was visiting Strasbourg to deliver a lecture. This is something that you and I must face alone. Your man Louis must stand by and alert the authorities in case... in case—"

She stopped short, but it was unnecessary for her to complete the sentence. Both she and I knew full well what would be the consequences of failure.

"But what are we to do?" I asked. "If it is the plates and the columns which are acting to attract the monsters here, then it seems that we are to remove them from their positions. That much seems obvious to me. My concern is how we are to do this without being attacked or otherwise assaulted by the monsters, which, by their sound, are in the room, and are no longer confined to the Untime."

"I had in mind," said Agathe, "some sort of shield that we could use within the Untime. I am convinced that such a shield would prove effective in our world, but in the Untime, it is possible that it would not prove to be so useful—"

"But of course, we do not have such a shield. Would it be simple to make one?"

"Simple," she said, "provided we have the materials, most of which we can take from the University stores. The only items that we would be unlikely to find there would be some aluminium sheets, a few millimetres thick, and half a metre on a side."

"I can procure those easily, or better, ask Louis to bring them from a supplier," I told her. "Let us tell him, and then you and I will prepare the rest."

Louis was accordingly located in the café, where, to my relief, we discovered him drinking nothing stronger than coffee, and we dispatched him to the supplier for the aluminium sheets, for which Agathe gave precise dimensions. We impressed upon him the need for haste, and provided him with money with which he was to impress this need on the merchant.

My wife and I returned to the University, and requisitioned the components that she considered to be necessary for the production of the shields against the monsters of the Untime.

Once in her office, we set about the production of the shields. We constructed three; one for each of us, and one use by for Louis, on his return. My skills as a craftsman had come on remarkably in the time since I had commenced work on the Untime machinery, and Agathe commented favourably on my skills.

Louis returned with the aluminium plates at precisely the time we were ready to install them, and the shields were soon finished. Agathe inspected them and pronounced them as being fit for the purpose for which they were intended.

"I believe that if we use them in the following fashion, covering our hearts and vital organs, that they will provide us with the strongest defence against our opponents," she told me.

It was now time to explain to Louis, as far as possible, what was happening.

Agathe took up the story. "Louis," she began, "what you have been building over the past few days is possibly dangerous to us all, as it attracts energies which are as yet little understood by most scientists. However, I am convinced that I do understand them as well as anyone here in this University, which is to say, as well as anyone in the world, and what we are building here with the shields is a defence against these energies.

"My husband and I will enter the room, and will attempt to dismantle the apparatus on which you have been working. Once we have done this, the energies which have been released will no longer be a danger. However, you must stay outside, and use this shield for protection if necessary should any of the danger leave the room. Should we succeed in our attempt to contain the energy, all will be well. If we fail, and we do not emerge within ten minutes of our entry, you are not, under any circumstances, to enter the room, no matter what you hear. Even if you hear my husband or me calling for assistance, you are not to enter the room. Instead, you are to give this envelope here to the Prefect of Police as soon as possible and to obey any instructions that he may give you. Do you understand all of this? Is this all clear to you?"

"I understand, Madame."

"Good. Then, Jules, if you have finished the third shield, we shall be on our way."

"What is in that envelope that you gave to Louis?" I asked as we walked towards the workshop.

"It instructs the Prefect to place dynamite around the building, and destroy it," she answered briefly.

The words filled me with horror. "Would that be necessary?" I asked.

"Can you imagine a better method of ensuring the safety of Paris? No, not merely Paris, the safety of France and the entire world? There is no alternative." She pronounced these words with an air of finality that admitted of no argument.

Though I loved Agathe, and I believed that I knew her character as one of the sweetest and most gentle of women, this steely resolve was something that filled me with a sense of some trepidation, as, I believe, it would any man.

However, it was now time for us to enter the chamber. Agathe and I held a hurried colloquy regarding our tasks. I was to remove the electrum plate, since that was relatively heavy, and was within my reach. Following this, she was to seize and disassemble the crystal columns that supported the plate. As soon as we had both completed our tasks, we were to leave the room, ensuring that any denizen of the Untime would remain there, and not follow us. In the event of one of us being attacked by the monster or monsters within the room, the other was to first proceed with the dismantling of the apparatus before attempting rescue.

These rules were proposed by Agathe, and though I was far from content with them, given that it exposed my dear wife to possible danger, I was forced to agree that they were necessary.

Before we entered, I embraced my darling, mindful of the fact that it might be for the last time, should some misfortune befall either her or myself, and whispered an endearment in her ear, which I will not repeat here, and which she returned. I removed my jacket, loosened my collar, and rolled up my shirt sleeves, in order to provide myself with greater freedom of movement. Agathe likewise adjusted her dress. Then, holding our shields before us, and engaging the switches that passed the electric current from the accumulators through them, we motioned to Louis to unlock the door.

It was I who entered first. I stepped inside the room quickly, allowing room for Agathe to follow me before Louis closed the door behind us.

I looked around the room, where there was no monster to be seen, but the hideous roars were almost deafening, now that the door was no longer between us and the portal to the

Untime. The sound echoed around the walls, and it was impossible for us to determine from what direction it proceeded.

It was Agathe who drew my attention to the pool of liquid on the floor, in the corner opposite to that where the apparatus stood. The pool shimmered slightly, and, was it my imagination? a faint smoke seemed to arise from it. A familiar foul stench seemed to emanate from it, and any doubts I might have entertained regarding the presence of the monsters from the Untime now vanished completely.

However, even though there was now, to my mind, sufficient proof that we had been visited by these creatures, there was no sign of the hideous being itself. Had it, I wondered aloud, escaped the room through an open window or some such, and was now roaming the streets of Paris in search of its prey?

I posed this question to my wife in one of the infrequent lulls in the continued bellowing of the Untime demon, and Agathe was forced to wait for another such before replying.

"No, I believe that they will be bound to the immediate vicinity of the apparatus, at least until they have become accustomed to the conditions of our world."

That gave me a little comfort, but then I reflected that this meant that the horror was still likely to be close at hand, and we were almost certainly in imminent danger.

I looked more carefully at the apparatus, in an attempt to discover any clue that would inform me of the present whereabouts of the monster. As I glanced upwards, I remarked an unusual shadow on the ceiling, and on following the shadow, to my unspeakable terror and disgust I perceived Dagon, or its twin, seemingly gripping the ceiling with the suckers on its tentacles, and crouched, upside-down (if such a being can be said to have correct and incorrect orientations), seemingly in expectation of being able to fall on us and destroy us. The attitude reminded me of nothing so much as a monstrous house-lizard or gecko in wait for its prey.

Wordlessly, I pointed to the loathsome thing, and Agathe followed my trembling finger, shrinking back in reflexive horror as she perceived its oppressive bulk. She extended her shield towards it, and turned the dial that increased the force of the repellant field. I was gratified to see that this had some effect. The monster seemed to shrink into itself a little, and the bellow changed to an angry snarl, which appeared to contain an element of pain.

Agathe flinched a little at the sound, but she showed herself to be a woman in a million. There are many men whose nerve would have snapped and who would have fled at the mere sight of what we were facing, but my courageous wife, after that first reaction, not only stood her ground unflinchingly, but advanced on our adversary, slowly and inexorably. The monster snarled and shrank into itself, seemingly becoming smaller as every step brought the shield closer to it.

While my Agathe was directing her shield at Dagon and thereby weakening it, I moved to the apparatus, and started to loosen the bolts that secured the electrum plate. This was not a difficult task, and was soon accomplished, following which, I moved to lift the heavy plate from its mountings. I was so engrossed in my task, which required my full attention, that I failed to notice that Agathe had moved significantly closer to me while I was engaged in loosening the bolts.

As I lifted the heavy metal plate that was my goal, the sudden weight of it in my arms, though I had been expecting it, caused me to stagger slightly and fall against Agathe, who happily managed to maintain her balance. The snarling sound from Dagon changed to an angry roar once more, though, and I noticed with horror that in my clumsiness, I had managed to detach the cables from the accumulators to her shield, which was now therefore failing to repel the beast.

I immediately let fall the electrum plate, which rang with a bell-like tone as it hit the floor, and, holding my shield high, interposed myself between Agathe and Dagon. Immediately, the monster halted its advance toward us.

"Take the crystal columns, and flee, my darling Agathe!" I cried. "Do not concern yourself with my safety, but save yourself."

"I cannot do that," she answered me. Brave woman! One in a million, but I could not let her sacrifice herself for me.

"No, no, my dearest Agathe, you must let me face this alone. You are the only person in the world who comprehends the solution to this danger. Leave me now and live, to save the world from this horror!" I shrieked, making myself heard only with difficulty over the roars of the monster, which continued to increase in volume.

Agathe regarded me, with horror in her eyes.

"I cannot!" she exclaimed.

"You must," I retorted. "Do not think of me, but think of others. Think of what will happen should these beings invade our world. You, my dear, are the only hope for this world."

My dear wife's face showed her reluctance, but she approached me, and bestowed a kiss on my cheek – a kiss that, although brief in duration, held within it all that wifely devotion could inspire. As soon as she had done this, she moved behind me, and after a few seconds, I could hear the door opening and shutting behind her.

I was now alone in the room with the monster. From what Agathe had told us earlier, the accumulators in our shields would furnish us with protection for no more than fifteen minutes at full power. I estimated that half of that time had already been used, with the result that I would have to work fast to accomplish my goal.

I determined that it would be impossible for me to remove both the electrum plate and the crystal columns from the room in the same operation, and determined that I would first remove the columns, and then, if it seemed practical, I would re-enter the chamber and retrieve the plate from the location on the floor where I had let it fall.

Each of the four columns which had supported the plate was fixed by a helical screw thread, which required many turns before the column could be removed from the assembly. I was conscious of time passing, and the diminution of charge in the shield's accumulator as I worked. I was forced to perform the operation single-handed, on account of the need to keep the shield raised against Dagon with the other hand.

All the time, the fearful snarls continued, and the sweet scent that I had noted earlier was now totally replaced by the foul sewer stench that I remembered so well from our previous encounter in the Untime. Smoking ichor dripped from the monster's hideous mouth, and the forked black tongue flickered in and out, coming so close to me on occasion that I could not avoid flinching from it.

Though my task would have been easier had Agathe been there to protect me with her shield, I did not regret her absence for one instant, rejoicing instead in the fact that she and her knowledge and skills would be saved, and she would be able to protect the world from the loathsome invaders.

At length, I completed the task of dismantling the columns. I gathered them together under one arm and turned towards the door. At that very moment, my shield seemed to cease to function. Dagon's snarls turned once more to roars, and it drew closer to me. I realised what I must do to survive, and threw the shield to the floor before running towards the door, Dagon's stinking breath hot on the back of my neck.

As I reached the portal, I felt one of the tentacles reach out and wrap itself around my wrist. With a desperate lunge, I freed myself, but I noticed that the suckers that adorned the beast's appendages had drawn blood. I wrenched open the door, and hurled the crystal columns through the doorway as another tentacle lashed out and wrapped itself around my ankle, dragging me helpless to the floor.

Chapter VIII

As I lay, my face down, on the floor, I felt myself being dragged backwards into the room by the inexorable tentacles of Dagon. My hands vainly scrabbled for purchase on the smooth floor, but there was nothing to impede my journey – into what? I shuddered as I recalled Professor Larmartine as I had last seen him in the Untime, awaiting a hideous fate in the mouth of Dagon.

I screamed – and I know not what I screamed, or how often, and resigned myself to a death that would not even permit of a grave where Agathe could console herself for my loss.

But I was saved – by Louis and Agathe, who

between them, using Louis' shield, advanced on Dagon, and drove it back. The grip around my ankle relaxed as Dagon drew back in seeming terror at this resistance, and the roaring changed to a snarling, and then to a whimpering. I half-crawled, half collapsed through the doorway, followed by the trusty Louis and my dear wife.

Agathe said to me at a later date that she had never before beheld a face on a living man as pale as was mine at that time. I felt myself to be completely exhausted, and found myself unable to rise.

"You are safe now, Jules," she assured me. "Safe." She cradled my head in her lap, as one would a baby, and I took strength from her strength as she did so. "Louis," she commanded him, "go to the café and bring brandy here. Go quickly."

I rested, breathless, and could hear, above the sound of the blood pounding in my ears, the sound of Dagon's baffled roars. I fear that I then lost consciousness, and the next thing that I remember was the taste of brandy in my mouth, as the good Louis forced the neck of the bottle he had brought from the café between my lips.

I sputtered and coughed, and attempted to sit up, but was prevented from doing so by a stabbing pain in my lower arm. Looking, I saw a mass of circular welts, corresponding to the place where I had been seized by Dagon. The flesh of my ankle, having been protected by my nether garments and by my hosiery, had escaped this damage, but it was still painful, and I suspected that it had been severely bruised.

I listened carefully for sounds within the room, but could hear nothing.

"What has happened?" I asked.

"I believe it has returned to the Untime," said Agathe. "The plate and columns are no longer in place, and therefore cannot act as a binding focus."

I was forced to believe her in this regard, because I was unable to understand the principles on which the apparatus worked.

"Should I go to retrieve the electrum plate?" I asked, eventually struggling to my feet.

"I will do that, monsieur," said the faithful Louis.

"You should take your shield, in case there is still some danger," Agathe told him. He took it, entered the room, and reappeared within half a minute, smiling, and bearing the plate.

"It stinks in there, it does. Stinks like a bloody sewer – begging your pardon, Madame. Here's the plate, anyway."

It was a relief to know that those parts of the apparatus which, according to my wife, formed the "binding focus" for the Untime's monsters were now disassembled and no longer posed any danger to us, and I said as much.

"Not at all, Jules," she answered me. "Menton's patients had no such apparatus, and they had the nightmares that you, Louis, and Jean-Paul all suffered, to the extent that some of them have lost their minds." Louis looked concerned at this, as well he might. "It is clear," she continued, "that there are those whose natural defences against the Untime are naturally weaker."

"Maybe," I hazarded, remembering the unfortunate Mlle. Duplessis whom I had encountered with Doctor Menton, "such people are what we usually refer to as being 'psychic'. Remember that I told you that she saw ghosts."

At this, Louis interrupted excitedly. With Agathe's permission, he had taken a drink of the brandy ("to wash the stink out of my mouth" as he explained it). "Why, Jean-Paul is always seeing ghosts," he exclaimed. "As I told you, he doesn't drink more than a glass, or perhaps two, of an evening, but he's always seeing things that aren't there."

"Such as?" I asked.

"He sees people when no-one else does, and he is always going on about feeling that he's being watched from behind, even when there's no-one else in the room."

A feeling of nameless dread swept over me. "We must go to visit him immediately," I said to the others.

"Why?" asked Agathe.

"I do not believe that I am psychic, but I believe Jean-Paul to be in danger," I said. "Quick. There is no time to be lost. Come, Louis, you must show me where he lives."

"I will stay here," Agathe told me. "If for no other reason than that this electrum plate may prove a temptation to some passer-by."

I embraced her, and Louis and I left her standing guard. I hailed a cab, which took us to the quarter where Jean-Paul and Louis lived. We struggled up the stairs to the apartment on the fifth floor where Louis and his wife lived.

A woman answered the door. Her hair was dishevelled, and her eyes were red, indicating that she had almost certainly been weeping.

"Now then, Marthe, stop that," said Louis, not unkindly. "What's the matter?"

"He's gone!" she wailed.

Louis' face took on an expression of horror. "Dead? Jean-Paul is dead?" he asked incredulously.

"I would that he were," she answered through a storm of weeping. "Come. See for yourselves. Are you a doctor?" she asked me, appearing to notice me for the first time.

"No, I am not," I told her, "but I have an idea what may be ailing your husband, and I believe that there may be a cure. Tell me, is he in a dark room now?"

"Why, yes, monsieur, he is," she said. "When the sun rose this morning, he said it was agony for him to endure it. If I didn't know him better, I would say that he had taken too much to drink last night, but I was with him all evening, and I know for myself, because I saw with my own eyes, that he had one glass of red. One solitary glass, monsieur."

"Lead us to him," I ordered.

As I had feared, the unfortunate Jean-Paul was in the state in which we had discovered Mme. Jabotte, the poor wretch in the asylum. Though alive, in the technical sense of the word, his mind was obviously far away, and he seemed unaware of our very presence. Even when Louis, whom he obviously knew well, and who was a good and trusted friend, addressed him, there was no response. A kiss on the cheek from his wife was likewise ignored.

"We will take him to the University," I informed his wife.

"Will the doctors there know what is wrong with him?" she asked.

"It may not be a doctor who is needed here," I told her, but refrained from giving any further explanation.

I removed my muffler and placed it around the unresisting man's eyes. "I do not wish to place him under the strain of the daylight during our journey," I explained. Strangely enough, my action seemed to import some confidence to the wife, who seemed to believe from this that I possessed some knowledge and expertise regarding her husband's condition, and would be able to effect some improvement.

We led the unresisting Jean-Paul to a cab. He seemed to possess no volition of his own, but was content to act as we guided him by gripping his arms and by steering him, automaton-like, to the vehicle. It was, of course, useless for us to give him verbal instructions, as he appeared to be completely unconscious of them, or indeed, of our very existence.

When we returned to the Sorbonne with the blindfolded Jean-Paul, I explained the situation to my wife, who listened with concern, but expressed her doubts as to whether she would be able to ameliorate his condition.

"What do you expect me to do?" she whispered fiercely, out of earshot of Louis. "I fear that you have built up the poor wife's hopes in vain, to say nothing of those of his friend."

"I had imagined," I said, "that you would be able to use the principles of the shields which repelled the Untime monsters to drive out the monsters from his mind."

She sighed. "My dear Jules, I have not performed any calculations to determine whether such a thing would be possible."

"What do we have to lose?" I asked. "Could we not simply hold the shields, with new accumulators, close to him, and trust that they will have the requisite effect?"

Agathe appeared to consider this. "It would do no harm, I suppose. Louis, take this," and she scribbled a few lines in a notebook, and tore out the page, "and go to the stores of the Physical

Science department. We need three new accumulators, of the type we used for these shields. And they must be fully charged," she added.

Louis departed, and she turned to me. "Well, husband mine, you may have something in this idea, now that I come to consider it, but we must not be disappointed if it fails to produce results."

"Of course," I said, and we waited for Louis' return. The unfortunate Jean-Paul stood, motionless as a statue, my muffler still bandaging his eyes. "Should we remove the muffler when we apply the shield?" I asked her.

"I do not think that it matters unduly," she told me after a few seconds' thought. "To be safe, I suggest that we leave the muffler in place. We saw the effects of light on one of these sufferers at the asylum, did we not?"

Louis returned, bearing three accumulators in triumph. Having ensured that the shields' settings were at their minimum, and that the contacts which activated them were open, we connected the accumulators.

"Louis, we will need you to assist your friend," said Agathe. "Take your shield and stand behind Jean-Louis, and present your shield to the back of his neck, at about twenty centimetres' distance. Jules, I wish you to stand in a position where you can present the shield to his left temple at about the same distance. I will do the same for the right temple."

We moved into the positions prescribed by my wife, and she continued giving us directions. "I think it will be wise if we do not use full power, at least at the start. When I give the word, set the dials on your shields to the halfway mark, and then make contact, before presenting the shield to Jean-Paul, maintaining the distance of twenty centimetres as far as is possible." She gave these orders in a clear, calm, confident voice, and I had no doubt whatsoever in my mind that all was clear to her, and we would succeed in our attempts at curing the unfortunate victim of the Untime.

She gave the word, and we presented the shields as instructed. There was no visible effect for a minute or so, but Louis excitedly reported that he had observed one of the fingers on Jean-Paul's right hand starting to twitch.

"Then let us increase the power of the shields," said Agathe. "Take the power setting to two-thirds of full." We did so, and the effect was nothing short of miraculous. The previously almost catatonic figure came to life with a start.

"What the ____?" came the oath, and Jean-Paul's hands tore the muffler away from his eyes. "Halloa! Where am I?" he asked us. He looked around him and recognised the surroundings of the Sorbonne. "How did I get here?" he asked in puzzlement. "What are those strange things you are holding?" he asked, looking at the shields we were lowering.

"Thank God you are with us again!" exclaimed Louis. "We thought you had left us."

Jean-Paul scratched his head. "I remember now. I was dreaming. It was a nightmare of monsters and terrible things. I woke up, and then— Did I fall asleep again? And I was at home? How did I get here?" he repeated.

It was Agathe who answered him. "You have been ill," she told him. "The effects of your nightmare caused you to fall into a trance-like state. Happily, Louis here and my husband visited your house, and brought you here so that we might bring you back to us using these," indicating the shields.

"My wife!" exclaimed Jean-Paul. "She must have been worried."

"She was distraught," I told him, "but she will be delighted to see you again in this state of health."

"Will this happen again?" the worried Jean-Paul asked us. "I fear to ever sleep again, in the event that I may once again encounter the monsters and fearful things that I met in my dream last night. I dare not close my eyes."

"I have every confidence that it will not," Agathe assured him. "We now know why you were suffering from these terrible dreams, and we now know how to prevent their recurrence."

Jean-Paul appeared to be considerably relieved by these words, as one might expect, and we sent him back home, in the company of Louis, assuring them that, although their services would not be required on the morrow, they would still receive their pay for as long as it was deemed they might be required in the future.

CHAPTER IX

AGATHE was, of course, delighted that her calculations and theories had been proved to be correct, and that her shields had been successful in repelling the creatures of the Untime. She expressed her appreciation of my conjecture that the shields would prove effective in the cure of those unfortunates who were afflicted by these monsters, and readily acceded to my proposal that we visit Menton and attempt a cure of his patients.

She was quick to point out, though, that our efforts had not eliminated the threat that our world faced from the Untime, and it would be necessary to devise a method of either preventing them from discovering portals to our world, or even destroying them completely.

"For this," she said, "I may need the assistance of Schneider. He is more familiar with some of the more recent writings from outside France which concern themselves with the problems of temporal distortion, and I believe that this phenomenon may be the key to the method of removing this danger."

I confess that I failed to understand fully what she meant by the term "temporal distortion", but forbore to enquire further, knowing that any explanation would almost certainly leave me in a state of greater confusion than before.

In the meantime, we determined not to work any further on the apparatus, but stored the crystal columns and electrum plate against the time when they would be re-installed in the Portal, as Agathe had named the apparatus.

When Schneider did eventually return from his visit to Strasbourg, Agathe and I presented him with a full account of what had transpired, to which he listened with an expression of intense interest.

"I suppose I must congratulate you, Madame," he said at length, "that your theories regarding the links between the Untime and our world have been proved so correct. Also," he added in my direction, to my mind in a somewhat sardonic tone, "that your husband proved to be so skilful in interpreting these theories, and turning them into a practical reality."

I replied. "We need your assistance, however, in devising a suitable defence to prevent such monsters invading our world, either through the minds of such unfortunates as Menton's patients, or any other means. Failing that, some weapon which will destroy them, making it impossible for us ever to be threatened by them again."

"The complete destruction of a species is something that may well be beyond our powers. We have no knowledge of how many of these creatures there may be, how they reproduce themselves, or any matters related to their lives. For that matter, we have no knowledge even of their origins. Are they natives of the Untime, or, like us, have they entered from another world and are using the Untime merely as a stepping stone?"

"So you are suggesting that we merely block their route to our world?"

"Indeed."

"There is an alternative," Agathe broke in. "It

might be possible for us to inflict such damage on these things that they consider the invasion of our world to be unprofitable, in terms of the effort they must expend, and the losses they would suffer."

"You are assuming," retorted Schneider, "that these beings will reason in the same way as human beings, and not, for example, as do ants, which seem to regard the loss of individual members of the community with as little regard as do we when hairs are pulled out by a comb."

"It is surely worth the attempt," I said. "Though the being I encountered in the Untime was certainly not human, it was exhibiting emotions and feelings which corresponded closely to some human traits."

"Very well, Monsieur Gauthier." said Schneider. "Very well, Madame Professor," he said, turning to Agathe. "You and I must work together on the design and construction of a destructive weapon."

"Madame Professor?" I enquired.

"Why, yes," replied Schneider, smiling. "The University has approved the appointment of Madame Gauthier to this post. I was appointed to be the bearer of the good tidings. My hearty congratulations to you," he bellowed, and bent forward to bestow a hearty kiss on the cheeks of my wife, who was too amazed to do anything other than respond. To my astonishment, Schneider produced three glasses, which he proceeded to fill from a bottle of champagne which he had been carrying in his case together with some scientific papers, and he proposed the health of my dear Agathe as Professor Gauthier.

My feelings were, as you may imagine, a little mixed, but I can truthfully say that I was proud of my wife's accomplishments, and delighted that they were being recognised by such an authority as Schneider.

I was unable to follow the arguments with which they debated the wisdom or otherwise of the different approaches that might be taken in developing equipment that might be used to fight the monsters, but felt myself on firmer ground when it came to discussing the composition of the party which was to enter the Untime.

It was natural that I should be one of the party, and, I felt, it was equally natural that I should not wish Agathe to expose herself once more to the dangers of the Untime. However, I was overruled on that last point by Agathe herself, who proclaimed that she would be well able to withstand any of the horrors that she might encounter there. She further pointed out that one scientist who understood the theoretical principles of the Untime should remain in our world.

"For," she explained, "if the worst should befall the expedition, and the members are unable to return to this world, there must be some knowledge of the Untime remaining here in order for future generations to guard against its dangers. Professor Schneider's words in these matters would carry infinitely more weight than would mine, despite the recent honour that the University has done me, and I therefore propose that I should enter the Untime, and that Professor Schneider should remain here, to pick up the torch should I fail."

This calm acceptance of the perils involved in a visit to the Untime chilled me not a little, and Professor Schneider was clearly impatient to experience the Untime for himself, but Agathe's logic admitted little argument, and he was reluctantly forced to accept her conclusion.

"Also," my wife added, "I believe that Louis should also accompany us in our expedition, should he wish to accompany us. He has already shown his courage and willingness to face danger, and he is far from unintelligent. Jean-Paul has shown himself to be far too susceptible to the dangers of the Untime, and he should not be included in the party."

"Very well," said Schneider, though he appeared to be displeased with the decision that he not be included in the expedition. "We will make our plans for three explorers, then."

"What shall we do with the apparatus, and the workshop containing it?" I asked.

"Why, nothing," replied Schneider. "We must lock it, and leave it until we are ready to do battle against the monsters."

"Believe me, Jules," said Agathe, "I believe there is no risk of the Untime monsters threatening us now that the crystal columns and the plate which they supported have now been safely removed."

"I trust you are correct in that regard," I answered her. "As, I am sure do poor Jean-Paul and his wife." I addressed Schneider. "I fear that I and my wife have put ourselves in the wrong with Doctor Menton, owing to the way in which his patient was disturbed during our visit to the asylum. Would it be possible for you to be the bearer of glad tidings to him, that there may be some cure for his patients?

"I will certainly do that," he answered. "Indeed, the sooner the better. With your permission, Madame Professor, and yours, my dear Gauthier." He bowed and left the room.

There was a silence for a short while, during which I regarded Agathe's face, which displayed some internal torment. The next words that she uttered came as a lightning bolt. "I believe I heard my father's voice while we were battling the monster," she reported. She had turned very pale, and she almost stammered as she said these words, clearly fearful of my mocking response.

"You have been under a severe strain," I told her. "You should rest."

"No," she insisted. "It may seem ridiculous to you, but I heard his voice, as clearly as I am hearing yours now."

"How can you have done?" I replied. "Quite leaving aside the fact that your father is—"

"Yes, of course I know that you last saw him in the jaws of the monster. But you were saying that aside from that there is some other matter?"

"Indeed. While we in that room, the monster was roaring and snarling continually. There is no way that you could have heard anything else.

Why, I was nearly deafened by the noise."

Agathe regarded me, a strange expression playing about her lips. "Jules, you must not think I am mad, or that I am out of my senses, but it was in those bestial roars and snarls that I heard my father's voice."

I regarded her with horror. "You have indeed been under a strain," I told her. "Those bestial sounds were nothing but the cries of a brute. There was no meaning or sense that could be attached to them."

"And yet, I tell you, I did hear his voice!" Her own voice rose in pitch as she made this claim, outlandish and improbable as it was. "I could hear him, even in the howling of the monstrosity. His voice was almost lost, but it was him. I swear it!" Her voice broke with the last words, and she fell, sobbing, into my arms.

"My darling," I told her, as I embraced her, and dried the tears from her face, "you must rest. This last week has been too much for you."

"But you must believe me, Jules, you must," she said. "It may be difficult for you to credit this, but I recognised his tones. There was no doubt in my mind."

"The monsters have affected you, too," I told her. "But rather than making their way into your mind through dreams, as they did with me, and with Doctor Menton's patients, they attempted a more direct approach. You are presumably made of sterner stuff, and they needed another tactic to attack you."

"How could the monster imitate my father's voice so precisely? And how would it know the pet name by which he called me when I was an infant?"

Though I considered that Agathe was guilty of misinterpreting her memories, I was reluctant to say this to her. Her voice bore the tones of complete sincerity, and I determined that if she was indeed deceiving herself, it was of such a level of deception that it could not be gainsaid. I was reminded of an elderly man I had once interviewed, who insisted to me that he had taken part in the Battle of Waterloo as a hussar. This despite the fact that his certificate of birth offered evidence that he had been but ten years of age in 1815, as confirmed by all his neighbours. When faced with these contradictions, he merely shrugged them off as being irrelevant, or lies put about by his enemies. The only course of action open to me in that case had been to go along with his story, and pretend to believe it, as I now did with Agathe.

"And what did your father's voice say to you?" I asked her.

She looked up at me, her eyes still filled with tears. "Why, he implored me to join him," she said.

"But how?" I asked, forgetting that I had promised myself that I would humour her in her fancies. "Surely you must realise that your father is in the Untime?"

"Yes, that is where he wished me to join him. 'Ga-ga,' he said to me, for that is the name I gave myself when I was but an infant. 'Ga-ga, you will join me in the Untime. You must join me. I am lonely here,' are the words he used to speak to me. They were in his voice, and they were his phrases. Oh, Jules, my dear, I see that you do not believe me." Once more, she started to weep, and this time, she buried her face in her hands, and would not suffer me to comfort her.

I began to fear for her, and wondered if perhaps it might be as well to summon Doctor Menton, or some such doctor, who specialised in the care of nervous disorders. This delusion, if that is what it was, had obviously taken hold of her mind in a way that was most disturbing to behold.

I determined to find out more. "My dear, where was your father when you heard the voice you believed to be his?"

"You are humouring me, Jules. I can tell it from your tone. Even so, I will answer your question, and you may determine for yourself whether I am mad or not. For I know what you are thinking, and I can understand why you believe this to be so. But it is not so, I tell you." She paused, and wiped her eyes with her handkerchief. "That beast that attacked us, my poor husband, the one that you named as Dagon, that monstrous thing was my father!"

Chapter X

HER speech chilled me to the very bone. To say I was horrified by these words of hers would be an understatement of the first order. I looked at Agathe, but there was nothing of the lunatic about her face, other than the effects of her distraught weeping.

"Why should it not be so, Jules?" she asked me. "You yourself said that you knew the beast in the Untime to be a devourer of souls. You saw my father about to have the very life-force sucked out of him by the monster. If we believe the soul to be immortal, where should it go in such a case? The answer is clear, is it not? It will find its way into the beast that devoured it, there to remain. What more natural than that it would seek me out and attempt to speak to me?"

What indeed? I asked myself. It was clear that Agathe had been able to find a rational explanation for the sound of her father's voice – one indeed, for which I was unable to discover any counter-argument, at least without some considerable additional effort.

"Very well, then," I said to her. "You have indeed put forward a convincing argument. But let me present a question that occurs to me on this matter. You will admit that this Dagon is a devourer of souls?"

"Yes."

"And that the soul is immortal, it would appear."

"It would indeed appear that this is the case."

"And yet you are proposing to destroy this creature? What, then, will become of those souls that have been devoured? And let us assume that Dagon, too, has some sort of eternal spark as part of his constitution. What happens to that?"

"I do not know, Jules. Perhaps that is one of the reasons why I am so troubled," she told me. "But suppose this. Perhaps these monsters that subsist on souls are not themselves immortal, but that the souls that give them sustenance are. In that case, where would those poor souls go on the death of their host? Why," she said, answering the question she herself had just posed, "they would become as ghosts in the Untime, manifesting themselves to us in our world from time to time. You know well how, when we were in the Untime, we ourselves were taken as spirits when we ventured too close to this world. Why should not the same be true of incorporeal spirits that have somehow survived their bodies and now inhabit the Untime?"

Again, I could find little with which I could disagree, monstrous as her argument seemed to me to be. I could only nod silently in agreement.

"So you understand, Jules? You truly understand?" There was something of her father's passionate nature in that appeal. With just such a phrase and intonation had he explained his theories, often wild-sounding, but subsequently proven correct, to me. I nodded again, and this time added some words of agreement to my gesture.

"Then I am happy to have convinced you," she smiled. Her face then turned serious again. "But, as you say, we are determined to rid our world of these monsters, even if it means their destruction, and I cannot bring myself to countenance such an eventuality."

This was very much akin to her emotions when we previously entered the Untime on the track of her father, whom we suspected of being capable of destroying the fabric of our Universe through inadvertent meddling.

"I understand, my dear," I told her. "But we must think of the whole world, and not just of ourselves in this instance." A further thought occurred to me. "Let us assume that you are correct in your assumption that your father's spirit – his soul, if you will – is still in existence. That his consciousness survives in a form that is capable of perceiving us, and even of communicating with us. But it is trapped, possibly alone, possibly with other souls or spirits which have been consumed, in the being of the monster. Can that be a pleasant experience? Surely, if the monster is destroyed, and the souls it has devoured are set free, that would be a release and a relief, not a hardship of any kind?"

"You may be correct," she admitted. "I will have to consider this. But I must beg you to say nothing of this to Schneider, or to any other person. Despite my elevation in rank, and his obvious pleasure in seeing this, I believe that a large part of his delight comes from his promotion of me, and he sees me more as his protégée, than as a scientist in my own right, with original ideas of my own. Also, it goes without saying that you must not inform anyone, especially the workmen, of this. Promise me this, my dear Jules."

"I promise," I told her, and sealed the bargain with a kiss.

Chapter XI

THE next day, Agathe and I were taking our morning meal of bread and coffee, when the maid announced the arrival of Professor Schneider.

"At this hour of the morning?" I said, somewhat incredulous. "Schneider is far from being the earliest of risers. Show him in."

I was unprepared for Schneider's appearance. Somewhat unkempt at the best of times, he appeared positively dishevelled as he entered our modest dining-room.

He apologised to Agathe as he entered, and made a vain attempt to smooth his hair, which stood out in all directions, as if he had experienced a powerful electric current.

"Will you please sit down and take some coffee?" Agathe invited him, as soon as he had seemingly recovered himself a little. He accepted the offer, and seated himself at the end of the table, facing us. A cup of coffee was placed in front of him, and he drank it off before starting to speak.

"It is Menton!" he exclaimed at length.

"What of him?" I asked.

"He has entered the Untime!" Schneider replied. "And not his mind only, as was the case with his patients. Menton has taken himself off to the Untime in his entirety. He is nowhere to be found."

"How do you know this?" asked Agathe.

"I received a message early this morning from his housekeeper. She told me that following my visit to him last night, Menton took himself to his library. She could hear him pacing and talking to himself, but when she knocked on the door and requested entry, she was abruptly, even rudely, turned away by Menton. Fearing the worst, and, I fear, prompted by an over-zealous natural curiosity, she continued to listen at the door. She could make out little of his mutterings, other than my name being repeated, as

well as yours, Gauthier, together with a word
she did not recognise or understand."

"The Untime?" enquired Agathe.

"Exactly so. When I mentioned the word to
her, she recognised it immediately. I had been
forced, you understand, to give a reasonably
detailed explanation of the Untime and its
workings to Menton in order to convince him
that there could be some hope for his patients
and their recovery. Though I regard him as a
fool and a rogue in some respects, especially
as regards his association with that Viennese
quack, I confess that he was quicker of understanding than I gave him credit for. He certainly
seemed to grasp the basic principles of the
Untime with little difficulty."

"A fool, then, but not an unintelligent one?" I
asked.

"Precisely. The housekeeper, Mlle. Jacquard by
name, told me that the sound of his voice, and
the constant repetition of certain words and
phrases, convinced her that she was the housekeeper of a lunatic. I may add," he said with
one of his sardonic grimaces, "that this woman,
being employed by Menton, has had the misfortune to come into contact with many such
madmen and madwomen. Her word on these

matters may be taken as quite authoritative, I feel."

"How long did this ranting and raving continue?"

"Mlle. Jacquard tells me that this went on for some three hours. I left him at ten precisely, by the way, so this all ended at one o'clock or thereabouts."

"Ended how?" I asked him.

"His voice apparently had risen in volume, and the frequency of the repeated words had also increased. Her fear was sufficient, she told me, to prevent her from retiring for the night, as she normally would have done some hours previously."

"Fear of what? Of her master's having lost his senses?" asked Agathe.

"Exactly that. Who, after all, would wish to sleep in the same house as a raving lunatic? In any event, the voice rose to a climax, and then there was a loud sound—"

"An explosion?" I asked, mindful of the sounds that had accompanied Professor Lamartine's experiments.

"She described it as being more of a 'pop' than a violent explosion," Schneider answered. "Following this, there was silence, she said,

and she feared that her master was injured.
She thereupon attempted to open the library
door, but it was locked. The poor woman then
discovered my card, which had been left in the
sitting-room where Menton and I had held our
discussion, and came round to see me and to
tell me what had occurred. It appears that she
could think of no-one better in whom to con-
fide," he concluded with a shrug. "My apartment
is at no great distance from Menton's dwelling,
however."

"And then?" Agathe demanded, pouring him
another cup of coffee, and offering him a crois-
sant, which he accepted and devoured.

"I took myself to Menton's, and was forced to
break down the door. I confess I was prepared
to find a cataleptic body, or even an unconscious one. My fear was that I would discover a
cadaver, but I was totally unprepared for what I
did discover."

"Which was?" I could not refrain from asking.

"Nothing!" Schneider positively revelled in
the word. "There was no sign of Menton anywhere in the room. The door was locked, as I
say, with the key in the lock on the inside of
the door, which forms the only entrance to the
room."

"The windows?"

"Do you seriously imagine that I did not consider that? There are two casements, opening onto a balcony. Both were fastened securely, with their catches being on the inside, and there was no sign of their having been opened."

"It may seem over-romantic to make such a suggestion, but there is no hidden chamber or closet in the room?" I ventured.

Schneider laughed. "I considered myself foolish for imagining that this might be the case," he answered me. "However, I felt that it should be considered as a possibility, and I therefore questioned Jacquard as to whether she was aware of the existence of such a feature in the room. As I had suspected, the answer was in the negative. However, I was not prepared to take her word for it, and I searched the room diligently, but could find no trace of such a hiding-place. The search took some considerable time. I commenced at perhaps three o'clock this morning, and have only recently concluded." He yawned. "Forgive me. I am not accustomed to being awakened by a shrieking harridan in the small hours of the morning. Mlle. Jacquard is no doubt an excellent housekeeper, but she suffers from a tendency to hysteria when excited, and the effect is wearing on the nerves."

"So your conclusion is that Doctor Menton has entered the Untime?" asked Agathe.

"Previously, I would have said that such a thing was impossible without an apparatus such as your father used," answered Schneider slowly, "but the experiences of Menton's patients, not to mention your recent work, and your own experiences, have shown me that the Untime may indeed be closer to us than we previously imagined. Indeed, it may well be too close for comfort for many sensitive souls."

"But why would he do such a thing?"

By way of answer, Schneider withdrew a piece of paper from a pocket inside his coat. "I discovered this on the desk in the library. Jacquard confirms that it is Menton's hand, with which she is, naturally, familiar. Here, read it." He passed it over, and Agathe and I read the following extraordinary document.

"Since my conversation with Schneider, I am convinced that the Untime, as he terms it, holds the secrets of what Freud has termed the subconscious. To discover the tangible scientific proof of his theories would put me at the forefront of the profession, and would establish my position in history for eternity. Though Schneider seems to have held in the past to a physical and mathematical model of this extraordinary state, he would now appear to regard it as at least partly controlled by the mind of the percipient. I therefore propose to engage in an experiment of self-mesmerism, whereby I can weaken the barrier between myself and the Untime, and thereby enter it at will. As to the dangers that Schneider describes, I believe they are negligible in my case. Though Schneider ascribes the troubles of some of my patients to monstrous beings that he claims inhabit these dimensions, my mind is of stronger stuff than theirs, and I am confident of returning to our world from this Untime as the bearer of new discoveries, and the hero of the age."

"What an amazing story!" I exclaimed. "When did you discover this?"

"It was before I had made the search of the chamber for hiding-places," Schneider said. "I read it, and my first thought was, quite frankly, that Menton was playing some kind of elaborate practical joke. I had warned him quite explicitly of the dangers of the Untime, pointing him to the experiences of his patients, but as you can see from his writing here, he claims that he is composed of stronger fibre than they."

"It is a document of extraordinary naivety and arrogance," said Agathe. "And to be honest with you, I find it hard to believe that following the explanation of the monsters to be found there, anyone would wish to enter the Untime on such a whim as he describes here."

"Vanity, my dear, is a strong spur to many, and overcomes caution in many cases," I pointed out to her. "Menton seems to be a man of considerable vanity and ambition."

"But tell me, Professor Gauthier," Schneider asked Agathe. "In your opinion, is it possible for a man to enter the Untime in this way, not merely with his mind, but his body also?"

"We know that the monsters seem to be able to invade our minds at will. I would hesitate to call what you are describing as an impossibility, but I would conjecture that it would take a very strong effort of will for it to be successful."

"An effort of will such as that driven by ambition as described here?"

"I have never met such a single-minded purpose," said Agathe, "but I would imagine that such a spur would be sufficient."

I interrupted their discussion and addressed myself to Schneider. "What explanation have you provided to the housekeeper regarding her master's disappearance?"

Schneider smiled. "I told her that I believed her master had gone out without informing her, having argued with me earlier in the evening."

"But the door? The windows locked on the inside?"

Schneider continued his smile. "I was able, with the aid of a little sleight of hand, to demonstrate to her that the windows were indeed unlocked, and that Menton had therefore exited the room in that way. She was naturally surprised at this supposed method of egress, but Menton is apparently a man of strange whims."

"And when he fails to return?" I asked.

"You believe he will not?"

"I believe that he will become disoriented and will fall a prey to the monsters in the Untime," I said, simply.

"I agree with my husband," said Agathe. "I believe that his vanity and pride will act as an attracting force for the monsters. He will be unprepared for them, and he will be swallowed by them. I have little sympathy for him, even so, given the way in which he treated that poor woman in the asylum."

"I suppose it is our duty to attempt to return him back to our world," I said. "As it was to persuade Agathe's father to return to us from the Untime. Let us pray that our efforts will meet with a greater success this time."

Schneider sighed. "You are correct, Gauthier. I am not enamoured of Menton, as a man or as a scientist, but common humanity, if nothing else, demands that we attempt to save him from himself."

"In that event," said Agathe, and I knew that she was also considering the fate of her father, "we have little time to lose. We know that the shields work against the monsters."

"But will they work in the Untime?" asked Schneider. Here, he and Agathe went into a debate which left me with little comprehension of its contents, but at the end of which, both turned to me with a worried expression on their faces.

"Professor Schneider is of the opinion, and I concur with him on this," Agathe said to me, "that the shields we used to repel the monsters and to drive them from Jean-Paul will be of no use to us when we actually enter the Untime. This also means that there will be no way in which we can develop any form of attack against them which can be used there."

"You must rely on the strength of your mind,

as you did the last time," Schneider added. "Since the Untime is essentially a non-material plane of existence, it will be almost impossible for a physical defence, such as these shields, to work, and hence no form of attack, either."

I considered the effort I had expended to defend Agathe and myself against Dagon on the previous occasion that we had entered the Untime. It had been a gruelling and arduous experience, and I had then received the assistance of Professor Lamartine, without whose aid I almost certainly would have been unable to gain the upper hand in the conflict. I pondered the matter for some time.

"Agathe," I enquired, of her, "would it be possible to create a smaller version of the Portal that we assembled in the workshop? One that could be disassembled, and carried with us into the Untime?"

"Why, yes," she answered me, frowning. "I suppose such a thing might be possible. But why would one require a Portal to enter a state when one is already in that state?"

"It occurs to me," I said, "that although the shields and the methods of attack may not work in the Untime itself, it might be possible for us to track the beasts to their world of origin, and attack them there. If you will remember, though, we did not leave the Untime completely on our last visit there, due to the difficulty of returning. If, however, we carried with us a method of re-entering the Untime once we have left it, and hence returning here, we could tackle the monsters on their own ground, without the limitations that would be posed by the nature of the Untime."

Schneider stroked his beard as he digested my words. "There is one major problem that I see with your plan. Other than its total impracticability, that is, with regard to the production and transportation of a temporary Portal. If you are to use this theoretical Portal to re-enter the Untime, and you fail to achieve the goal of exterminating all the monsters, why, since you have no way of you bringing with you the Portal, you will have left behind you an easier method for these beasts to enter the Untime and from there to ravage our world at will."

It was true. I had not considered this implication of my plan, and I confessed my failure. Agathe, however, seemed deep in thought, her head bowed. With a start, she raised her head.

"I have it!" she cried. "A small charge of dynamite and a clockwork trigger is all that is needed. "

"How so?" Schneider appeared to be a little puzzled.

"Why, the clockwork trigger would be set by the last person to pass through the Portal on his or her way to the Untime, and the dynamite would detonate a minute or two after that, thereby sealing the route and preventing any from following. The design of a small Portal would be simplicity itself, given the principles that I believe are involved."

I considered the matter, and could see little flaw in the idea. Neither, it seemed, could Schneider. "I can see that this plan would have its merits," he said at length. "It is not without its dangers, of course."

"More than the Untime itself?" I asked.

"Very true, Gauthier. Since the whole affair is a madcap scheme to begin with, I see no reason why you should not refine the insanity with an idea such as this." Noticing the look on Agathe's face, he hurriedly added, "I apologise, my dear colleague. I meant no offence there. Pray pardon my strange sense of humour."

"Such a mechanism which permits its own destruction is easy to prepare, I believe," said Agathe. "I myself lack the necessary skills, but I

am sure that you will be able to locate a suitable
expert to enable the production of this device,
Professor Schneider."

Chapter XII

THOUGH the original apparatus that had been developed by Professor Lamartine to enter the Untime did not permit the users to carry metal objects on their person, his daughter's improved version imposed no such restrictions on the users, employing as it did different principles to achieve its ends.

Agathe and Schneider were therefore free to develop the weapons that they felt would best fulfil the purpose of inflicting damage on the monsters, without the constraints that were originally considered to be needed. We also determined that the shields which had previously proved so effective should also form a part of our equipment.

After only a day of fevered consultations, Agathe presented me with the plans for a device that reminded me of a trident used by some fishermen in the Greek islands for spearing fish, with some complex electrical devices at each end. The end which was to be used to attack the monsters comprised two prongs, which were to make contact with the flesh of the opponent before a switch was thrown on the handle. According to Schneider, the electrical signals to be transmitted were of a frequency that he had calculated would cause maximum damage to the monsters' metabolisms.

Agathe explained to me that although the length of the device was a little under two meters, it should be constructed in such a way that the length of the main shaft could be extended with additional tubes, so that it could reach a total of a little under five meters in length.

"If you can locate these aluminium tubes," she said to me, "it should be easy to carry this through the Portal and into the Untime."

The procurement of the components and the assembly of the weapons was a simple affair, since I had already requisitioned the parts. I was aided by Louis, to whom we had explained our plans, and he readily assented to join our expedition. I like to think that the money we offered him formed only a small part of the reason for his assenting so readily.

When the devices were ready, and assembled to the joint satisfaction of Schneider and Agathe, the little expedition prepared to move against the monsters of the Untime. It would be impossible to take protection against all conditions that we might encounter there, but based on the descriptions of the monsters, Schneider was able to make some deductions regarding the nature of their natural environment.

"Their size, and hence their surface area, would argue that they come from a warm environment."

I had sufficient knowledge of these things to understand his meaning; that small animals have a proportionately greater surface area than their larger cousins, and accordingly lose heat faster. For this reason, warm-blooded animals such as mammals and birds tend to be larger, the closer their habitat is to the Poles, as the German naturalist Bergmann discovered. However, for invertebrates, who take their heat from their surroundings, rather than generating it themselves, the converse is true. A large body is more efficient for such creatures, such as we believed the Untime monsters to be.

I intended suggesting to Agathe that she dress lightly, but she anticipated my thoughts, and indeed, went beyond them.

"Do not be shocked, Jules," she said to me, "but I think it would be best if I were to travel dressed in man's attire. If you can lend me a shirt and a pair of your trousers, I believe that will be most practical."

"Indeed so," I said. Schneider, being of a somewhat Bohemian nature, did not appear to be unduly surprised or shocked by this suggestion, though I wondered what effect this mode of dress would have on the good Louis when he beheld it for the first time.

"What else can you deduce about the habitat we are about to visit?" I asked Schneider.

"I am guessing, though this is a guess rather than a scientific deduction," he said, "that they inhabit a moist, if not a positively wet, world. From the texture of their skin, and their general appearance, I think we may safely assume this to be the case. Also, the world from which they come is likely to be composed of lighter materials, or to be smaller than our own."

"I am assuming that you believe the gravity

on their world to be less than on this," said Agathe, "given the size and general form of these beings."

"Indeed so," said Schneider. "However, it would seem that the suckers on their tentacles possess great strength. This is apparent from your description of the beast hanging from the ceiling, supporting its own weight by means of these appendages."

"I can vouch for that from the way in which my limbs were seized and torn by them," I added, somewhat ruefully. "I was able to experience their strength for myself at first hand."

"It may be," mixed Schneider, "that unlike vertebrates, the intelligent force is not concentrated in the brain and central nervous tissue, but is distributed throughout the body. This appears to be somewhat the case with octopuses and other cephalopods, for example. However, from what you describe, any attack to the head will almost certainly prove to be a decisive blow. The tentacles may be described as being peripheral."

"What," I asked Schneider, "do you make of the scent and the stench that alternate, attracting and repelling by turns? After the visit to the Untime where we met Dagon, I had marked it as a purely mental effect, present only in my own mind, but after the monster had invaded the workshop, it was clear that this was actually a physical effect as well as a mental one. Even Louis complained of the stink after he had entered the room and the monster had departed."

Although I had addressed my question to Schneider, it was Agathe who answered me. "It seems to me, Jules, that Dagon, like ourselves, has some limited interaction between the Untime and our world. There are paradoxes in what we experienced, and I believe they are linked in some way to the quality of the perception."

"How do you mean?" I asked.

"For example," she continued, "when my father and you entered the Chamber of Deputies, but remained in the Untime, my father childishly flicked balls of paper at the Deputies, did he not?"

I chuckled at the memory, though indeed I had been somewhat perturbed, if not actually vexed, by the sight of the eminent Professor Lamartine behaving like a schoolboy "cheeking" his masters.

"And yet," she went on, "when you and I

visited the aboriginal natives of Australia, they seemed unable to see us and when the spear was thrown at you, it had no effect on you. You never felt it, as I recall."

"And yet, in the Untime, though I was well aware that the battle between myself and Dagon was being fought on the mental and not the physical plane, it nonetheless appeared to me to be physical, and the darts and other missiles that it hurled at me produced the sensation of pain."

"It is precisely for these reasons," answered my wife, "that I have concluded that the Untime, though it is indeed connected to the dimensions and temporal space that we inhabit, is very closely tied to our consciousness. Without consciousness to either experience the effects of the Untime at first hand, or to observe its effects on inanimate matter, I believe that the Untime as we experienced it could not exist."

"I concur," said Schneider. "I was previously of the opinion that the Untime was a purely mathematical phenomenon, but thanks to what I have learned from Professor Gauthier," (it still gave me a start to hear my wife referred to by that title) "I must conclude that there are some non-physical aspects to the Untime. It disturbs me, though, as a man who has been dedicated to the physical sciences, that I cannot discover the equations that govern this state and provide us with the definitive solution to its nature."

"They may well be beyond the power of today's mathematics," Agathe mused. "I have visions of a mathematics where there are no definitive solutions, but rather an infinity of such."

Schneider shuddered in horror, though whether this was real or pretended, it was impossible to say. "I trust that you will wait until after my decease before unleashing this horror on the world. I cannot conceive of a world or a universe without the certitude and firm foundation provided by mathematics."

"Be that as it may," I said. "If we do not make a move soon against the monsters of the Untime, there may be no world or universe left to us."

"Well said, Gauthier!" exclaimed Schneider. "Ever the man of action. Very well, then, I would suggest strongly that you and Louis prepare yourselves for the journey, including garbing yourselves appropriately. It will only be a matter of thirty minutes at most, I am sure."

CHAPTER XIII

I T was a matter of some hours, however, before
we considered that we were ready. Some of
this delay was due to the good sense of Louis,
who provided to have a remarkably far-sighted
head on his shoulders. It was he, for example,
who insisted that we take with us a supply of
food and drink for our stay in the Untime.

"I don't know much about this Untime, except
what I've heard you talk about, monsieur, but it
strikes me, if you don't mind my saying so, that
you don't know as much about it as you might."

"That may well be true, Louis," I said to him.
"And if so, what your advice?"

"Well, we don't know how long we're going

to be there, do we? And what we're going to meet, except for some of those stinking horrors. But we may spend a long time looking, and we might get hungry and thirsty."

"True," I admitted.

"And though, like I said, you may not know a lot about the Untime, and I know even less, I'm willing to make a small wager with you, monsieur, that there's no place there where a man can refresh himself with a good glass of wine or absinthe, or even buy himself a meal."

"So," said Agathe, "we take food and drink with us to the Untime?"

"Exactly, Madame Professor. If you will give me the funds, I will arrange with the café to supply us with suitable provisions."

He was gone some thirty minutes, during which time Agathe took advantage of his absence to change into some of my clothes. The effect on Louis when he returned was stunning.

He stopped and let out an involuntary whistle. "I beg your pardon, Madame Professor, but the effect is—" He seemed to stop and grope for a suitable word to describe his impression of my wife in male attire. He finished with a rather lame "—very fitting and becoming."

"Why, thank you, Louis," Agathe smiled. "I feel

that this is a very suitable dress for the occasion, don't you?" She shot him a smile, which would have melted the knees of a stronger man than Louis. I confess that I, too, with Louis, found the sight to be charming, and I strongly suspected that even Professor Schneider was not immune to the charms of my wife, dressed for action as she was.

"Very suitable indeed, miss – Madame Professor," he stammered.

"Less of that," said Agathe. "While we are in the Untime, we can do without the Monsieurs and the Madame Professors and the like. I am Agathe, my husband is Jules, and you are Louis. Is that clear?"

Poor Louis was obviously a little taken aback by this. "Why, yes, mad— Agathe," he answered, clearly a little ill at ease.

"And I?" enquired Schneider, smiling.

"Why you, sir, remain the great Professor Schneider," I told him. "Let us see what you have brought us, Louis." On inspection, it proved he had done well in his foraging expedition, with bread rolls, ham, and a sliced cold chicken forming the foundation of our rations. As well as several bottles of mineral water, and two of red wine, he had also included a small flask of brandy and one of rum.

"We will have no opportunity to recharge the accumulators in the Untime," Agathe reminded us. We must therefore ensure that we carry sufficient for at least three charges each of trident and shield."

It fell to Louis and myself to be the principal beasts of burden on this expedition, and by the time we were carrying our loads that contained the heavy accumulators that Agathe insisted were necessary, I began to despair of ever moving again.

"Do not worry," said Agathe. "As we use up the accumulators, we may drop them, and your load will be lighter."

"Also, monsi— Jules," added Louis, "we may well have eaten and drunk many of our provisions by that time, and that will also lighten our load."

Indeed, as well as the accumulators, and the smaller Portal which we would use to make our return from any world we visited from the Untime, which contained within it the mechanism for its own destruction, the sturdy Louis was also carrying a large coil of rope, and various basic tools, such as a hammer and a saw. These were of his own choosing, and he simply explained that as a workman, he was happiest when he was with these. It fell to me to carry many of the scientific instruments that Schneider suggested we take with us into the Untime, though I personally felt that we would have little opportunity to use them, and mentally resolved to find an excuse to leave them behind. What use, I wondered, would a barometer be to us in the Untime?

Agathe was carrying relatively little in the way of equipment, other than her own trident and shield, and one accumulator for each. In addition, she also carried the small detonators for the dynamite charges which would destroy the Portal carried by Louis when it should become necessary to do this. I did not grudge her that relative ease, however. It would be a remarkable woman indeed who ventured into the Untime, and I was, as on so many occasions, proud to call her my wife.

We had arranged with Schneider that as soon as we had re-assembled the Portal with the electrum plate and crystal columns, and used it to enter the Untime, he should immediately disassemble it, to prevent Dagon and its minions from entering our world. As for us, we were aware from our previous experience that it seemed easy for us to re-enter our world, though it appeared that the monsters required some aid in the form of the Portal to enter.

Agathe had speculated that it was easier for a being to enter its own world from the Untime than any other, but she had no evidence or theory to back this supposition.

Be that as it may, we were now ready to enter the Untime, and to save the world from its monsters.

Chapter XIV

WITH a feeling of dread regarding what me might find inside, we unlocked and opened the door to the workshop for the first time since encountering Dagon. The smell had almost vanished, but there was still enough to catch at the throat. Schneider, who was experiencing this for the first time, sniffed disdainfully, but refrained from comment.

The ichor that Dagon had left behind was gone, but a greenish crusted deposit lay on the floor, where the pools of vile liquid had previously lain. Schneider appeared curious, and seemed about to pick some from the floor, but I warned him that it was probably venomous, and advised him strongly against touching it with his bare hands.

"Remember," said Agathe, as we replaced the electrum plate, prior to re-attaching the crystal columns, "that this must be disassembled as soon as the last of us has passed into the Untime."

"And who is to be the last?" I asked. Somehow, we had failed to determine the order in which we should enter.

"You should be the first," said Agathe. It seemed clear to me that she had already determined this matter. "You are the most experienced traveller in the Untime. Then Louis, since he is carrying so many of the supplies, and I will bring up the rear. Once we are in the Untime, things will be different, and we may rearrange the order. But, Professor Schneider, you are sure that you will be able to disassemble the Portal speedily?"

"I am sure," he replied gravely. "Let me salute you, intrepid travellers." He stepped forward, and embraced Agathe, then myself, and then Louis. He appeared to be overcome with emotion. "At times like this, I regret my atheism," he said, with a rueful smile. "I wish you all Godspeed, whatever the meaning of that phrase may be. I trust I will see you all, victorious against the enemies of this world, and safe."

It was time. I faced the Portal, gripped my trident, and braced myself, ready to enter the Untime, and whatever horrors lay within it.

One step, and I was once again in that mysterious green haze that enveloped me, with the strange lack of perception, coupled with the omniscience of time and space that was part of the Untime. From now on, I will often use terms such as "turned", "moved", "listened", "spoke", and so on to describe my actions within the Untime. However, you should be aware that these are mere figures of speech, which merely approximate to the actual actions that took place there. I was alone there for a matter of a few seconds only, and then I was aware of Louis' presence. Though it was meaningless for me to speak, I nonetheless attempted to communicate with him through the power of thought, reassuring him that what he was experiencing, though strange, was indeed the natural state of the Untime, as had been explained to him earlier.

To my relief, I could make out an answering thought from Louis, and I was pleased that this stolid working man had the courage and common-sense of a true son of France – enough to maintain his composure, even in the midst of the strangest conditions ever to be encountered by human beings.

I was then aware that Agathe had entered the Untime and joined us. I turned to observe the workshop from which we had come, and saw, through the faint green haze that lay between my vision and the world from which we had just come, the form of Professor Schneider, who had already removed the electrum plate from the Portal, and was in the process of removing the first of the crystal columns.

I indicated this to Agathe, and she appeared pleased that Schneider was fulfilling his function. She turned her attention to the third member of our party.

"How do you feel, Louis?" she asked him. "I trust that the sensation is not too uncomfortable for you?"

"By no means," he said. "Indeed, the weight of my load seems to be less here than it was back there."

I had hardly remarked this until he pointed it out, but what he said was true. The heavy load of accumulators and other equipment was scarcely noticeable.

As previously, once in the Untime, I had the

sensation of omnipotence. This feeling was one which I had previously encountered while in these mysterious dimensions, and it was this, in my opinion, which had finally turned the brain of Professor Lamartine, Agathe's late father, persuading him that he was to be the ruler of the nation, and hence of the world. Louis, too, remarked it.

"I feel I could go anywhere," he said, "even out of this world onto strange new worlds, such as those which orbit other suns. And there is something else strange, that it is hard for me to express, but seems to me to be connected with the idea of Time. It seems to me, absurd as it may seem, that I could move backwards into the past, or forwards into the future. Is this what you mean by the Untime?"

"Indeed it is, Louis," I told him. "But do not step out of the Untime completely, because it will be hard, if not impossible, for you to re-enter. By all means observe from the safety of the green mist that surrounds you, but do not leave the mist, unless we all leave together, with the aim of returning."

"I understand," he said. "To tell you the truth, it is more than a little disturbing."

"You are correct, Louis. It is truly disconcerting,

is it not?" Agathe answered him. "But do not fear. Both Jules and I have been here before."

"In point of fact, Louis," I told him, "you are currently with the most experienced guides to the Untime that you could ever hope to encounter. For there is no-one else, to my knowledge, who has explored this mysterious dimension." I forbore from mentioning poor Agathe's father, who had seemingly met his end in this state, or Doctor Henri Menton, whose whereabouts and fate in the Untime were unknown to us. I also remembered little Marie, the child whom Lamartine had callously thrust into a seemingly endless loop of time in which she was forever trapped.

I could sense that Louis was curiously restless about something which he appeared reluctant to express, and I asked him if there was anything about which he wanted to converse, or whether he had any worries.

"Well, Jules," he said, using my given name with what appeared to be something of an effort, "there is something that I have always wanted to do, and which I have always regretted the impossibility of doing. That is, since I first heard about him, I have always wanted to see the great Emperor, Napoleon Bonaparte. This, despite my name, which was given to me by my parents."

I smiled to myself. On our previous trip, Agathe had expressed the desire to see Cleopatra of Egypt. Louis now wished to view Bonaparte. Was it possible that we all wish to meet a great historical figure whom we wish to emulate?

"I am not Cleopatra, and I have no wish at all to be her," Agathe told me, in what appeared to be a tone of some grievance. Too late, I remembered that thoughts in the Untime are not always as private as one might wish them to be. I had no way of knowing whether Louis had been aware of this exchange or not, but, good fellow that he was, he gave no sign as to whether he had perceived anything.

"Do we have time to visit Napoleon?" I wondered.

"This is the Untime," Agathe answered me. "We have as much time or untime as we could possibly desire. Where would you like to see him, Louis?"

"I have always wanted to see his return from Elba," replied Louis. "That famous occasion at Grenoble when he opened his coat and invited the soldiers to shoot him, but they refused to do so, instead joining his forces."

"I have wondered about that occasion, too," said Agathe. "Let us go there together. Are you confident that you can follow us, Louis?"

"I believe so, Madame," replied Louis. I was amused that he appeared to find it hard to use her name, but continued to address her by her title.

"Jules will lead," she declared, "as he did when we entered the Untime. You will follow him closely, taking care not to lose contact, and I will follow you. Remember, Louis, that at no time must you leave the Untime, as it will prove almost impossible to return."

"I am worried," Louis confessed. "Is this safe?"

"It is safe as long as you follow our instructions," I assured him. "The real danger is not from the Untime itself, but from some of the beings that inhabit it."

I took the steps that would lead us to Grenoble, where we might see the Emperor, and we found ourselves by the side of a country road outside the city. The faint green mist still enveloped us, as we stood, surrounded by soldiers, who were obviously expecting the arrival of Bonaparte.

We were clearly invisible to the soldiers, who wore the white cockade of the Bourbons on their hats, but it seemed that our presence was noted. Several of the infantry shuffled uneasily, and shot cautious glances in our direction, but apparently without actually perceiving us. Their officer's horse was extremely restless, and kept whinnying and champing at the bit, tossing its head, and trying to move away from the location from which we were observing the scene.

"Are we ghosts or something?" asked Louis, obviously more than a little awed by the reaction that we were provoking.

"That may be closer to the truth than you imagine, Louis," I told him. "We provoked a similar reaction when we entered the Untime previously, and it was our conclusion that what in our world we often call "ghosts" are in fact visitors from the Untime."

"Well, well," and I could make out an amused chuckle. "Fancy me being a ghost, and me not even dead yet! That is a strange one, to be sure."

Despite the distraction that we obviously provided, a cloud of dust on the road claimed the attention of the solders, and we could hear the excited chatter of the crowd, chatter which their officers seemed powerless, or perhaps unwilling, to check.

The dust cloud grew larger, and it was possible to distinguish the sound of horses' hoofs and the jingling of harness as it did so. At length, we could make out some shapes in the dust, which resolved themselves into the shapes of cavalry.

"It is the Imperial Guard!" exclaimed Louis. "The Emperor's favourite regiment, all of them hand-picked by the Emperor himself. One could not wish to see a finer body of men." The dust cloud grew larger, and we could distinguish more features in it. "And there he is!" said Louis, in a state of great excitement. "The Emperor himself. Long live the Emperor!" he cried, seemingly forgetting that his shout would be inaudible outside the Untime.

And indeed, there on his horse was the familiar figure of the Little Corsican, riding, it seemed, a little uncomfortably on account of his unmentionable complaint, but stern-faced, and waving his hat.

The stir in the ranks grew louder and more insistent as Bonaparte approached us. I was struck by the air of authority that he exuded. His face, stern but kindly, swept over the soldiers massed in front of him, seemingly taking in every face. He held up a hand, and the cavalcade stopped.

As Bonaparte spurred his horse forward, the ranks of hussars parted, until the Emperor was directly in front of his guard, facing the troops wearing the emblem of the man who had sworn to destroy him. He stood in his stirrups, and addressed the soldiers facing him.

A profound silence fell over the crowd. His voice was harsh, and yet clear. It was the voice of one used to command, and it carried, if the reaction of the soldiers gave any clue, to the furthest row of the massed army before him.

"Soldiers of France!" he began. "I, your Emperor, stand before you once more." He tore open his greatcoat, and displayed his tunic. "Which one of you will shoot his Emperor?" he demanded, pointing to his chest. "Who will be the brave man who will shoot me? Eh?" he added, with a little laugh.

There was a stir in the ranks, and the men on either side of us shuffled. Then came a shout from near us. "Long live the Emperor!" was the cry, and instantly, it was taken up by all the men. I glanced at one of the officers on horseback near us, to see how he would take this near-mutiny by his men, and to my astonishment, I saw him wave his hat in the air, and cry out in support of the Emperor, together with his men.

Then I saw the sight that was recorded in all the history books, and which I had dismissed as legend. The soldiers tore off the white Royalist cockades from their hats, throwing them to the ground and trampling them underfoot, and, from the interior of their hats, where they had secreted them, the tricolour cockades emerged, to be re-attached to their hats. In the space of a only a few minutes, the host which had been ranged against Napoleon was now his army. Breaking ranks, the soldiers pressed forward to the Emperor, who sat astride his horse, gazing down at the troops with a stern but affectionate gaze. His hussars were vainly attempting to keep him from being pressed by the soldiers, who were gazing up with adoration at their leader. Tears flowed down the grizzled cheeks of some of these veterans, who held up their tri-colours to the Emperor, shouting phrases like "I had this at Austerlitz!", "This was at Marengo with me!" and the like.

It was clear that Napoleon was moved by the adoration of his troops. It seemed to me that a tear came to his eye, but he re-buttoned his overcoat, and it was impossible to see his face clearly. He rode his horse forward towards us, the troops clearing the way before him. About five metres from us, though, the horse shied, and stopped, and refused to move forward.

Bonaparte appeared irritated by this, and urged the horse to go forward, but to no avail. It was clear to me that the animal had sensed our presence, and was refusing to move towards us.

The Emperor then displayed his ingenuity and talent for improvisation, which had stood him in such good stead throughout his career. Realising that the horse was not going to move forward, he swung himself from the saddle, helped by an aide, and made his way on foot to the front file of soldiers. Seeing one, he greeted the man by name, reminding him that they had fought together at Jena, and embracing him, kissing him on both cheeks! With such a memory, and such a personal touch, who could fail to follow this leader? I could see for myself how he had conquered, not only the nations of Europe, but also the hearts of his soldiers.

It took me some effort of will to prevent myself from joining in the adulation surrounding Bonaparte and enlisting in his army. As for Louis, I could sense, thanks to the peculiar properties of the Untime, the excitement with which he saw his childhood hero, and listened to his words.

"Do not leave us!" I said to him. "We need you here."

"I am aware of that," he answered, "but is not this splendid to see and to hear?" Adoration showed in his voice. Agathe, however, appeared to be unmoved by the scene. On my making enquiries of her after our return, I discovered that she was sickened by the thought of these men worshipping, as she put it, a man who would lead them to death and defeat at Waterloo. But for Louis and myself, the spectacle of these smartly uniformed men and the emotions aroused by Bonaparte worked powerfully on us.

At last, Napoleon moved on, followed by the troops who had just renewed their allegiance to him.

"Let us go," I said, and we moved back into the Untime, from where we were free to move anywhere in time or space.

"Where next?" I asked Agathe. "Do you choose a time or space that you would like to visit?"

"I have always wanted," she told me, "to see Jeanne d'Arc, who fought bravely against the invading English, before she was so unjustly handed over and burned as a witch. Let us go to the siege of Orleans."

"Very well," I said, and we used the strange powers of the Untime to transport ourselves to the scene where Jeanne was inspiring the French to resist the English besiegers. Fighting beside her was Gilles de Rais, who won such acclaim in the battles he fought alongside the Maid of Orleans, only to end his life with such ignominy after being found guilty of the most horrible crimes against nature, too foul to be listed here.

We found ourselves once more at the side of an army, the soldiers of which were, excepting their attire and arms, almost identical in facial characteristics and general demeanour to those of Napoleon's loyal army. Truly, there may well be a "universal soldier", whose general attributes differ little throughout the ages. It is quite likely that those who fought at Marathon or at Cannae would pass unnoticed were they to be put into modern uniform and armed with a Chassepot.

At the front of their ranks, I saw a slight figure in armour, grasping a banner, and beside that, a larger figure whose arms displayed on his surcoat were or, a cross sable. Both their backs were turned, and I was unable to see their faces, much as I wished to examine them.

In all the paintings and illustrations I had seen of Jeanne, she had been represented as a noble and spiritual young lady possessed of considerable beauty. It was therefore with some surprise that I beheld her face for the first time when she turned to face us.

It was the face of a young girl, true, but a face of such plainness that it can only be described as "ugly". Her features were irregular and coarse, and displayed few external signs of intelligence or even of personality. Beside me, I heard Agathe catch her breath.

"Is that her?" she asked me. "The saviour of our country?"

"I fear so," I said. I looked closer at the face, searching for the signs of the spirituality which must surely be there, given her reported visions and her ability to lead the armies of France. Alas, I saw none of that; merely a look in her face which in some sense corresponded to that of the wild-eyed fanatics who infest some of the poorer areas of Paris, plucking passers-by by the sleeve, and confiding in them the most extravagant and imaginative fantasies. I shuddered to think that this poor girl had become the symbol of my country's resistance. What, I asked myself, did she possess that had given her such power over the nobles and the royalty of France, who had permitted her to lead the armies in this way?

"There is something there," Agathe answered my unspoken thoughts, of which she was, of course, cognisant. "Look at the eyes again."

I looked, but was still unable to discern anything that would induce me to trust her as my leader. "Perhaps I am insensible to such things?" I suggested.

Suddenly, the Maid spoke, and the voice, coming from such an unexpected source, was that of an angel. In her uncouth, ungrammatical Old French, she exhorted the soldiers in tones that would move a stone to action. Now I understood her power, and listening to her, without looking at her face, I could even imagine myself following her into battle.

While she was speaking, her companion de Rais turned towards us. In contrast to Jeanne, he was positively good-looking, but I have seldom, if ever, seen such evil apparent in a face. It seemed the mask of a very devil.

Beside me, Louis shuddered. "Jules, Agathe," he said, "let us go from here. I smell death and destruction. Not like that which Napoleon carried with him, which brought glory to those who suffered, but a foul ignominy and shame. I am glad to have seen the Maid of Orleans, and even more glad to have heard her, but she is surrounded by violence, perversity and evil. I feel somehow unclean being here."

I looked with astonishment at Louis, whom I had always regarded as the personification of stoic materialism. To my surprise, Agathe agreed with him.

"You are right, Louis. We must depart this place and time."

"And where to now?" I asked.

Chapter XV

"IT is time," Agathe told us, in a voice that admitted of little argument, "that we went in search of the monsters."

"And of your father and Menton," I added.

"I have hopes," she answered me, "but they are not high."

"But where are we to start looking?" Louis enquired, looking around him with an air of perplexity. "It seems to me that we have no chance at all of discovering anything in this strange world, unless we first know where it is, as we did with the Emperor."

"I think you may have underestimated the inventive powers of Professor Schneider,

Louis," Agathe told him, withdrawing from her knapsack a device which seemed to resemble a compass, but which was attached to an electrical accumulator of the same type that we would use to power our shields and our tridents when necessary.

"What is that?" I asked her.

"Why, based on what we know of the monsters and the Untime, and based on his mathematics, Schneider believes that this device will lead us to the monsters."

"How does it work?"

Agathe gave me a smile in which pity seemed to be mixed with her affection. "My dear Jules, if I were to begin explaining now, it would take hours before you would understand."

"I did not mean the principles by which it works," I answered her, a little impatiently. "I was referring to the method by which it is operated."

"Oh, that is simple enough, if Schneider is to be believed," she answered, airily. "I close these contacts here, and slide this lever to adjust the sensitivity of the apparatus, and the needle will then point in the direction of the nearest monster. The position of the lever gives some indication of the distance between us and the monster."

"Very well, then. And what do we see now?"

My dear wife said nothing in direct answer, but manipulated the controls of the device, and after the space of about a minute, straightened up and pointed with a firm finger. "There," she exclaimed. "I believe there is one of the monsters in that direction."

We set off, still within the green haze by which I perceived as the Untime. I do not pretend to understand how Schneider could have calculated the workings of a device to predict direction in a state where the concept of direction and dimension had little or no meaning, but it seemed as well to take this route as any.

In the Untime, the concept of time likewise has little or no meaning, but it seemed to be some hours before Agathe held up her hand and signalled that we should halt. For my part, I was glad of the rest, and I saw that Louis, whose burden was considerably heavier than mine, also seemed glad of the respite, despite the reduction in weight of our burdens.

"I believe we are now very close," Agathe said to us.

"Is the beast in this green fog, or can we step outside into the open air?" Louis asked.

"I believe we will have to go outside, and this will be a test of our Portal when we return," Agathe answered him.

I wondered silently if we would actually return, should we find ourselves engaged in combat with one of the monsters.

"Let us step out," Agathe said to us. "Jules, then myself, then Louis. Take your shield, and have it ready, but wait before turning it on."

I stepped through the green misty barrier into the strange world. The warm air was breathable, though I was immediately aware of the floral scent with which I now associated the monsters. The ground underfoot appeared to be of simple white marble in its natural state, but worn smooth by the action of millennia of wind and rain, or so I surmised. I looked around us in the light of the bluish sun that lit the scene, but was unable to see any sign of such a being. Agathe and then Louis joined me, and they in their turn searched for the beast.

"It must be near," Agathe told us, "if Schneider's assumptions are correct."

I became conscious of Louis suddenly freezing in a rigid pose, his finger outstretched. "Look!" he cried.

My gaze followed his pointing finger, and to

my horror, I perceived not just one, but a number of the Dagon-horrors. The nearest of them was moving in our direction, but happily we appeared to be unobserved by the others of the party. The sweet flowery scent that initially announced the arrival of these monsters before it was replaced with a sewer-like stench was intensifying.

"Make sure that you are able to turn on your shield quickly, should it prove advisable to do so," I warned Agathe and Louis. The nightmare vision approaching us was as foul and loathsome as before. The putrescent skin with which it was covered glistened in the feeble light that illuminated the scene through a ceiling of thick mist, and from its beak-like jaws a vile black liquid dripped and steamed. Louis made a face of disgust as the first whiffs of the putrid stench that we had previously remarked reached us. A wordless screaming roar became apparent, and the monster thrashed its tentacles, seemingly resulting from a sense of anticipated exhilaration regarding the expected combat.

Some distance away from us it stopped its advance, but continued to rage and roar against us, while still snapping its beak, and waving its appendages at us in a menacing manner.

"Do you hear your father?" I half-whispered to Agathe.

She shook her head. "No, but I hear another voice that sounds strangely familiar."

It was my turn to shake my head, in a kind of bewilderment. "How can that possibly be?" I asked her.

"Listen," was her only answer to me.

I cocked my ear and listened to the creature's roaring screams, but could make out little that was intelligible. I said as much to Agathe, but she simply bade me listen a little more closely.

"Ah! I have it!" I exclaimed suddenly. "There were some words in French. Disjointed, and I could make little sense of them, but even so."

"I can hear nothing, Jules," complained Louis. "Only this hideous roaring in my ears. But yes, wait... 'Join us', I hear, and 'we will rule together'."

"That is what I hear, too."

"But what of the voice in which these words are uttered?" asked Agathe, who had been watching the monster with a wary eye, and had continued to grip her shield. "I am positive that I recognise it."

Louis shrugged. "I cannot believe that you are able to distinguish an individual voice from that noise," he said.

"No, it is not a question of hearing the sound of the voice, as of being presented with a mental image of the speaker," she answered him.

As she spoke, a clear picture flashed into my mind. "It is Menton, the alienist!" I cried.

"Why, you are right, Jules! By chance we have come across the monster in which his mind is now trapped. We must rescue him."

Louis coughed. "Pardon me, Agathe, but the words that I heard did not sound like the words of one who wished to be rescued. Rather, it sounded to me as though he was content with the state of affairs, and wished us to join him."

Agathe shuddered. "Jules, do you think you are able to contact Menton, if it is he?"

"I will do what I can," I told her, though in truth I had little idea as to how I should go about such an undertaking.

I decided that the matter was best attempted by my concentrating my mind, and attempting to focus my thoughts on the monster. The content of these thoughts was that I wished to know the monster's intention, and to rescue Menton from its clutches. I had no way of knowing whether my thoughts were having any effect, or indeed, whether they were being perceived by the creature, and I was about to desist in frustration, when I received what can only be described as a blast of thought. On the previous occasion when we had entered the Untime, I had received similar mental buffets, but at that time, they had been more like shrieks of raw emotion. On this occasion, though, the content was much closer to words than to feeling.

"I do not want to be 'rescued', you fool!" was the message that I received, delivered with not a little apparent fury. "I want you and your companions to join me here!"

I enquired of Agathe and Louis if they too had received this message. They informed me that they had, but it did not appear that they had perceived it with the same force and clarity as had I.

"For what purpose should we join you?" I asked. Though I am reporting this as if it were a conversation, in truth, the exchanges were slow, even painfully slow sometimes, and were carried out mentally. I am endeavouring to put into words here some things which were not, strictly speaking, verbal, but more in the nature of feelings.

"To rule the Untime! See behind me, the first of my followers." The monster appeared to gesture with one of its tentacles its fellows. I counted four of them.

"How many of your kind are there?" I asked, with a sinking feeling. I had been hoping that the Dagon-monster that I had previously encountered was the only one of its kind. It was obvious from what I saw here that this was not the case, but if what was before my eyes now was the whole population of these beasts, then I considered that there might be hope that we might prevail.

"Many eights of eights," came the answer. This puzzled me, until I realised that the creatures, like our terrestrial octopuses, possessed eight tentacles, and their arithmetic was therefore presumably carried out on related principles. My heart sank. What were we three to do against so many of these horrors? One on its own had almost taken my life and that of Agathe, and had indeed taken the life of Professor Lamartine. We would certainly perish in the attempt to prevent them from invading the Earth, and our planet would then be inhabited only by the mindless husks of men and women, their souls stolen by these inhuman monsters.

Chapter XVI

"Bᴜᴛ how can you do this?" I asked. "Have you no wish to return to our world?"

"I shall return," came the chilling answer. "Never fear. I shall return — but as the ruler of the planet."

This was so similar to the megalomania that had afflicted Professor Lamartine that I was seriously alarmed.

"Tell me," I enquired, "by what means you have become the leader of this group?"

"It is simple. These beings feast on the souls of those whom they encounter, from the world which I used to inhabit – your world – and others. For the most part, these souls are of inferior intellect, and are easily absorbed by the—" and here he pronounced what I took to be a name which it is almost impossible to write, the sound of which was obscenely hideous. "Take, for example, those whom I was examining at the Pitié-Salpêtrière. None of those was a strong character or of striking intelligence. Their souls merely strengthen their host, without adding anything of value to it. As for me," he continued, "once I had entered the Untime, and perceived the situation, it was clear to me that the addition of my mind to one of these would clearly augment its mental capacity. I therefore placed myself in a position to be absorbed by the largest and strongest of them. The result stands before you. A being ready to lead by nature of superior strength and intelligence, ready to absorb and trample any daring to stand in our path."

As you may imagine, this pronouncement came as a blow. When I had previously struggled against Dagon, he seemed to be almost mindless in his fury. For all Schneider's disparagement of Menton, the fact remained that he was regarded as one of the most advanced alienists in Europe, and held a chair at the Sorbonne. His intellect, therefore, especially with regard to the manipulation of the minds of others, was therefore not to be ignored. The strength and native ingenuity of these monsters I had experienced for myself at first hand.

"So," the thoughts directed towards me continued, "will you and your companions join us on this great adventure. I would demand only that I lead, but you could certainly take the role of second in command."

"I must consult with my companions," I told him, in an attempt to buy time.

I explained the situation, as I saw it, to Agathe and Louis, who had been attempting, with only moderate success, to understand the "conversation", if it may be termed thus.

"Even you, who admire Napoleon, Louis," Agathe said to him, "can surely find nothing to admire in this? We must throw his request back in his face, and then destroy him," she declared stoutly.

"Indeed there is nothing," Louis answered her. "I would be a traitor to the whole human race if I were to throw in my lot with these — these things."

"I concur. We must destroy the Menton creature, even if we must then face the others, and thereby perish in the attempt. Prepare your shields and tridents." I followed my own words, and turned my thoughts towards Menton (for now I was compelled to think of the creature as the former professor of the Sorbonne).

"No! We will never join you!" I declared.

"Then you must prepare to lose your souls to me, but as slaves, not as partners, as it would have been had you joined me willingly."

With these words, the creature appeared to vanish in a green mist. I knew that it had left the world where we were, and had made its way into the Untime.

"We must follow!" cried Agathe. "Louis, the Portal!"

"There is no time to assemble the Portal," I told her. "We must enter the Untime through the strength of our will alone."

"But how?" asked Agathe.

I had no clear notion in my head on how to achieve my goal, but I knew that we must, at all costs, stop Menton in his madness and to do that, it was necessary to follow the monster. Somehow, and without conscious thought, I plunged into the Untime. There was a feeling of dizziness that would have lasted for only a few seconds, had I been in the usual world, and then I perceived the Menton creature before me. As I watched it, and once again breathed in the sickly stench that it secreted, I became aware of Agathe and Louis joining me.

"How? What?" asked Louis.

"Never mind," I answered him. "Agathe, Louis, turn on your shields now, and have your tridents ready to attack." I closed the contacts on my shield and turned again to the monster.

"You followed me into the Untime without any mechanism," the Menton creature informed me. "Your mind is obviously stronger than I had reckoned. For the last time, will you join me? Not as a subordinate, but as an equal partner."

"No, I will not do so."

"You coward! You fool!"

With these words, the Dagon-monster unleashed a shower of fiery darts in our direction. I recalled the methods by which I had previously defended Agathe and myself from the Dagon-monster, and prepared to throw up a wall of ice to repel them, but to my amazement, I saw the darts halt in mid-flight, and drop, their energy spent, to the ground.

"It is the shields!" Agathe cried exultantly. "They are effective not just against the monsters, but against the monster's creations."

I saw that I would be able to summon up my

own offence, without having to concern myself with defence, as I had been forced to on the previous occasion, and I summoned up a mass of harpoons and flung them at the beast. Using its tentacles, it deflected most of them, but one or two struck home, and the creature gave a loud roar of anguish. Menton's voice seemed to thunder in my ears.

"You shall pay for this insult!" it screamed, and a rain of stones materialised over our heads and started to fall. Agathe and Louis raised their shields, and the stones ceased to fall and scattered instead harmlessly around us, with the exception of one stone, about the size of a tennis ball, which hit Louis on the right elbow.

Emitting a cry of pain, he bent to retrieve his shield, which he had dropped with the shock of the impact.

"I cannot hold it in my right hand," he gasped, his face white and sweating. "I am forced to use my left. I can feel my arm has been broken."

"Jules, keep attacking the beast," Agathe ordered me. She moved closer to Louis, and adjusted her shield to cover him as well as herself.

I extended my trident to its full length, and connected the contacts before lunging at the beast, shield in one hand and trident at the other. The three prongs of the trident made contact with the flesh of the Menton-monster, between the left eye and the beak, and a sizzling sound and a foul black smoke arose from that place.

The creature appeared to shrink back into itself and become smaller. Again and again I jabbed at my opponent, which made no move to attack me, flailing its tentacles in a seeming attempt to grasp the trident and withdraw it from its flesh, but as soon as it made contact with the metal, it recoiled. It screamed constantly in pain and terror. After some more strikes with the trident, the creature, which had been greater than the size of an elephant when we first encountered it, had shrunk to the size of a large dog. I summoned up my will to produce some method of destroying it utterly. I know not from where my mind plucked them, but I conjured up a host of flaming snakes, which fastened their fangs into the diminished being, which shrieked even louder, and shrunk to near-invisibility and then disappeared, along with the snakes. At the same time that it ceased to be visible, the screaming stopped, and we were left in near-silence.

Louis and Agathe looked at me in amazement.

"What did you just do?" Agathe asked me. "From where did you conjure up those snakes that finally destroyed the monster?"

"I do not know. They came from deep inside me, with no conscious thought. More to the immediate matter, where has Menton gone? Listen for his voice."

The three of us strained to perceive Menton's voice, or that of the monster which had just battled against us, but to no avail. There seemed to be no sign of the monster.

"Can it be," I wondered, "that when a monster that has devoured souls has been destroyed, the souls within it perish forever?"

"I do not know," Louis said, "and for my part, I hardly care."

The poor fellow appeared to be in considerable pain, and Agathe and I gently examined his arm, which appeared to be broken. We improvised a splint with some of our equipment, and, though I feared that it might impair his judgement, I allowed him a mouthful or two of the cognac from our supplies.

"Thank you," he said, wiping his mouth with the back of his hand. "I will attempt to use my left hand as far as possible, though I fear I will not be of much use at times."

I offered to carry some of his load, seeing that he was burdened with considerably more than was I, but the brave Louis refused my offer, informing me that he was happy to continue. I extracted a promise from him, however, that he would inform me if at any time he felt that he could not continue, and that he would hand over as much of his burden as appropriate.

In the exultation of having defeated the Menton-monster, I had momentarily forgotten its companions, and I came to with a start when I recollected them.

"They are not in the Untime, as far as I am aware," Agathe told me, after consulting Schneider's apparatus. "Should we leave the Untime to locate them?"

"I would do so," I said, "if I were sure of being able to return. However, I am unsure how we managed to re-enter the Untime just now, as I am unsure of the way in which I summoned those flaming snakes, or indeed, where those snakes and Menton have now gone. Remember that if we are to use the Portal to return to the Untime, we cannot bring it back with us, and we cannot leave it for others to use for the purpose of entering the Untime."

"Even so," said Agathe, "you have defeated

the strongest and most powerful of the monsters, my brave Jules." (my breast swelled with pride at these words) "The remainder of the monsters are surely weaker, and with their leader destroyed, their morale will surely have suffered."

"All this is true," I admitted, but it seems to me to be foolhardy to quit the Untime with no proven method of returning to it." Strange, you may be saying to yourself, that I should regard the Untime, that mysterious state beyond time and space, as a refuge, but to tell the truth, it appeared to me to be such at that time.

"Let me consider this," said Agathe, and her brow furrowed in thought. "I have it!" she said at length. "Louis, if Jules and I were to leave the Untime temporarily, would you be content to be here on your own until we returned?"

He appeared to be turning this proposition over in his mind. "Pardon me for mentioning the possibility," he replied, "but what would happen if you were not to return?"

"You merely have to will yourself back in Paris, in that room in the Sorbonne, or even in your favourite café," I told him, "and take a few steps to find yourself there. I would not recommend your café as a final destination, though," I added, laughing, "for your sudden appearance there might cause the customers to wonder about the contents of their absinthe."

"It was not of myself that I was thinking. I was considering how I might effect a rescue if you somehow were trapped outside this strange place, alive, but unable to return."

"Louis," Agathe informed him firmly, "do you remember the time that Jules and I entered the room in the Sorbonne to dismantle the apparatus there, and you were to wait outside to summon Professor Schneider should we not emerge?"

"Naturally."

"This is the same. Should Jules and I fail to return to the Untime, it is your duty to return and inform Professor Schneider and the other authorities of what has befallen us. Under no circumstances may you attempt to rescue or save us, but you must save humanity itself by making your way back as soon as possible. Is that clear?" My wife spoke in a firm, but yet friendly, tone, and I could tell that Louis was affected by her words.

"I understand, Madame Professor," he said, in a formal tone, and gulped as he said it. "It is hard for me, but I will do my duty."

"Excellent," I told him, and was about to clap him on the shoulder, when I remembered his injured arm, and restrained myself.

"I believe that I know how we can return to the Untime without the full Portal," Agathe told us. "Louis, your pack, if you please."

He shrugged off the pack, and my wife searched through the components of the Portal that we had been planning to assemble to facilitate our return, and retrieved two crystal columns and a spool of electrum wire. "This will be sufficient for our needs, I believe," she smiled.

When I considered the large complex machinery that her father had developed to visit the Untime in the past, and the only slightly less complex apparatus which she had designed and constructed to allow us to visit the Untime on this occasion, I was astonished.

"This seems to be all too simple," I remarked. "Are you sure that this will prove sufficient to bring us safely back to Louis?"

"As sure as I was that our shields and tridents would have the effect that we desired," she answered.

I could not argue with this – my wife had indeed proved to us in tangible fashion that she understood and could interpret the principles underlying the Untime. "Very well," I told her, taking the wire and one of the columns, as she directed. "You have your shield and trident?"

My wife took my hand, and we stepped out of the Untime together to face the monsters.

Chapter XVII

It was not long before Agathe and I located the remaining monsters. There were three of them, but they seemed strangely quiescent, without the air of menace that had characterised the Menton-monster.

"I fear the worst," I said to Agathe, when she remarked that they appeared to be sleeping. "I believe that they are attempting to lull us into a false sense of security."

"You must talk to them, all the same," she instructed me. "You appear to have the gift of communication with them. The links between you and them are stronger than between them and either Louis or myself."

"Very well," I answered, "but what am I to say to them?"

"You must ask them about my father, of course!" she replied, with some impatience.

"Very well, then. However, remember that we were told there were many eights of eights of these monsters, and the population may be spread over the whole of the universe. I do not think we can expect to discover your father's location so easily. But I may, of course, be mistaken," I added hastily, as I saw a look of despair spread over Agathe's face.

I advanced towards the motionless horrors, with my shield active, and my trident at the ready, expecting an attack at any moment. Much to my relief and surprise, no such attack appeared forthcoming. The sweet scent that generally preceded these beings continued, with almost no interspersions of the foul smell.

As I drew nearer, I picked up a feeling of curiosity emanating from them. There appeared to be little of hostility in it, though it was mixed with another emotion, which eluded me at first, until I identified it as fear!

Fear! These monsters were frightened of me and Agathe!

"What do you want of us?" I received. This was even stranger than I had imagined. These creatures were asking me for directions.

I had no idea of how to describe Lamartine to them. Instead, somehow I managed to make them understand that I was searching for a being similar in general appearance to myself, who had appeared some time before, and had been devoured by one of their kind. I attempted to transmit an image of Lamartine to them through my mental powers, but I was not sure if my efforts had been in vain or not.

Their reply, as far as I could interpret it, was that they had never encountered Lamartine, or the monster that had devoured him, and I sadly reported this news to Agathe.

"I expected nothing more than this," she replied, although a little bitterness was apparent in her tone.

However, I was taken aback when the monsters seemed to be offering their services to us, to help us locate Lamartine.

"Why would you do such a thing?" I asked in astonishment.

"Why, we were following the one whom you eliminated," came the answer. "We are therefore now bound to follow you and to carry out your orders."

I laughed out loud. Here I was, having entered the Untime expecting to die in a battle against these foul creatures, and instead, I found myself at the head of a group of them.

I explained the situation to Agathe, who had been unable to follow all the developments. She was dumbfounded. "But if these creatures are so good-natured now, why were they so hostile to us before? And why were you and my father attacked so viciously and senselessly on the previous visit?"

"I do not know. Do you believe we can trust these creatures?"

"No matter whether we can trust them or not, how can they ever find us again after they have journeyed through the Untime to discover what we are searching for? And if they did locate my father, could they describe to us where to find him?"

"I do not know. Shall I enquire of them?"

"It can do no harm." She shrugged.

By now, I had acquired some facility at communicating with these creatures. Although their outward form was still altogether revolting and nauseating, once I was actually conversing with them, they proved to be less frightening and more accommodating than they appeared to the eye. Indeed, I received an impression of their desire for our friendship.

I was amazed to discover that, as some, such
as Fabre, have postulated is the case for ants,
that these creatures could be in communication with each other, no matter where in time or
space the others might be located. As a result, it
would be a relatively simple matter to identify
and locate the monster in which Lamartine's
soul now existed. I communicated this information to Agathe, who was likewise astounded
by the information.

"Their mental powers must be immense," she
exclaimed. "I wonder if they have acquired them
through exposure to the Untime, or whether
these powers existed before they started to
enter the Untime and therefore enabled them
to exploit the peculiar properties of that state."

"That, my dear Agathe, is a question that will
have to wait till another time."

I turned back to the creatures, and enquired
of them whether they were able to locate
Lamartine. The answer was in the affirmative,
and I therefore requested them to attempt to
locate him.

The result was extraordinary. The three creatures (by now, I was ceasing to see them as
monsters) formed a ring, facing inwards, and
linked their tentacles together. Amazingly, their

skins appeared to change colour, and suddenly I was hit by a blast of thought as they made the enquiry of their fellows. There is no better way for me to describe this phenomenon than as a blast, and I felt as though I had been unfortunate enough to be close to a violent explosion. I staggered, and my vision swam. I could see Agathe had likewise been affected, but as a result of my greater facility in communicating with the creatures, I was worse affected than was she.

To my further astonishment, once the roar of thought had ceased, the creatures were aware of my distress, and as far as I was able to tell, apologised for causing me pain. A far cry from the vicious all-destroying horrors that we had encountered earlier!

Agathe supported me and helped me to stand upright once more, and I was able to inform her that the being containing her father was currently in the Untime, and was the leader of a group that periodically visited our Earth.

"Then it really was my father whose voice I heard when the monster appeared in that room at the Sorbonne!" she exclaimed.

"It would appear that this is the case."

"Then my father is leading a pack of

these— these things, in an attempt to take over the Earth?"

I could do nothing but nod in silent assent.

CHAPTER XVIII

"WHAT are we to do?" Agathe appeared, for the first time since we had entered the Untime, to be in a state of despair. "It seems that if we slay the monster that swallowed him, as you did the one that devoured Menton, my father will be lost for ever. And yet," she lamented, "I fear for our world and all the people in it, if he is truly assembling an army of these – these things to take over the world."

I remembered Lamartine's almost maniac laughter when he and I emerged from the Untime for the first time, and his determination that it would be he who would rule the world, using the power of the Untime. It now seemed that his mania had not only increased, but had

acquired a greater potency through the employ-
ment of these creatures.

"We have an army of sorts," I pointed out, gesturing to the three former followers of Menton.

"I would greatly prefer it if we could prevent
my father from achieving his ends without
destroying him," Agathe said to me. "However,
I have no way of knowing if it is possible for
us to do that. Naturally, I feel it would be best
if we were somehow able to deflect him from
his purpose and separate him from the monster that has devoured him, and bring him back
with us. Even if he was still suffering from his
delusions, it is possible that we could find a
cure for him, I am sure."

"Before we start discussing this further, we
should return to Louis. Even if he has been
observing what has happened, I am sure that he
has no conception of the latest turn of events.
How are we to return to the Untime, though?"

"My calculations and theories lead me to
believe that if we hold the crystal pillars in
our left hands, and each of us takes one end
of the electrum wire with our right hands, we
will be able to re-enter the Untime without any
difficulty."

Accordingly, we grasped the crystals and wire

as Agathe had suggested, and willed ourselves back to the Untime. Although it seemed that we were approaching the Untime itself, and we were both aware of Louis' presence, we were unable to make any progress towards entering that mysterious state. After what appeared to be hours of strenuous effort, but in truth was probably little more than five or ten minutes, we abandoned the attempt, and retired, somewhat enervated by our exertions.

Agathe appeared to be more than a little downcast by this turn of events, and I myself was completely at a loss as to how to proceed.

"I do not know whether this would be any improvement," I suggested, "and forgive me if this is contrary to your calculations, but if we were to reverse the way in which we hold the items? That is to say, if we hold the pillars in our right, and the wire in our left hands?"

"We can but try," Agathe answered, and we attempted to re-enter the Untime, but with the same lack of success that had greeted our earlier attempts.

"How did we manage before?" Agathe asked, in frustration.

"I believe that we were in a state of terror and desperation at that time, and I am sure that this was a factor that contributed to a large degree to our success."

"How can we recapture that state?"

"We must use our wills to will ourselves through the barrier to the Untime. I am sure that you are right, my dear, when you say that we must use these crystal columns and the wire, but to my mind, the driving force behind our entry into the Untime must be our mental state. We must will ourselves into there. Think, Agathe! Think of your father! Think of the Earth and the millions of people there!"

"Oh, it is too horrible to consider," she said, and my brave Agathe appeared to be on the verge of tears.

"Do not despair, my darling," I told her. "Use your pain and your grief to propel you through the barrier to the Untime." As for myself, I feared for the future of our world, should Lamartine and his army of monsters ever come close to success in their plans. Once again gripping our columns and the wire, we attempted to rejoin Louis, and I saw Agathe disappear into the Untime. As for me, I found myself in a most uncomfortable position. My head, and my body to the waist, was in the Untime, and was bitterly cold, while the lower part of my body remained outside, and was at a usual temperature.

However, struggle as I might, I was unable to move either forwards or backwards. Louis and Agathe attempted to drag me by main force into the Untime, but it was as if I were being sucked into a bog or a swamp, from which there was no escape possible. Was this, then, to be the end of me, to perish in this half-state between the reality of a distant world and the Untime?

I had started to resign myself to my fate – indeed, I had already implored Agathe and Louis to leave me, and to return with all haste to the earth in order to save it – when I found myself freed, and in the company of my companions in the Untime.

I had no idea how the quagmire in which I had been trapped had disappeared so suddenly, until I turned, and became aware of the three beings who had formed Menton's entourage, waiting quietly near us.

Louis gasped, and reached for his trident, wincing as he momentarily forgot his injured arm.

"Do not do that, Louis," I warned him, holding up my hand. "These beings are not our enemies." I had no doubt that it was they who had been responsible for my release from the state in which I had just found myself.

"Not our enemies?" Louis asked incredulously.

"Indeed not," Agathe assured him. "In fact, they have already been most helpful in locating my father, and informing us of his intentions."

Louis gasped in astonishment, but seemed prepared to accept Agathe's statement.

For my part, I turned my mind to the monsters, and attempted to express my gratitude to them through the mental process that I had previously employed.

Within the Untime, I found that communication was much easier, and this applied not only to me, but to my companions as well who, while unable to converse with the beings with the same facility as I, were nonetheless able to understand at least the basics of my conversation with them.

I received the impression from our new friends (for I felt this was now an appropriate description of these beings, whose form had become no less loathsome, but whose attitude towards us was markedly different from that which we had expected from them in the past) that the move between normal space and time and the Untime was trivial for them. Not only were they able to make these changes with little or no effort, but they could assist others, as they had just assisted me.

"It will be easier for us and for you," they informed me, "if you allow us to swallow you so that we become one being."

I was horrified by this idea. I had seen Lamartine devoured by one of these things, and we had seen the result when Menton had likewise let himself be consumed. My worry had obviously communicated itself to these creatures, and they hastened to reassure me.

"Should you at any time wish to leave, of course you would be free to do so. You should not think of it as being any form of imprisonment. There are three of us, and three of you. Consider, with our abilities in this strange space, you would be far more powerful in your quest."

"But why would you want to do this?" I asked. "When your fellows have acted to destroy my species, it seems strange to me that you should choose to ."

"Because you chose not to destroy us," came the reply. "We were bound to our leader, whom you destroyed, and we have no doubt that you could likewise have eliminated us, had you chosen to do so. We owe you a debt of gratitude. We know of your quest from your thoughts, and we wish to help you."

"Let me consult with the others," I told them. I turned to the others, who had heard some of this last interchange, and had been unable to believe what they had heard.

"Are you seriously proposing, monsieur, that we should allow ourselves to be swallowed by these... these things?" Louis asked me incredulously. "Would we not lose ourselves in them?"

Agathe's question was less direct, but just as practical. "Since you seem able to discuss such matters with them, ask them if you would, Jules, what would happen to us should they succumb to an enemy, either in the Untime or out of it?"

I put these questions to the creatures, and received the following replies.

"As to the first, you would retain your own identity, as you saw when you met and conversed with the one whom you eliminated. It seems to us from what we have observed that you all have strong personalities, and we would be unable to best you in that regard should a conflict of wills ever occur."

I communicated this to Louis, who heard my words, and shook his head sadly. "I cannot believe this, but I will be guided by your decisions," he said, turning to Agathe and myself.

Next I posed Agathe's question to the creatures, who informed me that they were not completely sure, but they believed that should they
be defeated in the Untime, as I had defeated the
Menton-monster, then they would perish irre-
versibly, and those minds within them would
likewise perish. However, were the incident to
take place outside the Untime, those who had
been devoured by the creatures, as well as the
"souls" of the creatures themselves, might well
survive, though my informants were not as sure
of this as I would have liked.

Again, I relayed my findings to the others,
and announced my determination to try the
idea for myself, in other words, volunteering
myself as a meal for one of these creatures. "You
must return to our world should the experiment prove unsuccessful," I warned them, and
extracted their solemn promise that this would
be so.

To say that I was nervous regarding this would
be an understatement. But it was not courage
that led me to take this step – it was fear – fear
of what would happen to our world should
Lamartine and his monsters succeed in their
fell purpose. Agathe embraced me, and Louis
clasped my hand as I turned to the monsters

and announced my intention.

"We are grateful that you have placed your trust in us in this way," the largest of them said to me. "Are you ready?" and on receiving my nod of affirmation, bent its hideous beak towards me.

The beak opened, and I could no longer see Agathe and Louis, their mouths contorted by horror and astonishment, as I disappeared within the monster.

Chapter XIX

ONCE inside the monster, I took stock of my surroundings. Firstly, I could see, through the creature's eyes, which were very different from our own. I could see colours which our human eyes cannot see. Later I was to learn from Schneider that these are the "infra-red" and "ultra-violet" waves that travel through the æther, and which are believed to be perceived by certain animals. Not only were these previously unknown colours visible to me, but the vision itself was of a far greater acuity and sharpness than attainable by human eyes.

Next, I was able to communicate almost perfectly with my host, in as easy a fashion as I

was able to communicate with others in Paris.
I learned the name that these creatures gave to
themselves, which I can best write in our language as "Blève", but the initial sound was close
to the sound of a child's balloon popping than
to our "b", and the last closer to the rustling
of dry leaves in the breeze than to any sound
produced by a human throat. For the sake of
simplicity, therefore, I will continue to use this
clumsy transliteration which serves to describe
the whole tribe of these creatures, as well as
acting as the word used to denote a single spec-
imen. My host also provided me with his (or
her, since gender did not seem to be a concept
that was readily understood by these creatures)
own personal name, but it was impossible for
me to pronounce it, and I cannot even begin
to attempt to transcribe it into our sounds. I
therefore asked if he (I had determined to see
this creature as masculine) would mind if I
addressed him as "Georges", and received an
affirmative answer.

In addition to being able to communicate
with Georges, I also became aware of others
of the Blève; not merely those other two who
accompanied Georges, but also of those scattered throughout the Untime. The impression I

received regarding them was similar to being in a crowd of people, where one is fully aware of the presence of many, but it is difficult to distinguish individuals, let alone establish communication with them.

In addition to sound and sight, my olfactory sense was greatly enhanced. I have mentioned previously the floral scent and the sewer stench emitted by these creatures. Using Georges' senses, though, I was able to discover minute differences between the scents emitted by the other two Blève. Furthermore, these scents were not only distinct from each other, but changed constantly in a subtle fashion that had previously been impossible for me to discern. Although these scents continued to change, there was a distinct timbre to the scents which marked them as proceeding from an individual. The closest I can come to providing an analogy is to compare this phenomenon to that of the human voice. Each of us has a distinctive nature when we speak, by which we may be recognised, whether we speak in a quiet gentle tone, or raise our voices in anger. In the same way, it seemed to me that the Blève distinguished individuals by their scent. On my enquiring of Georges, he confirmed that this was indeed the case, and further informed me that the changes in scent marked different moods. The abominable smell of the sewer was an extreme example of this, and showed anger and aggression in the individual emitting it.

Although Georges' senses were undeniably superior to human senses, it seemed, from what I could gather, that his reasoning powers were inferior to ours, and he confirmed this.

"Your strength of mind is greater than ours," he told me, "and that may be one reason why some of us have attacked you in the past. They wished to absorb your fellows and thereby acquire the use of their mental powers. You will note that you and I are still individuals, and neither of us has lost his identity, but at the same time we are able to work together. You may share the sensations that I experience, and at the same time, I am able to make use of your reason, as indeed I am doing now."

These last words caused me to start. I had not been aware that Georges was employing my mental faculties, and I found the idea to be more than a little disturbing. Georges was conscious of my disquiet, and hastened to reassure me of his honourable intentions.

"Have no fear," he said. "Making use of the

reasoning portion of your mind causes no harm, as far as we know, even when you are unaware of the procedure taking place. However, if we wished to access your memories and emotions, that would be a very different matter. I have heard that if I were to attempt to read your memories, you would instantly be aware that I was attempting to do so, and were I to force myself into that portion of your mind without your permission, it would be extremely painful for you. Indeed, among the Blève, such an action is regarded as particularly heinous, and is strictly forbidden."

"I am glad to hear it," I answered, and indeed, I was delighted to find that the awesome mental powers of these creatures were restrained by a code of morals. Now that I was better accustomed to the situation, I found the experience of sharing a body, no matter how unprepossessing its appearance, with this alien mind to be an enlivening and even inspiring experience.

"I am glad you find it to be so," Georges told me, and I could almost imagine a smile accompanying these thoughts.

"Indeed I do," I replied. "Now, if you will be kind enough, I would like to leave, and inform my wife and my friend of what I have experienced, so that they may join your companions."

"Nothing easier," replied Georges, and before I realised what was happening, I found myself disgorged, and facing Agathe and Louis once more. They regarded me with some horror, mixed with fear.

Agathe was the first to speak. "You are alive, Jules!" she exclaimed, and threw her arms around me in a fond embrace.

Louis continued to regard me with a kind of wonder. "I admit that I never expected to see you alive again," he told me. You may find it hard to believe, but a tear stole down the honest fellow's cheek at the sight of me.

"But what is it like?" asked Agathe.

I proceeded to tell them of what I had experienced, as I have written just now, and the concern and worry that had been visible on their faces slowly vanished as I told them of my conversations with Georges, and the augmentation of my senses.

"You appear to be describing the greatest adventure that a man could imagine," said Louis. His apprehension now seemed to be replaced by a sense of anticipation. "Why, were these – what did you call them? Blève? – any more attractive in their appearance, the whole of humanity would be fighting to join them."

"Hardly that, Louis, I feel. Many would prefer to keep the form that Nature bestowed on them. But there is one thing that occurs to me." I mentally turned to address Georges. "My friend," (and yes, you may marvel at this expression, but I had come to trust this strange being) "My friend, I wish to talk in private with my companions. May I humbly request you not to listen to our conversation?"

"Naturally, Jules," Georges replied.

I turned to the others. "I wish to impress something of great importance on you both. These beings have powers far beyond those that we possess, it is true. However, our mental powers and strength of mind far exceed theirs."

"And this is important?" Agathe asked.

"It is extremely important, I believe. They are highly susceptible and will be quick to take their mood from us. When I was absorbed by Georges just now, I concentrated on honesty and openness, and it appears to have paid mighty dividends. He is now our friend, and will help us in our endeavours. But if another, with anger or some other destructive feeling in his heart is to be absorbed—"

"Such as Menton and his overwhelming

ambition?" suggested Agathe.

"Yes, indeed. Or even, forgive me, your father, with his wish to rule the world. Such a mood would transfer itself to the host, and would cause it to become hostile and violent. We must therefore keep a rein on our feelings if these beings are not to transform themselves into the enemies of humankind." I went on to explain a little more about the importance of scent in the lives of the Blève. "If at any time, you discover Georges, or one of 'our' Blève emitting the foul smell that we have met in the past, you must communicate with the one who has been absorbed and from whom the smell is emanating, and ensure that peace is restored."

"I understand," said Agathe, and Louis nodded his assent.

"Then are you ready for the greatest adventure of your lives?" I asked them.

Neither answered, but both silently signified their readiness, and I advanced to Georges, and the other two to the other two Blève.

"Welcome back," said Georges as I took my place, which by now felt familiar and comfortable. Even as I relaxed, I was conscious of Agathe and Louis being absorbed by their Blève. Almost immediately, I could sense Louis' sense of wonder as he discovered his enhanced senses, and took in the new sights and sounds and smells.

I had previously informed Agathe and Louis that the language and names of the Blève were not easy for us to pronounce, and that I had dubbed my Blève Georges, advising them to do something similar, should their hosts be agreeable to this.

It was easy for me to communicate with Agathe and Louis, and soon my wife let me know that she had given the name of Marie to her Blève, in memory, as she explained, of the little girl whom her father had so cruelly perpetually consigned to the Untime some years earlier.

Louis, for his part, had given his Blève the name of Annette, as he felt some similarity of appearance between his mother-in-law and his new host. I could not help but chuckle to myself at this fancy of his.

Agathe continued to be in raptures over how she was able to see new colours through Marie's eyes, not to mention the ability to be aware of all the other members of the Blève.

After some time during which Agathe and Louis established their rapport with their hosts, we were ready, we felt, to make the journey to view Lamartine and his cohorts' attempts to take over the Earth.

Chapter XX

HOWEVER, even though we had decided to make our way to Lamartine, it took us some time before we were agreed on our actions once we arrived there. Agathe, naturally, wished to spare her father from any harm, and gave it as her opinion that she would be able to reason with him, and bring him back to our world where he might be cured of his folly and restored to his family.

For my part, I was less sure of our ability to achieve this end than was she, and it seemed to me that we should be prepared to destroy Lamartine, together with his Blève, if necessary. Once this was done, Georges, Marie and

Annette assured us, his followers would rally to our side, and would, if their lives were spared, be prepared to follow us, and to do our bidding.

Louis, sensible man that he was, held his peace, and indicated merely that he would follow whatever course of action we determined upon, and to lend his full support to it. The Blève remained silent during this discussion.

Agathe and I were still in dispute over this matter, when we became conscious of another Blève, which had joined us in the Untime. This stranger introduced itself to Georges, Marie and Annette as one of the "officers" in Lamartine's band, as far as I could interpret what it was attempting to tell us.

As we now knew, the Blève were able to detect the other members of their species throughout the Untime, and they had clearly detected the fact that Georges, Marie and Annette had absorbed new beings. In retrospect, it seems to me that we had already raised the alarm by our dispatch of the Menton-monster, which must have been remarked, even at the other "side" of the Untime.

I was startled when our visitor addressed us directly, rather than our hosts. It demanded to know who we were, with none of the politeness that had been shown to us so far, and with occasional whiffs of sewer-gas. It fell to me to provide the explanations, as once again I was the member of our party who was best able to understand the communications.

I explained that one of our party was the offspring of Lamartine, and that I had known Lamartine before he had become a leader of the group of Blève. As for Louis, I described him merely as our companion.

The officer appeared to consider this, and then asked us our purpose in visiting the Untime. My answer was that we had been concerned that some of the Blève had been visiting our world, and frightening some of its inhabitants. Our intention was to find out more, and if possible, to bring Lamartine back to our world.

"You cannot do that!" the visiting Blève protested. "He is our leader, and we must protect him. If there is an attempt to take him from us, we will resist it with all our might."

"How many of you are there?" I asked.

"Several eights," came the answer.

This was far more than our three, but it was not the many "eights of eights" that I had feared. Unless fortune smiled upon us in a way in which I was currently unable to conceive, I could not imagine how we might prevail against Lamartine and his "army".

"May we discuss matters with your leader?" I asked. "And will you give us your assurance that if we do talk, you will not attack us?"

"I cannot speak for the leader," came the answer. "But you are permitted to speak with him."

I relayed all this to the others, and asked them if it was their wish to make the journey to see Lamartine. As I had anticipated, Agathe was eager to speak to her father, even in this new guise, and Louis once again expressed his willingness to accept a majority decision on the matter. For my part, I was happy to accept the idea of a session of negotiation, since it seemed hopeless for us to think of using force against the numbers about which we had been informed.

I consulted Georges, Marie and Annette on the matter, and they were likewise in favour of us taking such a step, being naturally unwilling to face overwhelming odds in combat. Accordingly, we informed our visitor that we wished to talk with his leader.

I was amazed by the facility with which the Blève were able to move between different locations in the Untime. For us, it was easy enough, but there was always some sense of vertigo and disorientation when taking the single step that could lead to the other side of the Universe, or back and forth in time. For our hosts, there seemed to be no such inconvenience. We were transported through the Untime to an inhospitable scene, which I took to be on some distant planet.

The sight that met our eyes when we arrived at our destination was almost impossible to describe in its hideousness. A rugged landscape of jagged rock was all around us, with lakes or seas of what appeared to be molten metal in the distance. Not one, but two, red suns, low on the horizon, illuminated the scene, and the light flickered fitfully, as thick clouds, which appeared to be composed of something other than the water of our terrestrial clouds, passed in front of the suns. We found ourselves standing in a kind of amphitheatre, ringed by rough crags, and with a floor of relatively smooth rock, on which the Blève were massed.

Though I was now aware that the Blève were relatively harmless when unprovoked, and indeed, were possessors of a moral code, their individual appearance was still disconcerting, and frightening. To see perhaps fifty of them massed together in this way was such a sight as I never again hope to behold.

Georges was, of course, aware of my distaste, and I received the impression of a chuckle from him. "To tell you the truth," he informed me, "your appearance is none too pleasant to us." Standards of beauty are obviously not universal, as we may see from the differences of opinion on the matter between the various races on this earth, or indeed between individuals. How many times have we marvelled at a friend's choice of partner or spouse? How much more, then, would be the difference in what we term "beautiful" between us, and a race of beings that differ so much from us in almost every respect?

At the centre of the Blève, who seemed to be arranged in a pattern of concentric circles, was an individual who was obviously the leader of the group. He (I will use the masculine pronoun to denote the creature) was larger than the rest. His eyes spoke of menace, and his tentacles lay still, twitching occasionally, in contrast to those of his followers, which were thrashing wildly in a kind of apparent frenzied excitement. Thought it was impossible for me to be certain, it seemed to me that the Blève now before us was the same "Dagon" whom I had battled previously.

Remembering the role that scent played in the emotions of the Blève, I sought to determine the prevailing mood of the crowd. To my relief, the floral scents of the crowd appeared to be stronger than the occasional foul stench that marked anger or bad temper, but there were sufficient indications of the latter to give me pause.

Before we approached the leader, I suggested to Agathe and Louis, and to our Blève, that we human beings should leave the Blève, and present ourselves to the leader in our own forms. I had a number of reasons for suggesting this. Firstly, it is possible that the sight of Agathe might stir memories of his previous existence in Lamartine and this might aid us in the task of restoring him to our civilisation. Second, if combat were to take place, an event which I sincerely trusted would not transpire, we would be able to use our shields and tridents to full effect. Lastly, it seemed to me to be unfair to our Blève to expose them to the risk that they might incur were we to remain absorbed by them and become the target of the mob's fury.

Accordingly, we "dismounted", and prepared

our shields and tridents, though they remained unconnected to the accumulators.

We had previously determined that Agathe should be the leader in our approach to this Blève, and accordingly she placed herself at the front of our group as we approached it.

I could sense hostility proceeding from the monster, and the smell of the sewers had been becoming more and more common by comparison with the flowery scent, but when Agathe made herself visible to it, the flowers reasserted themselves, and I could sense the feeling of hostility starting to fade.

"I know you," I sensed. "You were my daughter, Agathe." The voice was unmistakably that of Lamartine, and I shuddered to perceive it from such a source.

"And I still am your daughter, Papa," exclaimed Agathe.

"I am transformed, as you can see," came the answer. "What I once was on earth has now passed away, and I am now in a new form – a form that is virtually immortal, and possesses powers beyond those of which I dreamed. See!" and the creature used its tentacles to mimic a human's expansive gesture, showing to us the crowd of Blève that surrounded it. "These are my followers. First, we will conquer the earth. It is a rich planet, richer in all manner of things than the planet of the Blève. Above all, it is rich in souls – souls which will strengthen us, and make us invincible."

A shudder ran through me as I heard these words. This was undoubtedly Lamartine, the same man who had exclaimed "god-like" to describe his first experience of the Untime and had, that very same evening, announced his determination to rule the earth. Now it seemed that his ambitions had spread considerably further, though what his ultimate aim in this might be, I had no idea.

"But, father—" began Agathe.

"Silence!" roared Dagon-Lamartine (as I will now refer to this being, since it seemed to partake of the character of both these). "You are no longer my daughter. I renounced all ties with you and with humanity when I entered this blessed state."

I marvelled to hear him say these words, given that he had fought so bravely and so hard against the monster that now possessed him in order to save the daughter whom he now disavowed.

"You must return to the earth," Agathe

implored him. "You are sorely missed, and your colleagues at the Sorbonne would welcome your explanations of the Untime."

"Ha!" was the only response to this. A silence fell, and the eyes of the monster locked on me. "Gauthier, it is you, is it not?"

I acknowledged that it was indeed I who stood there.

"Why did you attempt to hinder me from joining the Blève? I see that you yourself have discovered the advantages of joining them. Why do you not join me and rule the Untime alongside me.

I remembered that Menton had made a similar offer to me only a few hours previously, or so it seemed. For some reason, the idea seemed ludicrously amusing, and I started to laugh uncontrollably.

"What is so funny?" asked Dagon-Lamartine. "I fail to see why an offer of supreme power should be a cause of merriment." A whiff of the sewer stench accompanied these words.

"Let me ask you if you remember a Dr. Auguste Menton, of the Faculty of Medicine at the Sorbonne," I said.

"Yes." A scornful tone was apparent. "A quack when I knew him on earth, and a meddler in our affairs of the Untime. He attempted to 'cure' those whom my followers were absorbing. With a singular lack of success, I might add. What of him?"

"He entered the Untime," I told him. For all his disparaging remarks regarding Menton, it was clear, from the monster's reaction, that this news came as a surprise to him.

"How did he achieve that?"

"We are not certain, but we believe it was through the strength of his will."

"What was his purpose?" I began to feel that I was being interrogated by the Professor Lamartine whom I had known on earth. The rapid, aggressive style of questioning was certainly familiar to me.

"He believed that he could rule the world through the Untime," I told him.

Chapter XXI

The effect of my words was astonishing. The hue of the Dagon-Lamartine Blève changed to a vivid green. The foul stench returned, and the tentacles flailed in a demented manner.

"There is only room for one ruler of the Untime!" he declared.

I smiled to myself, hoping to hide my feelings, but I had temporarily forgotten the mental powers of the Blève.

"Why are you smiling?" he asked.

"Menton is no more," I informed him. "The Blève that absorbed him no longer exists, and Menton went with it."

"You observed this?" he asked, incredulously.

"Not only did I observe it, but I was the cause of it," I told him.

"Pah! How can a puny human go up against a Blève and win?" He paused a little. "In any event, how did you arrive here in the Untime with my daughter? And why are you together? And who is he?" indicating Louis with the languid wave of a tentacle.

"So many questions, father." It was Agathe who answered him. "First, we arrived here through a device of my own design. We determined to destroy your apparatus, as being too dangerous to exist."

At this, Dagon-Lamartine's tentacles started to tremble, and I could discern a sense of anger spreading through the being, accompanied by stronger bursts of the obnoxious smell.

"You dared to destroy my life's work?" he burst out. "My crowning achievement? The culmination of years of research? How dare you do such a thing? By what right could you perform such an action?"

"Schneider—" began Agathe, but she was silenced by a snort from Dagon-Lamartine.

"Schneider, indeed! When did that pompous nincompoop know the first thing about my work? What of him, anyway?"

"I was about to say, father," Agathe continued calmly, "that Schneider, Jules here and myself carefully considered the merits and advantages of exploring the Untime further. However, we determined upon reflection that, despite the obvious boon to historians and to others offered by access to the Untime, the possible dangers were too great. Accordingly, we destroyed the apparatus. Forgive me, father, but it appeared to be the wisest course of action for us to take."

"And yet you are here now. How does this come about?"

"When you and your Blève started to make their presence felt in the earth, we were forced to make our own arrangements to travel here. I reconstructed your apparatus from my memory of your notes, and was able to produce a simpler, yet still effective, version of it. As to why I am with Jules here, why, we were married soon after you – after you stayed in the Untime. He is my husband. Your son-in-law."

"And I suppose you have come here to seek a father's blessing on the union?" Dagon-Lamartine asked sarcastically.

"No, that is not our reason," Agathe replied. "We are come to take you home, father."

"Home? This is home, you little fool! The Untime, nay, the whole Universe is now my home. Do you not understand? I will be the ruler of the whole of the Universe in a very short time from now, thanks to my followers."

Agathe's face fell at the words with which she was addressed, and Louis plucked at my sleeve. "He is insane!" he whispered to me. "How can one man, or one being, be the sole ruler of the Universe?"

"How did Menton meet his end?" Dagon-Lamartine suddenly bellowed. This time it was I who answered.

"I defeated him, with the help of your daughter, and Louis here."

"You? A puny human defeated a Blève, which had absorbed a human mind? Tell me, what do you know of the Blève?"

"A little," I admitted.

"Then you are aware that they possess extraordinary mental powers, are you not? That they are able to move easily through the Untime? That they are able to produce and deploy powerful weapons simply through the power of their minds?" The rhythm of the catechism reminded me forcefully of Lamartine when he had been alive, and this gave me hope that the human part of this monster still retained sufficient of its original nature for us to be able to persuade him to return with us to our world.

"I am aware of these things, yes."

"Are you aware that, with all these powers, the Blève are, by our standards, feeble-minded?"

I felt that this was a somewhat unfairly disparaging description of the Blève, but simply nodded. I remembered that Lamartine, in common with so many of the faculty of the Sorbonne, were prone to apply this characterisation to the majority of their fellow-men, and that what they considered to be "feeble-minded" would often pass for normality with most people. On the other hand, though these professors tended to regard themselves as being above the common herd as far as intelligence was concerned, many of them were singularly lacking in what we might term "common-sense", and often needed considerable assistance to live their everyday lives.

"Well, then," continued Dagon-Lamartine, "when one adds the power of an intellect such as mine, or even one like that of Menton, to the undoubted talents of a Blève, the result is a super-being, which can transcend almost any obstacle. I therefore find it impossible to believe that you could have defeated Menton after he had been absorbed by a Blève."

"You may find it impossible to believe,

Professor," I retorted, "but I am telling you no more than the truth. The devices designed and prepared by your daughter have proved singularly effective."

"Hah!" was the incredulous reply. "Maybe you would like to show me how effective they really are?"

"Then I suggest that we move back inside the Untime."

"Very well."

For the Dagon-Lamartine creature and his followers, this move was trivially easy, but Agathe, Louis and I required the assistance of our Blève to make the transition.

"So," continued our adversary when all were assembled, "you wish to demonstrate these contraptions of yours?"

"The defensive shield only," Agathe told him. "We have no wish to harm you."

"Did you really think that your puny toys would be used against me? No, you shall try them against the bravest and strongest of my warriors, who recently absorbed a Roman centurion from Caesar's legions. A tried and tested cunning warrior, allied to one of the strongest and most powerful Blève in existence." He gestured towards a Blève, as big or even slightly larger than himself, whose features seemed even more hideous, and from whom proceeded a hideous stink that caused me to retch.

I shuddered inwardly. If this were the calibre of opponent that our world would be facing, then there would be no hope for us. Too late, I remembered that my thoughts were open to all, and Dagon-Lamartine opened its beak and emitted a bark of hideous laughter.

"Indeed you may fear me and my subjects," he said. "When our numbers are a few eights more, with souls seized from the Earth, there will be no force, anywhere in the Universe, that may stop us." He motioned for the centurion-Blève to step forward.

"Whether it is you or another," I told Lamartine, "I have no wish to use our offensive weapons."

An unpleasant chuckle came from the centurion. "Little man, when I was on the Earth, I won the corona muralis — the decoration bestowed on those who were the first to scale the enemy's ramparts, not just once, but five times. After I had killed my first hundred enemies, I ceased to count them any longer. Will you stand against me?"

Despite my earlier words stating that I would

use only defensive measures, I whispered to Agathe and Louis to prepare both their shields and tridents.

"I am ready," I told the centurion, connecting my shield to the accumulator, and stepping forward. As I did so, a rain of stones started to descend against me. I raised my shield, set at full strength, against them, and was happy to see them deflected away so that not a single one fell near me.

Next came a massive tidal wave of green foaming water, which raced towards me with the speed of an express train. Again, the shield halted the water, which vanished immediately it had been stopped in its path.

"Grapple with him, Flavius," came the voice of Lamartine.

"I cannot, master," was the answer. "I cannot approach him, and it seems that I am powerless to knock his device from his hands."

I was emboldened, and took a step forward. The centurion took a corresponding move backwards away from me. Again I advanced, and again he retreated.

"Enough!" commanded Lamartine. The centurion moved back to his former place, and I rejoined my companions.

"Intriguing," mused the Dagon-Lamartine creature. "Your invention?" he asked Agathe.

"Yes, father," she answered him. "I could remember a good deal of your notes on the Untime, and developed your principles a little further."

"And those?" gesturing towards the tridents that we carried.

"The shields that you just saw demonstrated are for defence only. These are for offence. It was one of these that destroyed Menton."

"Do you feel that, even armed with these, you could withstand a simultaneous attack by all my followers?"

"You would not do such a thing against your own daughter!" I protested hotly.

"I have told you before. I have no daughter now. I have cast off my earthly ties, and am now beyond human. It strikes me, though, that you have acquired a good understanding of the Untime and its denizens. I ask you one more time. Will you join me in my quest to rule the Universe?"

"We will not," Agathe declared emphatically.

Dagon-Lamartine appeared to be about to answer, when a small, childish voice entered the conversation.

"Mademoiselle Agathe?" it enquired.

"I know that voice!" exclaimed my wife, and to tell the truth, I also felt that I recognised it. "It is little Marie!" Agathe cried after a moment's thought. Little Marie, the small child whom Lamartine had callously consigned to the Untime, with no hope of return, was here!

"Where are you, Marie?" I asked.

"Here," came the answer, and I saw one of the Blève, somewhat smaller than the others, moving towards us. "I want to go home." The voice was unmistakably that of little Marie.

"And so you shall," Agathe told her.

"I also," came a voice from another Blève.

"Who are you?" I asked.

"I am Berthe Jabotte."

The name was somehow strangely familiar to me, but I was unable to place it precisely for a minute or so. Then I remembered that this was the name of the patient whom Menton had exhibited to us at the Pitié-Salpêtrière, whose mind appeared to have departed from her body.

"But you are still in Paris!" I exclaimed.

"I never entered the Untime in my body. For several weeks I suffered from terrible dreams in which these creatures continually appeared, and I was in terror. Then one night I went to sleep, and when I woke up, I was here, inside this creature – this Blève. It has been most kind to me and attempted to comfort me in my condition, but it is still very hard for me, and I wish to return." At this point, the voice broke into a fit of violent sobbing.

"You may not return!" Dagon-Lamartine thundered forth. "Neither you, not the girl. You are to follow me, and me alone."

"And if they attempt to return?" Agathe asked.

"Then they shall perish! In the sight of all, so that all may know of the futility of attempting to go against my wishes."

At this, Louis nudged me once again, and made the vulgar sign often used to indicate lunacy, twirling his finger against his temple. I could not help but nod in agreement. It seemed to me that Lamartine's wits were truly addled.

Without uttering another word, the Blève that had identified itself as the one which had absorbed Marie detached itself from the group and moved to stand by Georges, Marie and Annette. Suddenly, the figure of a small girl, scarcely more than an infant, stood beside the four Blève.

Marie, for it was indeed she, looked around her in bewilderment, and then burst into floods of terrified tears as she perceived the mass of Blève around her. Without speaking a word, Louis thrust his trident and shield into my hands, and moved towards the little girl, and scooped her up with his good left arm, before carrying her back to us and depositing her beside Agathe.

"There, there, my dear," my wife told her, gently ruffling her curls, and little Marie's sobs started to subside.

There was a bellow from Dagon-Lamartine. "Destroy it!" he directed the centurion, Flavius, which lunged forward menacingly towards the Blève which had previously absorbed little Marie. Instantly, my shield was energised, as was that of Louis, who had reclaimed it from me when he had left little Marie with Agathe.

Chapter XXII

Presenting our shields, Louis and I interposed ourselves in front of Marie's Blève,
and the big Blève known as Flavius stopped its
advance.

"Forward, Flavius!" Dagon-Lamartine urged
the monster.

"Master, I cannot," complained the centurion.
"These devices make it too painful to proceed."

"I order you to destroy that one!" Dagon-
Lamartine ordered, pointing to Marie's Blève.
"You will be rewarded."

Slowly and cautiously, our opponent started
to move towards us. Brave Louis and I turned
the power of our shields to their fullest possible

capacity, and presented them to the enemy. Agathe was fully occupied in comforting and protecting little Marie, and was momentarily unable to assist us.

"Chipwata," Dagon-Lamartine ordered another Blève, "circle round and attack from the rear."

With Louis only able to use one hand, and therefore being prevented from using both spear and trident together, it was imperative that we faced danger from only one direction. Although I had declared that I would use only defensive measures, it seemed that the time had come for me to reconsider this. Accordingly, I instructed Louis to cover the attack from the rear with his shield, while I energised my trident, albeit at the lowest setting, and prepared to meet Flavius.

My adversary advanced slowly towards me, and it was obvious that the shield was causing him considerable discomfort, if not actual pain. However, even at full power, it was clear that the shield would not restrain him for ever. Furthermore, at full power, the accumulator would soon be discharged. It was therefore necessary for me to act soon, and to take the offensive.

Flavius sent a shower of hailstones towards me, but the effect of these was easily negated by the power of the shield, and, snarling, he inched closer towards me. It appeared to me, though, that the effect of the shield was becoming weaker. As Flavius sent another rain of spears towards me, only half were stopped by the power of the shield, and one that was not halted passed very close to me, missing me by a matter of a few centimetres only. I determined that it was time for me to take the offensive, and moved forward, stabbing once with the trident, and the effect was as marked as it had been with Menton. Flavius seemed to shrink into himself, and become smaller and weaker. As I took a step forwards in his direction, he moved back fully twice that distance, and roared with a terrifying sound.

"Forward, you coward," Dagon-Lamartine snapped at him.

"I am no coward, master," came the reply, "but this thing, whatever it may be, is too much for me. With just one touch, I am weaker than I was. I fear with more touches I will lose all my power and strength." He did not advance, but stayed in place, making no further move towards me. However, I did not feel in any way confident that he would not launch an attack at any moment. The stench coming from him was almost overpowering, and it took all my resolve to stand my own ground.

"I would like to inform you," I told him, "that this trident is now at its lowest power setting. If you wish to discover what a higher power setting will do, I will oblige." I turned to Dagon-Lamartine. "Do you believe now that we defeated Menton?"

At that moment, my shield's accumulator gave out, and I had no spare on my person! Louis was carrying our supplies. Without, I hoped, betraying the panic that I now felt, I moved backward, brandishing my trident before me. Soon, I was back-to-back with Louis, to whom I explained my situation.

While still defending himself against the other Blève, whom Dagon-Larmartine had named Chipwata, Louis extracted a spare accumulator from his pack, with my assistance. I fear that with his damaged arm, the effort cost him considerable pain, but he bore the agony without flinching, and I was soon once more in possession of a fully working shield, which I presented towards Flavius, who backed away as I advanced.

"Enough!" came the order from Dagon-Lamartine. "Stand before me!" Both Flavius and Chipwata advanced towards their leader, and it appeared to me that they hesitated in their movements. I could sense fear coming from both the Blève, and had they been human, I would have said that they were trembling. Certainly their tentacles seemed to show some signs of extreme agitation.

"You have failed, both of you!" Dagon-Lamartine snarled at them. Without warning, a shower of pointed icicles fell from the sky, piercing the hide of the Blève named Chipwata. A steaming dark liquid spurted from the pierced flesh, and the Blève screamed in agony, with tentacles curling and uncurling almost too fast for the eye to follow. The beak opened, and more of the dark liquid dribbled out, as the creature sank to the ground, seemingly becoming smaller as it did so. Again, a rain of projectiles fell on the Blève, this time iron darts, which seemed to take the life from the monster, which dwindled to almost invisibility, as Menton had when I attacked him, before disappearing completely.

Flavius, the larger Blève, appeared to be distraught. "No, master," he cried, his distress evident in his tones. "I will do your bidding." So saying, he leaped at me once more, but I had not disconnected my shield, and the wall of fire that he launched at me was dispelled by the power of Agathe's science.

Though his last attacks had been powerful enough, now he was attempting to demonstrate his loyalty and obedience to Dagon-Lamartine, and the assaults were becoming more than I could withstand alone. Agathe was still occupied with comforting little Marie – and the events transpiring were not fit sights for little Marie's eyes – but the brave Louis once more stepped into the breach to assist me. With his shield and mine, we were more than a match for the assaults of the Blève, who nonetheless continued his frenzied attacks and once again, I felt that I was justified in using the trident, which I set at half-power.

This time, Flavius screamed with an intolerably human sound as the extended trident met his flesh. He shrank in size, and continued to do so as I thrust again and again. By now I had abandoned any idea of making only defensive moves, and was fighting for my life against a desperate and crazed opponent. The trident soon did its work, and the Blève shrank to nothing and disappeared, taking, I fear, the Roman soldier with it.

Damon-Lamartine appeared astonished and not a little frightened, from what we could perceive, shrinking back from us a little. His followers also backed away, allowing us more space around us, but I dared not relax my guard. By now, little Marie had stopped her weeping, and she and Agathe joined Louis and me. The three of us had our shields turned on at their weakest power, but we were ready to increase the intensity at any time.

"Flavius was my strongest warrior," Dagon-Lamartine exclaimed, with what seemed to be wonder in his voice, "and you destroyed him."

"Say, rather, that your daughter destroyed him," I told him. "For it was she who developed the shields and tridents that we used just now."

"Then I suppose I should be congratulating you, Agathe," came the answer, which appeared to have more than a touch of irony behind it.

"A toast," Louis said suddenly, retrieving the bottle of cognac from his knapsack, with some difficulty, owing to his damaged right arm. "To the destruction of our enemies."

An idea struck me regarding a plan by which we might be enabled to return Lamartine to our world safely. "A toast, indeed, Louis," I replied, and he passed the bottle to me. I flourished it in the air, ensuring that it was in plain sight of Dagon-Lamartine, and raised it to my lips, but without actually drinking.

"Is that cognac?" the Blève asked me.

"It is indeed," I replied. "Perhaps not of the very finest quality, but certainly of at least an adequate standard.

"It seems as though it has been so long since I was able to enjoy such refreshment," said Dagon-Lamartine, and I fancied I could detect a sigh accompanying these words.

"It would be a simple matter to correct that situation," I smiled.

Dagon-Lamartine appeared to be deep in thought at my words. "I understand," he said at length.

The beak of the Blève opened, and there before us stood Professor Rémy Lamartine, seemingly unchanged from the last time that I had seen him in our world. Agathe gave a gasp, and would have rushed to meet him, but I restrained her. "There will be ample time later," I told her. He walked towards our group, a faint smile, which appeared to be mixed with a certain amount of greed, and extended his hand to reach for the brandy.

"If you would be so kind," he said with the faint mocking smile that I remembered so well.

I forced a smile in return, and extended the bottle to him. "I regret that we neglected to bring glasses with us," I told him. "Perhaps some of the aroma will be lost."

"No matter," he answered. "I confess to being more than a little impressed that you brought brandy with you once more, though I seem to remember that the last time you and I ventured into the Untime together, it was Armagnac that you brought with you."

"So it was." I could not help but be amused by this memory of Lamartine's, and it confirmed me in my belief that my tactics would succeed.

"Your health," said Lamartine, and drank from the bottle. I could not help but marvel at the irony of one who had so recently ordered our destruction, and was now coolly drinking our health – moreover, using our brandy to do so. Even so, I smiled, and gave him to understand that all was well.

When he had been on earth, Lamartine, while not a drunkard in the strictest sense of the term, had never been noted for his abstemious nature. I was trusting that this facet of his personality had not weakened since his arrival in the Untime.

I was not disappointed. He took another generous draught of the spirit, and he appeared to sway. As I had guessed, his enforced abstinence from alcohol had weakened his tolerance. One more drink, and his eyes appeared to glaze over.

"Quickly!" I said to Louis, who had been watching the scene in amazement.

As I seized one of Lamartine's arms, and Louis the other, we dragged the semi-conscious Professor back to my Blève, Georges, who had been waiting with Annette and the other Blève, whom I suppose I must now call "big Marie" to make a distinction between the Blève and the little girl whom we were rescuing.

"Can you accommodate me and the Professor?" I asked Georges.

"Willingly," replied the Blève, "as long as you are able to control him when he awakens."

It should be noted that by this time, the brandy, even in the small quantities in which he had imbibed it, had rendered Lamartine unconscious. I therefore directed Georges to absorb the limp body with as much care as possible under the circumstances.

CHAPTER XXIII

GEORGES absorbed Lamartine, and I in turn was about to be absorbed, when Louis drew my attention to the Professor's followers, who had regrouped into their original formation in which we had first discovered them, and were advancing on us. I was happy to see, though, that Dagon, Lamartine's former host, did not seem to be leading them.

I interposed myself between Georges and the advancing horde, but to my surprise, it seemed that there was no animosity. I noticed that it was the Blève which had absorbed little Marie that addressed me with a surprising gentleness.

"Will you take care of the master?" it asked.

"And of the little one I protected?"

"You protected her?" I asked incredulously. This hideous monster had absorbed little Marie and held her prisoner in the Untime, and yet it was claiming that it had protected her.

"Of a certainty I protected her," it told me. "There are many dangers, both in the Untime and in the other worlds, that might harm her."

"More dangerous than you Blève?"

"Much, much, more dangerous. We Blève are peaceful by nature, and avoid conflict whenever we can, but if we are attacked, or if we absorb an aggressive spirit, then we have ways to defend ourselves, and even to attack if necessary."

I considered the first Blève that I had ever encountered, Dagon, who had sought to destroy Agathe and me on my last visit to the Untime, and had absorbed Professor Lamartine, but I did not seek to contradict this statement. "And these other beings that you describe?"

"They are far bigger and stronger than we Blève, and they are aggressive in the extreme. They seem to live for destruction and delight in pain and death."

This news made me shudder.

"Happily," my informant went on, "they can only exist in the Untime. There is no planet outside the Untime that can support them. We Blève find it easy to go between the Untime and other worlds, so it is easy to escape from these monsters."

I smiled to myself to hear this Blève, itself a fugitive from a nightmare, describe other beings as "monsters", but inwardly I thanked Providence that we had not encountered any such beings on our journeys through the Untime.

"But we are concerned about him who was our master," continued the Blève. "While he was our master, he commanded us, and we were bound to him. Now we see that you have defeated him, and our strongest fighters, and therefore we are no longer under any obligation to obey him."

I considered our three Blève, who had joined us following the destruction of Menton. "You are telling me," I asked, "that you Blève will always follow the strongest, who defeats his enemies?"

"That is so."

"It is not so unlike we human beings," laughed Louis, who had been listening to the conversation. "Consider Alexander the Great, Julius Caesar, and Napoleon. If they had been weaker in battle, do you think they would have retained the following that they did?"

"There may be something in what you say, " I
admitted. I turned back to the Blève. "What will
you all do now?" I asked.

"If you wish us to follow you, we will do. We
will return with you to your home planet if you
desire, and serve you there."

I had to laugh. For all the familiarity that I
had acquired with these creatures, the Blève
were still hideous to the sight. To bring a troop
of them to Paris would cause chaos. I had no
doubt that the Army would be called in to
destroy them.

"It is most kind of you to offer," I told it, "but I
do not think your services on our world would
be welcome."

Our conversation was interrupted by Agathe's
voice, proceeding from big Marie. "Jules, have
you forgotten the poor men and women whose
souls were stolen from them while she slept?"

I smote my forehead. Indeed, poor Berthe
Jabotte and the others had completely slipped
my mind. "Is there any way that this woman's
mind can be restored to her? And that of any
others whose minds have been taken?" I asked
the Blève.

"Of course," came the instant answer. What I

can only describe as a thunderstorm occurred in my mind, during which I felt dizzy and my head spun. "They have been returned," I was told.

"And you and your people will no longer attempt to visit our people and steal their souls," I commanded, in as firm a tone as I could muster.

"We will no longer do so," the Blève assured me.

It was time to leave, before Lamartine awoke and started to protest at his abduction. Once again, I prepared to be absorbed by Georges, when a sudden cry from Louis' Blève, Annette, caused me to look around.

Despite the assurances I had been given, two of Dagon's Blève, presumably angered by the disappearance of their leader, were moving fast towards me, and a shower of flaming darts was launched in my direction. I had disconnected my shield from the accumulator, and was therefore powerless to use it to deflect the attack.

"Courage, Jules!" I sensed from Agathe. "You attacked Dagon with nothing but your mind and came close to besting him. You are capable of repeating the feat."

I quickly threw up a mental wall to block the

attack, but this was not completely successful, and one of the darts struck me in the shoulder, causing me to stagger, and to lose my concentration as another dart hit me, this time in the thigh. The pain was immense, and I could no longer summon up the mental strength to defend myself. I closed my eyes and prepared to be absorbed by one of these hostile Blève.

With my eyes closed, I heard the terrifying bellowing scream of an enraged Blève, and prepared to meet my fate. Seconds passed, every one of which seemed an eternity, as I readied myself for the pain and terror that I knew was to come momentarily. Then the screaming stopped, and a blessed silence fell.

I opened my eyes to see Louis standing, seemingly dazed, beside me, pointing at the remains of three Blève.

"Three?" I croaked. "But only two attacked me, surely?"

For answer, Louis simply pointed back towards our Blève. Rather than the three who had been there before, only two now stood in that place.

"It was Annette," Louis said simply. "She disgorged me, and flung herself at your attackers, sacrificing herself to save you."

I could hardly believe it. A monster from my

worst nightmares had sacrificed its life for a being from another planet – one, furthermore, whom it hardly knew. It is not too much to say that tears came to my eyes.

"Why?" I asked Georges. "Why would your companion do such a thing?"

"Because you have been good to us," he answered me. "We have seen that you can destroy even the strongest of our species, even when they are augmented by one of your species. We have no doubt that you could have destroyed all of us here," and his gesture took in the assembled multitude of Blève. "However, you did not, even when you had the chance. Furthermore, you could have made us your slaves, and we would have been bound to obey you, but you did not. Your only requests to us have been to help your fellows, not for your own gain or aggrandisement. What could we do but help you?"

"I cannot thank you enough," I said. In truth, how could I display my gratitude to these beings, who had shown a degree of loyalty that was hardly believable?

"And now," said Georges, "it is time for you to return. We know that our appearance is somewhat less than pleasing to your people, and so we do not propose to accompany you," and here I received the distinct impression of a smile. Could it be that these creatures possessed a sense of humour?

"Thank you again," I said. "Agathe, and little Marie, please join Louis and myself. And Georges, if you would be kind enough to disgorge Professor Lamartine."

We were now five in number, ready to make our return from the Untime.

"Simply will yourself back in the room at the Sorbonne," Agathe told Louis, "and take your step into there, out of the Untime."

Chapter XXIV

THOUGH it could hardly be described as a familiar experience, the complete strangeness and novelty of moving from the Untime to our world was in some sense missing. As had previously occurred, we were all chilled to the bone. Agathe had previously calculated that this was due to some loss of energy as we made our transition, but it was impossible, as always, for me to follow her mathematics.

Little Marie, on beholding the room at the Sorbonne, gave a squeal of delight, and clapped her hands. "This is so much nicer than where I have been for so long," she told us. She looked around her. "Are there any biscuits?" she asked

Agathe. "It has been a long time since I ate a biscuit."

"You shall have all the biscuits you desire," Agathe told her. "But what of my father?" she asked me, regarding the supine and almost motionless figure of Professor Lamartine.

"He is still affected by the brandy," I told her, "and quite probably by the journey between the Untime and here. I think he will awake soon."

As if he had heard my words, the Professor stirred, and opened his eyes. He looked around him, and saw Agathe, Louis, and myself. Last of all, his gaze fell on little Marie.

"Is this a dream?" he asked Agathe, with an air of puzzlement. "Or have I been dreaming?" His voice was quiet and restrained, a contrast to the aggressive hectoring tone he had used in the Untime. His face was calm and untroubled, and it seemed that whatever madness had been affecting him had completely disappeared.

"What sort of dream?"

"I dreamed that I led a horde of monsters through the Untime," he answered. "I was determined to take over the world in my dream, I seem to recall." He paused and looked around him. "Where am I now?" he asked, as he regarded the room, and the apparatus that

Agathe had devised to transport us into the Untime.

"Father," Agathe said to him gently, bending down to be near to him. "It was no dream, or if it was, it was shared by Louis here, Jules, and myself."

Lamartine sat up slowly, and rubbed his eyes. "It seems like a dream." He looked at me. "Gauthier, you were there, were you not? You and I fought against a monster together, and you escaped with my daughter, and I was devoured and became one with it."

"Indeed we did," I told him. "That was two years ago or more."

"Indeed?" He seemed more than a little surprised by this news. "Two years. And in that time, you..."

"We destroyed your apparatus, Father," Agathe told him. "We judged it was unsafe to leave an open gateway to the Untime."

"Ah, dangerous indeed," mused Lamartine, and sat silently for a while. "There are things in there that can turn a man's mind." He seemed to come to with a start. "Gauthier, answer me honestly. We visited the Untime for the first time together, did we not?" I nodded in assent. "On our return from that first visit, did you believe I had changed in any way?"

"Quite frankly, Professor, you had become a megalomaniac. You had talked of ruling the world."

He sighed. "I did, did I not? I recall it now."

"Tell us, Father, of what happened to you after you had been absorbed by the monster following your battle with it in which Jules took part," Agathe implored him.

He mopped his brow. "It all seems so long ago, and, as I said, it seems more like a dream than reality. I was terrified when we were attacked and I was absorbed by the monster – the Blève." His pronunciation of the name was no better than mine. "Imagine my surprise when I came into contact with the creature's mind, and found it to be powerful in the effects it could produce, but yet easily controllable by the power of my will. I therefore determined to collect a following of these beings with which I could control the Earth."

"So you sent these beasts to invade the minds of sleepers and to steal their souls?"

He nodded. "To my shame, that is what I did. The Blève, as I am sure you saw, respect strength, and this was one of the best ways for me to show my strength, and to increase my power over them."

Something had been gnawing at the back of my mind, and I interrupted Lamartine's narrative. "Professor," I asked gently. "We came into contact with the Blève. Other than those who had been inhabited by warlike and aggressive human spirits, I found them to be surprisingly gentle and honourable beings, despite their hideous appearance. And yet, when you and I battled the monster that absorbed you, it was angry and wished only to destroy us, though we had done nothing to provoke it."

Lamartine sighed. "That is not strictly accurate," he corrected me. "You had done nothing to provoke it. I, on the other hand, had discovered these creatures, and had acted in an aggressive and unfriendly manner towards them, without demonstrating my superior mental capacity. The Blève that attacked us had been the subject of my teasing, as you may best describe it, and resented my actions. No doubt it considered all humanity as its enemies. As you observed, the Blève share many thoughts and emotions in common, and I therefore inadvertently tarred all of humanity with the same brush, which they regarded as being hostile and dangerous." He sighed. "I agree – the Blève, given kindness

and honourable actions, will return those feelings with generosity."

"More than you know," I told him, and
informed him of the final sacrifice that Louis'
Blève had made on our behalf.

Lamartine shrugged. "I am sorry that any of
this happened."

"Another question, Father. How did little
Marie here come to be with you? And you shall
have your biscuits soon, my dear, never fear,"
she told the infant.

"I have some in my pack," Louis smiled, and
passed one to Marie, who thanked him gravely,
and started to eat it, an expression of near-ec-
stasy on her face.

"You may remember," Lamartine answered his
daughter, "that perhaps Gauthier here informed
you of the fact that little Marie here was the first
to enter the Untime – involuntarily, I confess.
When I had been absorbed, however, the fact of
her being lost started to prey on my mind, and I
therefore determined that even if she were not
to be sent back to our world, a course of action
that I could see would bring its own set of difficulties and contradictions, she should have the
company of at least a friendly Blève."

"Gagar was very kind," said Marie. "That's what

I called her. She looked horrid on the outside, but she was nice inside. But I was lonely. Very, very lonely. Can I have another biscuit, please?" she added, with the charming inconsequentiality of the very young. Louis passed another biscuit to her, and she thanked him.

"And what would you have done, Professor, had you ruled the world?" Louis addressed Lamartine for the first time.

The question seemed to perplex him. "What would I have done?" He scratched his head. "Do you know, my dear fellow, I cannot tell you now. All seems as though it was a dream from which I have awoken, remembering only part of what went on in my mind. I would have done great things, I am sure," he laughed, "but I have no idea what they might have been." He paused and appeared once more to be in deep thought. "Did you say that it was two years since you and I entered the Untime together, Gauthier?"

"A little more," I told him.

"And what of me? How does the world view me now?"

"As far as the world is concerned, you perished in an accident with the diving-apparatus on which you had been working," I told him. "Your reappearance as Professor Rémy Lamartine would create a sensation, and not a particularly pleasant one," I am sure. "There is, however, currently another Professor Lamartine of the Sorbonne." I could not resist this slight teasing.

"Another Lamartine? An imposter! I will unmask him!" This was delivered with the energy of the old Lamartine whom I had known and admired before the arrival of the Untime in his life. "I am willing to bet the scoundrel Schneider is behind this."

"It is I, Father," Agathe told him. "I am now a full professor here." Lamartine's mouth fell open.

"Though Schneider was indeed helpful," I added, "the appointment would never have been made had my wife been unsuitable for the post."

"Your wife? I thought that, too, was part of my dream. So, my little Agathe, you are a married woman, and a professor. I may congratulate you, I suppose." And then, in a display of affection that I had not seen in him before, he embraced Agathe.

"Gauthier, I owe you and my daughter, and you, Louis, my profound thanks. I cannot say what would have happened had I remained in the Untime. Not only I, but the whole world might have been in serious danger, it seems to me."

I said nothing, but silently agreed.

Chapter XXV

To conclude, Lamartine declared that he would prefer to remain deceased in the eyes of the world, and accordingly adopted a new identity, and took himself to America, where he has been responsible for a number of patents under his new name, which I shall not give here. However, it is quite likely that you have used one or two of the devices for which he has been responsible. He still maintains correspondence with his daughter, though not his wife, and there is no evidence from his letters that he is troubled by the mental disturbances that had led to so many difficulties in the past.

Louis' arm and my injuries healed quickly,

within a matter of a few days. It is possible that injuries inflicted in the Untime are of a different nature to those inflicted elsewhere, or that the change out of the Untime speeds up the healing process. Agathe has no theories on the matter, and neither has Schneider, to whom we related the events that had taken place. He professed himself to be sorry that he had not accompanied us on our journey to the Untime, but I sensed a feeling of relief beneath his words.

He and I destroyed the apparatus that Agathe had designed, including the shields and tridents, but we retained the plans for all of these, which are kept in a locked safe in the Ministry of Justice, where they may be accessed by the authorities, should any further mischief come from the direction of the Untime. Louis, by the way, has become an invaluable assistant in Agathe's laboratory, and we are both pleased to have this brave fellow as a friend.

Agathe's work at the Sorbonne continues to bear fruit. I do not pretend to have an understanding, but I am proud and happy that the woman I love has achieved such distinction. As for me, old Simon, after a token show of resistance, allowed me to rejoin the magazine, where I continue to produce stories to entertain the public.

Berthe Jabotte, whose mind had been captured by a Blève, and returned to her, was released from the asylum following an examination by several doctors, at the request of Agathe, as were the other patients whom Menton had been treating. Unlike Lamartine, they had little or no memory of their time in the Untime, and none at all of the time that their bodies had spent in the asylum, being merely more than a little puzzled that a month or more had been missing from their lives.

And lastly, you may be asking about little Marie? She is now Agathe's and my little Marie. We determined that it would introduce too many complications were she to be restored after so long a period, and we therefore determined that we should adopt her. She has been a joy to us, and compensates us for our failure to produce a child of our own.

The Untime, let us hope, is now a thing of the past, as far as our world is concerned. The actors in this little drama have moved on, and mankind will no longer be troubled by it, or the monsters that inhabit it.

If you enjoyed this book…

Thank you for reading this story – I hope you enjoyed it.

It would be highly appreciated if you left a review or rating online somewhere.

You may also enjoy some of my other books, which are available from the usual outlets.

ALSO BY HUGH ASHTON

Sherlock Holmes Titles

Tales from the Deed Box of John H. Watson M.D.
More from the Deed Box of John H. Watson M.D.
Secrets from the Deed Box of John H. Watson M.D.
The Case of the Trepoff Murder
The Bradfield Push
The Darlington Substitution
Notes from the Dispatch-Box of John H. Watson M.D.
Further Notes from the Dispatch-
Box of John H. Watson M.D.
The Reigate Poisoning Case: Concluded
The Death of Cardinal Tosca
The Last Notes from the Dispatch-
Box of John H. Watson M.D.
Without My Boswell
1894
Some Singular Cases of Mr. Sherlock Holmes
The Adventure of Vanaprastha

General titles
Tales of Old Japanese
Balance of Powers
Leo's Luck
Beneath Gray Skies
Red Wheels Turning
At the Sharpe End
Angels Unawares

Titles for Children
Sherlock Ferret and the Missing Necklace
Sherlock Ferret and the Multiplying Masterpieces
Sherlock Ferret and the Poisoned Pond
Sherlock Ferret and the Phantom Photographer
The Adventures of Sherlock Ferret

About the Author

HUGH Ashton was born in the United Kingdom, and moved to Japan in 1988, where he lived until a return to the UK in 2016.

He is best known for his Sherlock Holmes stories, which have been hailed as some of the most authentic pastiches on the market, and have received favourable reviews from Sherlockians and non-Sherlockians alike.

He currently divides his time between the historic cities of Lichfield, and Kamakura, a little to the south of Yokohama, with his wife, Yoshiko.

Contact him at hashton@mac.com

www.ingramcontent.com/pod-product-compliance
Lightning Source LLC
Chambersburg PA
CBHW031605180726
48284CB00005B/1410